BRITAIN'S
SMARTEST
KID ...ON ICE!

BRITAIN'S SMARTEST KID
...ON ICE!

IVOR BADDIEL

SCHOLASTIC

Published in the UK by Scholastic, 2022
Euston House, 24 Eversholt Street, London, NW1 1DB
Scholastic Ireland, 89E Lagan Road, Dublin Industrial Estate, Glasnevin,
Dublin, D11 HP5F

Text © Ivor Baddiel, 2022
Illustrations by James Lancett, © Scholastic, 2022

The right of Ivor Baddiel to be identified
as the author of this work has been asserted by him under the Copyright,
Designs and Patents Act 1988.

ISBN 978 0702 31375 2

Printed by CPI Group (UK) Ltd, Croydon, CR0 4YY
Paper made from wood grown in sustainable forests and other controlled
sources.

13 5 7 9 10 8 6 4 2

www.scholastic.co.uk

To Soph

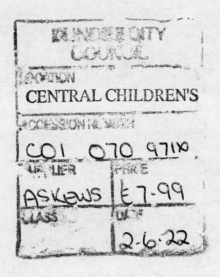

PART 1

GRAN HAS AN IDEA

CHAPTER 1

"*Hamlet*."*

"Carbon dioxide."†

"Lake Titicaca."‡

"Frank Lampard."§

"Wow!" said Mum, whose real name was Melissa.

"Amazing," said Dad, whose real name was Jonty. "Marsham, you've just won *Mastermind!*"

"He's a genius. He must get his brains from me," said Gran, who lived with Marsham, Jonty and Melissa, and whose real name was Elsie.

"I wouldn't say I'm a genius, Gran," said Marsham, a little embarrassed.

---

* What is Shakespeare's longest play?
† What gas makes up most of the atmosphere of Mars?
‡ What is the largest freshwater lake in South America by surface area?
§ Who is Chelsea's all-time leading goal scorer?

3

Marsham wasn't overly comfortable with being publicly labelled a genius, but the truth was, he was also pleased and proud. He *was* clever. Very clever. And, if he'd actually been taking part in *Mastermind*, he may well have won, but he wasn't. He was watching the show on television with his family.

Twelve-year-old Marsham Lucas loved quiz shows. He also loved his cat Tonks, building complex gadgets, playing – and devising – computer games, music, writing, magic, swimming and macaroni cheese, though not necessarily in that order.

It was quiz shows that Marsham loved most, though. He loved to feel challenged, and relished what felt like a battle going on in his brain to get the right answer. When he did, there was a delicious buzz of exhilaration. But even if he didn't, the soaking up of a new piece of knowledge was deeply satisfying, because he knew there would be a time in the future when he would be able to use that new knowledge. Ultimately, though, he was just a kid doing something he loved, and that was the best feeling in the world.

The other reason Marsham loved quiz shows so much was because Mum and Dad both had busy jobs. Mum was an architect. She had long, wavy hair, a kind face and always wore bright clothes. Dad worked in IT.

He *didn't* wear bright clothes, was bald and had quite a serious face. Because they both worked so much, sitting around the television with them, and Gran, was special; it was family time that they all enjoyed. And if he was really honest with himself, part of him liked basking in his family's amazement. Genius, though? He wasn't too sure about that.

"How do you do it?" asked Mum, Dad or Gran at least once every time they watched a show together.

Marsham had three responses. Sometimes he just shrugged. Other times he said, "It must be because I'm really an alien with a super brain." And occasionally he would say, "I guess I'm just good at learning things and remembering them."

That last answer was probably closest to the truth (the second certainly wasn't!), but it was dangerous because it usually led to Mum or Dad asking, "But then why...?" and that was when things got complicated, because of what had happened a year ago...

***

One year ago

"Come on, Marsham!" shouted Mum. "You don't want to be late for the first day at your new school."

Marsham certainly didn't want to be late, but he also didn't want to miss anything from his checklist. He'd brushed his short, black, straight hair, looked in his ears and up his nose for anything that shouldn't be there, cleaned his teeth three times, scrubbed his round, cheeky face until the flannel surrendered, buttoned and unbuttoned his shirt twice, knotted his tie five times (he had to wear a tie!), polished his size eight shoes (he had big feet for his age), and packed and repacked his bag in four different configurations.

"Ready, Mum!" he shouted, checking himself in the mirror one last time.

The mixture of nerves and excitement swilling around inside Marsham was making him want to laugh and cry at the same time. It was an odd feeling that lasted till lunchtime on the first day. He was sitting eating his sandwich on a bench in the school playground with two boys, Adrian and Nainan. They were in his class and the three of them had buddied up.

"Erm, Marsham is quite an unusual name," said Adrian through a mouthful of crisps.

"Yeah, I've never met anyone with that name before," said Nainan.

Marsham had faced this question many times and was expecting it. "Yes, it is an unusual name. It was the name of an old school friend of my father's and he's always liked it," he said, hoping he sounded casual but informative.

"I like it," said Adrian.

"Me too," said Nainan.

And somehow, in that moment, Marsham knew he'd made two good friends. The earlier feelings of nervousness began to seep out of him and were replaced by relief and curiosity, which, added to the excitement that was still there, made him want to laugh, explore and also sleep, which was another odd combination.

Over the rest of the week, Marsham discovered that Adrian and Nainan loved computer games just like he did. He also found out that Adrian loved football and military history, and Nainan was into cars and graphic novels.

They looked quite an odd trio. Adrian was tall and thin, with messy hair and a long face and big ears that made him look a bit like a beagle. Nainan, on the other hand, was quite broad and thick-set, with glasses and a face that made Marsham think he looked like a newsreader on television.

Most importantly, though, the three of them just clicked, and on the Thursday of that week, Marsham got the chance to show them his hidden talent.

"Hey, have you seen *The Q&A Kids?*" said Nainan.

Marsham grinned widely. He knew it well. It was

his favourite quizzing channel on YouTube, where two brothers, Paul (who was sixteen) and Marc (twelve), were asked and challenged to answer anything and everything! They also set their subscribers – all twenty-five million of them – a quiz.

"Yes, I know it," said Marsham.

"Let's do the quiz they set," said Adrian. "Bet I can get all ten questions right."

"You're on," said Nainan, pulling out his mobile.

Marsham said nothing.

The theme of the quiz in the latest episode was space, and as they gave out the answers, both Adrian and Nainan seemed confident.

"I got seven right!" said Nainan. "Beat that."

"Easy," said Adrian. "I got eight. Marsh, do you want to congratulate me now?"

"Yes," said Marsham. "Congratulations on coming second."

"No way!" said Adrian, but when Marsham showed him and Nainan the piece of paper he'd written the answers on – he'd got ten out of ten – his new friends were blown away.

"Wow," said Nainan. "Are you some sort of space freak?"

"Not really," said Marsham. "I just love quizzes."

"Cool," said Adrian. "But I'm still going to beat you next time."

The three of them laughed, and Marsham could almost sense the last of his nerves trickling away to be replaced by a feeling that he was going to be pretty happy at his new school.

On the following Monday, that all went very wrong.

"One last thing," said Ms Potter, the headteacher, at assembly that morning. She was a short woman with thick, fair hair and a face that said *I'm a reasonable person, but don't cross me.* "It seems we have welcomed a very bright new pupil to the school this year, Marsham Lucas. Where are you, Marsham?"

Marsham shyly raised his hand.

"Ah, there you are," said Ms Potter. "Your form teacher, Mr Bradley, tells me that not only did you get top marks on a maths test last week, you also got an A+ in your history essay. That's what we like here at Aylestone Vale. A great start, keep it up. Congratulations."

Ms Potter started applauding enthusiastically, which led to a dribble of applause from the rest of the school. Marsham knew he should have felt proud, but instead he had a strong sense that it might have been better if Ms Potter hadn't told the entire school how well he had done.

At lunchtime that day, he learnt why.

"Oi, Martian, or whatever your name is," said an older boy with slicked-back hair and non-regulation shoes.

The group of people with him laughed.

"If you're so clever, what's my middle name?"

Marsham's heart started racing and he could feel little beads of sweat popping out all over his body. He was with Adrian and Nainan and he could sense their discomfort as well.

"I... I don't know," he said, looking at the boy. "How could I possibly know?"

"You don't know?" said the boy meanly. "I thought you were a *genius*. Not much of a teacher's pet, are you? More of a teacher's little slug. Yeah, that's what you are! A *slug*."

He then started pretending to be a slug by making sucking and slurping noises with his mouth. The group around him, which had now grown, all started laughing and copying him.

"Don't listen to them," said

Adrian, but the damage had been done.

Marsham walked away feeling just one thing now: like he wanted to cry. Tears welled up in his eyes as he looked down, desperately hoping no one would see. Last week he'd loved showing his new friends how clever he was, and they had been impressed; if anything, they had liked him *more* because of it. Now people were being horrible to him about it, and he felt miserable and scared.

The rest of that week things only got worse. Lots of people made the slug noise when he walked past, and he was called Swotty McSwotface, Smarty Farty Pants, Clever Clot and other names.

By the end of the week, Marsham had made a decision. If that's what he got for being clever at school, then he wasn't going to be clever any more. From then on he made sure to only get average marks in all his tests and essays.

And his plan worked. A week later, people had forgotten all about him, and he hadn't been called any names or heard the slug noise since.

***

For a whole year Marsham had carried on being an average student, while at home he was still answering quiz show questions as if it were the easiest thing in the world. Mum and Dad couldn't understand why his school reports were so mediocre, so family quiz nights often led to The Question: "But then why aren't you top of the class at school?".

Then Marsham would give one of his three answers, and, for the past year, that had been that. But, unknown to Marsham, it was all about to change.

CHAPTER 2

The following week, Mum and Dad were working late, so only Marsham and Gran were watching *Mastermind*.

In actual fact, Marsham wasn't sure if Gran *was* watching the show; she seemed to be lost in her own world, no doubt thinking about her next "hobby". Gran had had many hobbies over the years, everything from pottery to juggling to cosplay. Some lasted a few months, some a few weeks and some just a day (feng shui – Mum and Dad had returned home to discover that every single thing in the front room had been rearranged. They weren't happy about it, even though they felt oddly relaxed).

So Marsham was quite surprised when this happened:

"In order to raise awareness of the survival of the world's ecosystems," said the host on the television, "the United Nations have designated May 20th as world *what* day?"

"Bee!" said Gran.

"Wow, Gran," said Marsham. "I'm impressed. How did you know that?"

"Bee! Bee!" shouted Gran.

"I don't think he'll be able to hear you, no matter how loudly you shout, Gran," said Marsham.

"No, there's a bee above your head!" screeched Gran.

Marsham froze. He'd been stung once before, and it wasn't nice. He looked up and, sure enough, crawling down the wall towards him, was a bee.

In situations like this there are traditionally two things you can do: remain calm, or panic. Marsham chose the latter, and jumped up, waving and flapping his arms about like a deranged windmill. Unfortunately, in doing so he knocked over his orange juice, Gran's chamomile tea and a large plant pot (containing a large plant). It resembled a disaster scene,

but, on the plus side, the bee did fly away.

The mess was cleared up before Mum and Dad came home, just in case they thought Gran had decided to try feng shui again, but that incident definitely made an impression on Gran: a few days later, she came into his room wearing a beekeeper's outfit.

"Gran? Is that you?" asked Marsham.

"Of course it's me," said Gran. "Can't you tell?"

"Not really. Not with that hat and veil on," said Marsham.

Gran tutted and took it off. "Is that better? Good. I've decided to keep bees because you need to learn not to be so scared of them … and also because we need to save the world's ecosytems. I'm getting my first hive tomorrow. But I didn't actually come in here to talk about that. Can I sit down?"

Marsham's room was quite small. He had a single bed, a desk and a chair, a set of drawers, a bookshelf, a cupboard and a beanbag in the corner. There were some music and computer game posters on the wall, some magazines on the floor, and a few board games and toys in a box by the bed. Gran didn't wait for him to answer and headed for the bed.

"Yes, of course," said Marsham. "But be careful of—"

"Miaaaooowwwww!" miaowed Tonks, who, up

until that point, had been having a lovely kip on the bed. Gran had rather ruined that by nearly sitting on him, making him jump up and dive off the bed. Now he was on the floor, looking at her as if to say, "I'll get you back for that!"

"So," said Gran, "you know there's a new series of that show you really like coming up, *Britain's Smartest Kid*?"

"Yes, I do," said Marsham, trying to sound casual. It was his favourite of all the quiz shows. He'd watched every series since he was five.

"They said on the television that this series is going to be the best yet, with loads of surprises."

"I know," said Marsham. "I can't wait to watch it!"

"Oh, I don't think you should watch it," said Gran.

"Why not?" asked Marsham.

"I think you should be *in it*," she said.

An unpleasant flutter cascaded through Marsham's body. This could be tricky. "Me?" he said, laughing. "They wouldn't want me. The kids on it are much cleverer; I wouldn't stand a chance."

"Don't be silly," said Gran. "You'd be wonderful! And anyway, I've been reading about it. You have to go through a selection process before you get to be on the show. You'd find out then if you were good enough, which you are."

That unpleasant flutter Marsham had felt was now heading towards full-blown panic. He had to think quickly. "Maybe," he said. "But the truth is, Gran, some of the kids who have been on that show become really famous. They're, like, celebrities, and then the newspapers do all sorts of stories on them and reporters follow them around. They found out that one girl from the series three years ago was a distant relative of the queen. She had paparazzi camping outside her house and following her around everywhere. It was awful for her."

"But you're not related to the queen," said Gran.

"No, but you know what I mean," said Marsham. "I'm happy just being famous in our family. That's all."

"I see," said Gran. "Hmm, yes, but what if. . .?"

"What?" said Marsham, a little rudely.

"Oh, nothing, just a thought," said Gran, rising from the bed. "Well, you can't blame me for trying. See you later."

After Gran left, Marsham sat at his desk thinking for a long time. He felt unsettled, but also something else that he couldn't quite put his finger on, as if she'd planted a seed in him that could either grow or wither away.

In truth, he didn't really mind the thought of being famous. It actually might be quite fun, and being on the show, if he got on it, would be amazing. *Then again*, he thought, *if the kids at school saw me, which they definitely would, that could lead to all sorts of problems.*

He could always just go along and see how he did at the selection process, though.

No, too risky, he thought. *Things have been fine for the past year. Why rock the boat now? I'm not doing it.*

CHAPTER 3

"I got to the dragon queen's lair last night," said Nainan, "but she has giant robot cockroaches protecting her, and they are really tough to get past."

It was the next day and Marsham was at school talking to his friends about *Dragon Queen Dynasty 5*, the latest computer game they were all into. It was morning break and they were under a tree they had christened the Tree of MAN, which stood for Marsham, Adrian and Nainan. The school had a lot of outdoor areas, so as well as a main playground, there were plenty of nooks and crannies, along with grassy areas with trees, and this quiet, fairly secluded corner was very much their patch.

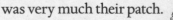

"I can't get past the fire-breathing centipedes," moaned Adrian. "I know I could do it if I got the laser catapult, though."

"You need five hundred galactic runes for that," chipped in Marsham. "And if you don't fire it correctly, it blows up and destroys your shield armour. You can't cope with that sort of weapon; leave it to the big boys."

"Hey, I'll have you know I'm almost five-foot-nine!" cried Adrian.

The three of them laughed. Over the past year their friendship had really grown and now they were tight as could be. Marsham had other friends, but Ade and Nain were definitely his crew.

"The new single from Steve and Eve dropped last night," said Nainan. "It's great. Have you heard it?"

"Not yet," said Adrian. "Aren't they the twins who were on *Britain's Smartest Kid* a couple of years back?"

"Yeah," said Nainan. "Hey, did you see the trailer for the new series? It's going to be brilliant."

"Can't wait!" said Marsham.

"Neither can I," said Adrian.

They fell silent for a moment. It was a little awkward; it felt to Marsham as if his friends were going to say something, but they didn't, and then they were quite literally saved by the bell.

The show didn't come up again at lunchtime, but that seed which Gran had planted, the one Marsham thought he'd got rid of, had now taken root again. It was nothing more than a small itch really, but it was unsettling and distracting, as if it was reaching into a part of Marsham that he didn't quite understand and didn't want to understand because that could make things difficult.

All afternoon he did his best to push the seed away and by early evening he felt he had pretty much succeeded, which of course was precisely the moment that Gran decided to return to his room. She wasn't wearing her beekeeping outfit this time, but a small bee was perched on her shoulder, just below her head of grey, candyfloss hair. Marsham felt himself about to panic.

"Don't worry about Bella, she's very friendly," said Gran. "She's a worker bee from my hive that was delivered this afternoon."

Marsham managed a mini-smile, but made sure to keep Bella in his sights. One false move from her and he would be out of the door in a flash.

Tonks was on the bed again, and he opened an eye, but Gran stayed where she was this time.

"I've been thinking," she said. "I'm sure you're

going to be famous one day, probably for inventing a time machine or a backscratcher that knows exactly where to scratch or something, but I can see why you wouldn't want to be famous right now."

"A backscratcher that knows exactly where to scratch?" said Marsham.

"Ooh, yes, it's so annoying trying to get exactly the right spot," said Gran. "It would be so much better if it just knew where to go. Anyway, the thing is, you might not want to be famous now, but what about if *you* weren't *you*?"

Marsham looked at Gran. Even by her standards, this seemed very odd. "Sorry, Gran," he said. "How can I not be me?"

"If you were someone else," said Gran, matter-of-factly.

"Riiiggght," said Marsham. "But I'm not someone else. I'm me."

"I know that. Dearie me, Bella, what *are* we going to do with this one?" said Gran. "What I'm suggesting is that you *disguise yourself* as someone else, then you wouldn't be you, and *you* wouldn't get famous. So you could enter *Britain's Smartest Kid*. As not you."

"Sorry, Gran," said Marsham. "Let me get this straight. You're suggesting I put on a disguise and enter

Britain's Smartest Kid with a different name?"

"By George, I think he's got it, Bella," said Gran. "And then, when the show is over, the disguised you can just disappear. It'll be a great mystery that only you and I will know the answer to. Oh, and my friend Ethel."

"Ethel?" asked Marsham, his brain spinning.

"Oh, yes, we're definitely going to need Ethel," said Gran.

CHAPTER 4

"Gran, do you really think that if I put on some glasses and maybe change the colour of my hair, no one will recognize me?" asked Marsham as he and Gran walked to Ethel's house.

Marsham didn't quite know why he had agreed to go there with Gran. She wasn't overly pushy or forceful; rather, she was the sort of person who just assumed you would do as she said. So she'd made all the arrangements and told Marsham they were expected at Ethel's on Saturday morning. It was a done deal. Of course he could have refused, but he was actually quite intrigued. At the very least, it would make a funny story to tell Adrian and Nainan at school on Monday.

"Here we are," said Gran as they approached the small cottage where Ethel lived. She'd completely ignored Marsham's question.

Gran rang the doorbell and shouted, "Coo-ee, Ethel dear, we're here!"

A short while later the door opened and a woman who, at first glance, looked much like Gran, ushered them in.

"Come on, come on," said Ethel. "The kettle's on and I've got some lovely teacakes from the supermarket."

Once they were inside, Marsham could tell that Ethel was a little younger and taller than Gran, with thicker hair. She was also wearing quite a lot of make-up and actually, thought Marsham, looked quite glamorous, as if she was going somewhere special, rather than just having a friend and her grandson round.

The cottage was very quaint and full of just the sort of trinkets Marsham would have expected an old lady to have: little china animals, small silver jugs and thimbles. There were also photos of people who Marsham presumed were Ethel's family and quite a few pictures of flowers.

"Ooh, you've got wonderful skin," said Ethel. "We can do a lot with that. Now come and sit down."

Ethel made a cup of tea for her and Gran, and put a glass of milk in front of Marsham, along with a plate of the aforementioned teacakes, which he didn't think looked all that lovely.

"Thank you for the photos, Elsie, they were very

helpful," said Ethel. "Based on them, I've come up with a look that I think will work well."

Ethel went over to a drawer and pulled out a folder from which she took a piece of paper. She laid it on the table.

Marsham looked at the drawing in front of him. It was of a boy with full, bushy brown hair, lots of freckles, green eyes, prominent eyebrows and quite a big pointy nose.

"Who's this?" he said.

"That's the you that's not you," said Gran, as if she was saying the most obvious thing in the world. "The you in disguise."

Marsham looked at Gran and then at Ethel. The two of them were smiling sweetly, which he found a little unnerving. He also felt somewhat uncomfortable. If this was a joke, Gran was taking it quite far. If it wasn't, perhaps she wasn't very well.

"But that person looks nothing like me," said Marsham. "I can't just become someone completely different. Unless you've got some sort of magic potion?"

Marsham was joking, and hoped it might raise a smile from his two older companions, but if anything it had the opposite effect and their smiley faces turned quite serious.

"Ethel," said Gran. "I think we're going to have to show him *the room*."

"I thought we might," said Ethel. "Good job I tidied it up last week. Come on."

Ethel and Gran stood up and began making their way upstairs. Once again it was just assumed that Marsham would go along, which he did, but he was now getting irritated by all this nonsense. He had a ton of homework to do, and there was a new daytime quiz show on at two o'clock that he wanted to watch.

Nonetheless, he traipsed up behind Gran and Ethel until the three of them came to a room on the first floor, next to a bathroom.

"Ready?" said Ethel.

"Erm, yes," said Marsham.

Ethel opened the door. "After you," she said.

Marsham walked in, but it was too dark to see anything.

"The light's on the left," said Ethel.

Marsham found it and switched it on. It took his eyes a moment to adjust, but then they widened; his jaw dropped and his brain went into overdrive. The entire room was a treasure trove of film posters, props, scripts, photographs and letters.

There were posters from some of the biggest films

of all time: *Star Wars*, *Alien*, *Mad Max*, *Back to the Future*, *Jurassic Park* and one called *The Thing with Two Heads*.

There were framed photos of a woman who looked a lot like a young Ethel with some very big movie stars and directors. Marsham was sure one of them was Steven Spielberg.

There were also framed letters of thanks from the likes of Harrison Ford, Sigourney Weaver, Michael J Fox,

Tom Cruise and Jane Fonda.

Most impressive, though, were the props. Marsham didn't recognize them all, but there was a lightsaber, a hoverboard and a very scary-looking alien.

There were also stacks of wigs and a variety of noses, fingers, toes, ears and other body parts, and over in the corner was a mirror surrounded by light bulbs.

For some reason, the first thing Marsham thought was: *I wonder what it was like in here* before *Ethel tidied up.*

"Wow!" said Marsham. "What *is* all this?"

"Oh, these are just a few things I picked up over the years," said Ethel nonchalantly.

"Things you bought?" said Marsham.

"Not exactly," said Ethel.

"Oh, for goodness' sake," said Gran. "Come here, Marsham."

Marsham followed Gran to one of the film posters. At the bottom there were the names of the people who had made the film: the director, the producers, the cinematographer and many others.

"Have a read through that," said Gran.

Marsham scanned the text. There were a lot of names, but eventually he came to "Head of Make-Up". By that it said *Ethel Salsby*.

"Ethel Salsby," said Marsham tentatively. "Is... Is that you, Ethel?"

"I suppose it might be, yes," said Ethel.

"So you worked on all these films?" said Marsham.

"Yes, I did," said Ethel. "And quite a few more. Sci-fi

films were sort of my speciality, but I did others as well."

"Oh, she didn't just work on them," said Gran. "She helped make them the huge spectaculars that they were. Ethel's a genius. She could turn you into an alien if you like. Or a monster, a giant squid, or a robot. She could make it look like your face has been cut in half, your hair is alive, or your ears are speaking. So I don't think it'll be too much trouble turning you into a boy who is not you. Now, sit down in front of that mirror and let her get on with it while I make a fresh pot of tea."

Marsham didn't quite know what to say. He was blown away. Could it be that Gran's plan just might work? He felt excited, but also something else: guilty. He knew people of Gran's age must have had jobs and done things when they were younger, but he'd never really thought about it. To him they were just . . . old.

"Sorry, Ethel," said Marsham. "I didn't know. When Gran said. . ."

"Oh, don't you worry," said Ethel. "I could tell you thought this was a waste of time earlier, but why wouldn't you? You didn't know."

"You could tell that?" said Marsham.

"Oh, yes," said Ethel. "I'm good like that. I remember when I first worked with Meryl Streep.

Everyone thought she was so relaxed and laid back, but I could tell she was covering up her nerves. Now, do as your gran says and sit down. This won't be my biggest job, but it'll still take a while."

Marsham felt a little as if he'd been ambushed, but in a good way. He loved the *Star Wars* films. His dad had shown him the early ones when he was six, and he must have watched each of them at least ten times.

He sat in the chair facing away from the mirror and, over the next hour, as Ethel prodded, scraped, pulled, washed, rinsed and stuck things to him, she told him all about the adventures she'd had with some of the world's biggest stars, including the time she'd raced Eddie Murphy and Sylvester Stallone down some rapids in a canoe, and beaten them!

It felt strange having things done to his face, especially when it involved sticking things to it, like when she fitted the prosthetic nose, but Ethel's stories took his mind off all that.

"There," she said just after she'd carefully put some contact lenses in Marsham's eyes. "What do you think, Elsie?"

"Ooh, yes, Ethel, very good," said Gran, who had been watching proceedings and who, for once in her life, had stayed pretty quiet. "You definitely don't look like you now, Marsham."

"Ready?" said Ethel.

A thrilling jolt of anticipation went through him. It was like the moment just before he opened a big birthday present.

"Yes," he said.

Ethel swung the chair round and Marsham looked in the mirror. There in front of him was the boy in the picture he'd seen earlier. It was uncanny! It was identical! Marsham was blown away. Ethel really was a

genius. He was so impressed. This was his secret disguise, and it almost felt like a superpower. He could do anything as this person and no one would know, apart from Gran and Ethel. It felt delicious and exhilarating.

"Well, what do you think?" said Gran.

"Awesome!" said Marsham.

"Great," said Ethel. "And how does it feel?"

"A bit odd, to be honest," said Marsham. "The wig is quite tight, and the nose feels heavy, but I'm sure I'll get used to it."

"You're going to have to," said Ethel. "The trick is to try not to feel too self-conscious, and just relax. You're not usually aware of your nose or your hair, so do your best not to think about them."

"Right," said Marsham.

The room fell silent. It wasn't awkward, but there was definitely an elephant around, and Marsham knew what it was.

His mind started racing and his heart started beating.

Looking like this, nobody would know who I was. I really could enter the show. I'd be there, in the studio, facing questions for real, not just in my house. I might even win! But what if the other kids on the show really were much cleverer than me? And what if someone at school found out? And who knows: the nose could fall off in the middle of a round. It feels risky, it feels dangerous, it feels terrifying. . . It feels like the most exciting opportunity I've ever had.

The him who was not him, but was still him, looked at Gran and Ethel.

"I'll do it!" he said.

CHAPTER 5

"Gran?" said Marsham.

He was sitting at his desk with Tonks, who was annoyingly lying on top of the computer keyboard. Gran, who had come in to discuss Marsham's secret new identity, was sitting on the bed.

"Yes," said Gran, who thankfully hadn't brought any bee buddies along this time.

"Why does Ethel keep her film stuff in that room?" asked Marsham. "Why isn't it downstairs, where everyone can see it?"

"Ah, well, you see, Ethel is a bit like you," said Gran. "She doesn't like the idea of being famous either, and, even though it's not quite the same, she prefers keeping that part of her life private now. It's tiring, answering lots of questions, and people can be quite intrusive. She doesn't want every person who delivers something to her house to know all about her life."

"I guess not," said Marsham.

"She's quite shy, really," continued Gran. "But she still loves films and film stars. She's cuckoo about all celebrities, in fact. At the moment she's in love with that Ben Shephard, and if Idris Elba came into the room, she'd go weak at the knees." Gran giggled at the thought. "Right, come on," she continued. "Let's go through your story once more before we fill in the application form."

"OK," said Marsham. "My name is Daniel Phillips. I'm homeschooled by my parents, who are explorers. They're currently away in the Ecuadorian cloud forests searching for a new species of toadstool, which is why you have taken over for the time being."

"Good," said Gran, but then she paused. "So you're absolutely sure you don't want to tell Mum and Dad about this just yet?"

Marsham had thought about this a lot. On a simple level, the fewer people who knew the truth, the better; but it *wasn't* that simple. He didn't think Mum and Dad would buy his not-wanting-to-be-famous story as easily as Gran did. They would ask why he couldn't just enter as himself, and then things would get tricky. They would also probably think being disguised was too dangerous – what if the show found out? Could he go to prison? (Marsham had actually worried about this a bit himself.) No, it was better to keep this just between himself, Gran and Ethel.

"Yes, absolutely sure," said Marsham. "So, Daniel's birthday is January 31st, he was born in Winchester, his email is Danielpquizmaster@syrinx.com and he now lives at 28 Tancry Road in London."

"That's right, that's Ethel's address," said Gran.

"Daniel has extremely good SATs scores, his IQ is 130, and he has won prizes for quizzes in magazines, on the radio, and he has helped his dad's pub quiz team to victory many times. I'm also going to say he likes military history and graphic novels; I can borrow some stuff from Adrian and Nainan. And also calligraphy, along with some of the things I really like as well. Oh, and he has a cat called Piffle."

"Excellent," said Gran. "Let's hope that's enough to get you a place in the selection process. Go on, fill in the form, no time like the present."

Marsham turned back to his computer.

"Sorry, Tonks," he said. He gently pushed Tonks, who reluctantly gave up his spot on the keyboard.

Marsham pulled up the show's website. There was a link that read, "Do you want to be on the show?" A big part of him was screaming, YES! But he was still nervous about it. There were a lot of *what if* questions going round his head. It was frustrating as he liked questions with *definite* answers: he was good at those. The answers to these questions were anyone's guess. But then one particular *what if* question came to the fore.

What if I don't do this, will I regret it?

Once again the answer was a resounding YES.

Twenty minutes later, he was faced with another link to click on: "Send".

"Come on, then, what are you waiting for?" said Gran, who had been flicking through one of Marsham's gaming magazines. "Just press it!"

To Marsham though, it was huge. He'd spent the last year keeping his head down, not drawing any attention to himself. Despite the fact that he'd be in disguise, it still felt massively weird and challenging. It was a step into the unknown, and that is always frightening.

Marsham was grappling with his indecision when suddenly Tonks jumped back up on to the desk and put her paw on the computer mouse.

"Whooosh!" went the computer.

For a moment Marsham was horrified, but then he started laughing. Tonks had made the decision for him, and it was definitely the right one.

"Did you see the goal Lukaku scored last night?" enthused Adrian. "He beat three players and then back-heeled it past the keeper. Amazing!"

"I saw a couple of kids trying that in the playground this morning," said Marsham.

"Yeah, and now they're in the school nurse's office with sprained ankles," said Nainan.

The three of them chuckled. They were eating lunch in the school canteen: a big, bland functional room about as far from the Great Hall in Hogwarts as you could imagine, but then Aylestone Vale was just an average comprehensive and not a magical school for wizards.

"Did you do anything else over the weekend?" asked Nainan.

"Nah," said Adrian. "It was a pretty lame one."

"Yeah," agreed Marsham. "Though that new quiz show wasn't too bad."

Marsham hoped he'd sounded chill and matter-of-fact, because the truth was, he was bursting to tell his friends about Ethel's room, Daniel Phillips and entering the show. He wanted to shout it from the rooftops so that everyone in the country could hear, and some people in France as well. He knew, though, that it was just a reaction to the fact that he couldn't tell anyone, not even his closest mates. But he was still surprised at how difficult it already was. He couldn't crumble at this early stage. *If* he got on to the show, Adrian, Nainan and pretty much everyone else in his school would be talking about it. That would make things a lot tougher than they were now.

However, that "if" was pretty big. Marsham knew the show would probably have thousands of applications that would take a long time to sift through, but every day that went by without him – or rather, Daniel Phillips – hearing back, was agony. It made Marsham realize just how much he wanted this. It was complicated, though. This was an amazing chance to show everyone who he was and just what he could do, without actually showing anyone who he was and what he could do.

As the days went by, he worked on Daniel Phillips. He practised making his voice sound different, a little lower and fuller, and he read online articles about military history, as well as teaching himself calligraphy.

It was enjoyable, but he was doing it against a backdrop of nervous impatience, and at times it toppled over into hopelessness and he started to think that it was all a waste of time.

Ten days after he'd sent off the application, he was walking home from school when an email popped up in Daniel Phillips's inbox. The subject was *Britain's Smartest Kid*.

Marsham's heart almost flew out of his mouth. He stopped and let out a yelp, which startled two women nearby and made a pigeon fly off. Holding his phone tightly, as if letting go of it would mean losing the email, he took off and ran the rest of the way home.

"Gran! Gran!" he shouted breathlessly as he almost fell through the front door.

"Oh, Marsham, you frightened the life out of me."

It was Mum. Marsham had expected her to be working in the attic room that had recently been converted into a home office which she shared with Dad.

"Sorry, Mum," he said. The wind had been well and truly taken out of his sails, and he was concerned that Mum might ask why he was so keen to see Gran, which was precisely what she did.

"Gran's having a nap upstairs, I think," said Mum. "Why do you want to see her so badly?"

"Oh, it's nothing," he said. "I just found out something really interesting about bees, erm, and also, erm, my Geography teacher, Ms Jubb, wants to buy some honey from Gran. Isn't that great?"

"Yes, I suppose so," said Mum a little suspiciously.

"I know it's not really, really big news," said Marsham. "But I was just being silly when I came in, you know, pretending it was more important than it really is. I thought Gran might find it funny."

"I'm sure she would have," said Mum. "But she might also have jumped out of her skin like I did, so maybe think of something else Gran might find funny next time. She might be awake now. Why don't you go and knock . . . *gently*?"

"I will, thanks, Mum, sorry," said Marsham as he made his way up the stairs. He still wanted to charge up and burst into Gran's room, but he took his time and knocked softly when he came to the door.

"I'm up, come in," said Gran.

"Gran!" hissed Marsham, entering the room – he was whispering, but loudly – "I got an email!"

"Oh, that's nice, dear," said Gran. "I got one earlier from a company offering me a stairlift. Fifty per cent off. Sounds like a bargain."

"No, Gran!" said Marsham. "I don't mean any old

email, I mean, I got one from the show! Well, I didn't. Daniel did."

"Crikey!" said Gran. "That is exciting! What does it say?"

"I haven't opened it yet," said Marsham.

"Well, what are you waiting for?" urged Gran. "Let's take a look!"

Marsham nodded and braced himself. His whole body suddenly felt as if it was pulsating. He hadn't ever known excitement like this: full of hope and expectation, but also danger and fear of disappointment.

"OK, here goes," he said.

He got the email up on his phone and opened it.

Congratulations! Your application to be considered as a contestant on the new series of *Britain's Smartest Kid* has been approved. We look forward to seeing you for the selection interview on Saturday October 20th.

There followed details of the time and place and other bits of information about the interview, but Marsham didn't read them.

"Yeessss!" he shouted, dancing around Gran's room. "I'm on the show! I mean, Daniel is . . . on the selection show . . . I mean interview."

"Well done, Marsham," said Gran. "I knew they wouldn't turn you down. They know a brilliantly clever boy when they see one, and soon you'll be the champion!"

"Easy, Gran," said Marsham, his heart still racing. "It's only the selection interview; I've got to get through that first."

"You will," said Gran.

"I hope so," said Marsham. "Oh, I can't wait to tell Nainan and Adrian about thi—"

Marsham stopped. The news was great, but it was clearly going to be difficult not telling anyone about getting to the selection interview. If he actually made it on the show, keeping it secret was going to be like trying to keep a very wild cat in a very small bag.

CHAPTER 6

"Just off to that over-sixties Beekeepers' Conference, Melissa!" Gran shouted up the stairs. "Marsham's coming with, to help carry my smoker and my hat and veil!"

"Bit of an early start, isn't it, Mum?!" came Marsham's mum's voice from upstairs. "It's only seven."

"Well, you know what they say," shouted Gran. "The early bee catches the worm! Bye!"

"Erm, OK," said Melissa, who, even though she was well used to Gran's idiosyncrasies, still sounded a little confused. "Have a good time!"

"We will," said Gran. "Don't work too hard!"

She turned to Marsham, who was waiting by the front door with a backpack. "Let's go," she whispered.

The two of them left the house and walked to the

bus stop. Twenty minutes later they were at Ethel's cottage. Gran rang the doorbell.

"Ooh, hello Elsie, hello Marsham," said Ethel from an upstairs window. "I'll be right down."

Five minutes later, Marsham was back in *the room*, in front of the mirror. It was the day of the selection interview. Almost three weeks had passed agonizingly slowly since the email had been sent. It hadn't helped that trailers for the new series of *Britain's Smartest Kid*, featuring the host, Selina Constantin, had been appearing more frequently on television.

Selina had hosted the show for the past ten years, in which time she'd been christened "The Nation's Headmistress". To be fair, she was quite a glamorous headmistress, but still, not many people would dare mess with her. She was a big woman, large all over, and that included her personality. She gave off an air of confidence, the sort of person who thinks they are always right, and, infuriatingly, usually are.

The trailer that most people were talking about featured Selina saying, "We've already found Britain's smartest kid," after which the camera cut to a young goat walking along a narrow wall. It then cut back to Selina, who said, "But despite being extremely smart, I don't think she could answer any of my questions.

Don't worry, though, when the new series starts, we'll have plenty of kids who can, along with plenty of surprises. That's the new series of *Britain's Smartest Kid*, coming soon."

Nainan had particularly liked it and kept playing it on his phone whenever he got the chance. Marsham decided the best tactic would be to go overboard, so laughed heartily every time, sharing their excitement.

"Right, Marsham, love," said Ethel. "Are you ready for this?"

"Ready as I'll ever be," said Marsham.

"Well, I never," said Ethel. "That's exactly what Jack Nicholson said to me the first time I worked with him. Now just relax and let me do my *thang*, as you young people say these days."

"Wow, you worked with Jack Nicholson?" said Marsham.

"Four times, I think," said Ethel. "Charming man. Now, keep still and be quiet; we need to leave in an hour, and if you keep yabbering away I'll never get it done."

Marsham did as he was told and fifty minutes later – having done it once, it was a little easier for Ethel this time – he had disappeared and Daniel had taken his place.

"Amazing," said Marsham, looking at himself. He

was as enthralled as he had been last time, only now he would be trying out his disguise in public, which felt wickedly exhilarating.

"Now then," said Ethel, "you need to know a few things about wearing prosthetics. You have to keep as cool as possible. Heat and sweat can cause big problems."

Ethel opened a drawer in her dressing table and took out a small, hand-held fan.

"This is your best friend. I'm bringing three, along with extra batteries. The lights in TV studios can make things very hot, so we need to cool you down whenever we can."

"Got it," said Marsham.

"Also, itchiness," went on Ethel. "I've tried to apply everything as smoothly as possible using the best products, but, as the day goes on, you will get itchy. Try, try, try not to scratch. If it becomes unbearable, I can put some talc on a powder puff and manipulate the area as best I can."

"Yup," said Marsham.

"I'm also bringing my suitcase with," said Ethel, gesturing to possibly the biggest suitcase Marsham had ever seen.

"Are you going on holiday after the interview?" said Marsham.

"Yes and no," said Ethel. "It contains all my bits: spares, adhesive, cotton buds, make-up, brushes, you know. It might seem odd bringing it along, so I'm going to say that I'm heading straight to the airport after the interview."

"Ooh, lovely," said Gran. "Where will you say you're going?"

"I thought Majorca," said Ethel. "It's lovely at this time of year. Now, your wig is fitted securely so shouldn't be a problem, but don't put any undue pressure or tension on it. If you can't answer a question, don't tear your hair out, if you get my meaning. It's a quiz show, though, so I can't imagine you'll be moving about all that much."

"Roger that," said Marsham, who was listening attentively.

"Similarly, your contact lenses should be fine, but avoid rubbing your eyes. And if they are irritating you, I've got some drops in the suitcase."

"Gotcha," said Marsham. "Thank you, Ethel."

"Yes, thank you, Ethel," chimed in Gran. "Right. Time to head to the TV studio! Ready . . . Daniel?"

"I'm ready," said Marsham, in the voice he'd been practising for Daniel.

"Excellent," said Gran. "And you can tell Marsham

all about it when you get home."

"Oh, he'll be the first to know," said Marsham. "Let's do this."

PART 2

SELECTION

CHAPTER 7

"Why is my Cassandra by a *window*? It's well known that the sun's rays can cause mental distress!"

"No, Mahendra, the chemical formula for glucose is not $C_3H_8O_3$! That's glycerol, obviously! Glucose is $C_6O_{12}O_6$!"

"Is there somewhere Bertie can go to meditate? He can't do anything unless he's meditated for forty-five minutes."

"Will there be toilet breaks? Jiaying simply won't be able to concentrate unless she knows she can go to the toilet!"

Marsham, Gran and Ethel were in the TV studio building: a large, nondescript brick construction behind some car showrooms. They had just walked into a room about the size of a school gym. There were chairs all around the sides and a big "Registration" sign at the end, under which was a row of tables with people seated behind them. They'd been told to go there by someone at reception, which was a short walk away. (Ethel had left her suitcase there.)

Within approximately five seconds of entering the room, they felt as if they were in a parallel universe where parents thought that nothing was good enough or safe enough or clean enough or anything enough for their children and made sure that anyone and everyone knew about it in no uncertain terms. Or rather, terms that were loud, screechy and rude.

And the objects of these sustained attacks were the staff of *Britain's Smartest Kid*, who were doing their best to reassure parents that their delicate offspring would be fine and were in the best possible hands. For the most part, their message wasn't getting through.

To make matters worse, there was plenty of gawping and swooning as well, not least from Ethel: Marc from *The Q&A Kids* was there, posing for selfies with his brother, Paul – he was too old to be in the competition, the upper age limit was fourteen; and a famous actor

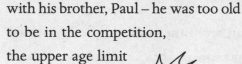

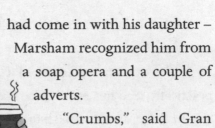

had come in with his daughter –
Marsham recognized him from
a soap opera and a couple of
adverts.

"Crumbs," said Gran
loudly, over the noise. "If
this is what the parents
are like now, whatever will
they be like when the show
actually starts?"

"Well, hopefully there won't
be as many of them – quick! There!"
shouted Marsham, pointing to a space by one of the
tables that a tall woman wearing ferocious spectacles
had just vacated, dragging a young boy along behind
her.

"Good luck!" shouted Ethel. "I'm going to find
somewhere to sit down, my feet are killing me."

They got to the table in the nick of time, beating
a rotund man with a walking stick by a matter of
milliseconds, and stood facing a young woman who
looked as if she had been set upon by a pack of wild and
really quite unreasonable dogs.

"Yes?" she just about managed to force out of
her mouth.

"Hello, I'm, erm, Daniel Phillips, I'm here for my interview."

As the woman looked up, Marsham and Gran could practically read her mind: *These people aren't shouting at me. Are they about to? I don't think so, they seem fairly normal and they're standing politely and waiting. Thank goodness.*

Seconds later, she had rearranged her features and smiled as if she'd just had the quickest makeover of all time.

"Yes, of course!" she said. "And this would be . . . your mother?"

"Oh, my dear, you are funny," said Gran. "I'm his grandmother. His parents are searching Ecuador's cloud forests for a new species of toadstool, so I've brought him along. My friend Ethel is with us."

"How interesting," said the woman. "Now then. . ." She began scanning a list of names on a clipboard. "Yes, here you are, Daniel. You're number 19. Take this and find somewhere to sit down, if you can. You'll be told what to do shortly."

She smiled broadly and handed Marsham a badge with the number 19 on it.

"Thank you," said Marsham, pinning the badge to his shirt. "Come on, Gran."

Marsham and Gran headed off, with the woman

clearly thinking *there are some nice people left in the world,* *hallelujah,* before instantly being accosted by a short woman carrying a huge, overflowing bag who opened with, "What provisions have been made for children with sinusitis? My Sebastian suffers very badly from it, and stress makes it worse! What are you going to do about it?"

They found Ethel and watched as the chaos continued for another few minutes. Marsham focused on the other children. If he made it on to the show, he would be up against some of them. He spotted a girl with her hair in pigtails wearing a blue smock. She was sitting down and reading a book titled *Advanced Economic Theory.* She seemed perfectly at ease with herself and not at all bothered by the chaos all around.

I'll bet she doesn't have to pretend to be not so clever at school, he thought, as a pang of jealousy swept over him. *In fact, I bet none of the other kids here do.*

It was a frustrating thought, but then Marsham spotted a slim, broad-shouldered man with dark hair and a prominent chin stride confidently into the middle of the room.

The man stood on a chair, cleared his throat, and said, "Could I have everyone's attention, please?"

He might as well have been invisible and saying it from

the moon, thought Marsham. If anything, the mayhem only increased.

The man said it a little more loudly.

Then he said it again, and again, and again, each time getting louder and louder, until eventually: "COULD I HAVE EVERYONE'S ATTENTION, PLEASE?"

He must have finally hit the right decibel because, magically, the room quietened down.

"THANK YOU – sorry. Thank you. My name is Khalid, and I am the executive producer of *Britain's Smartest Kid*. It's our pleasure to welcome you all here today, and believe me, we will make sure that all your needs are catered for. The interviews will be starting very soon, but for now could I ask candidates one to twenty, and *only* the candidates, to make their way to the canteen."

The silence lasted about half a second before a barrage of shrieked questions were lobbed at Khalid.

Why does my son have to wait is the canteen dairy free how long will the interviews last is there a washroom near the canteen are you single can I go to the canteen to get a drink if my daughter is number thirty-eight why can't I go with my son when will number sixty-six be called we have a train to catch. . .

"Oh, wow, I'm 19, that's me!" said Marsham. "This is it; it's happening!"

"Calm down, Marsh— *Daniel*," said Gran. "Remember what Ethel said about keeping cool."

"Me?" said Marsham. "I'm as cool as a cucumber at the North Pole. I'm just excited!"

"Of course you are," said Ethel in a way that Marsham knew meant she could tell exactly how he was feeling: about as cool as a cucumber roasting on a bonfire.

CHAPTER 8

To get to the canteen, Marsham walked out of the registration room, back to reception, and then along a corridor going the opposite way. The canteen was at the end. As he made his way there, he was breathing heavily, his mind flipping between thinking it was a stupid idea that he was there, to reassuring himself that he "had this", to wondering if the canteen would have his favourite: turkey-and-pickle sandwiches on rye bread. He could also feel an itch by the side of his prosthetic nose that he really hoped wouldn't get worse.

He got to the door of the canteen and was met by a relaxed-looking man with short hair, stubble and a prominent nose ring.

"Hello, you," the man said, chirpily. "I'm Gavin. How are we today?"

"Erm, *we* are good," said Marsham.

"Awesome," said Gavin. "Now, I see you're number 19, which means you're" – he scanned a tablet he was holding – "Daniel Phillips, right?"

"Absolutely, that's me, I am Daniel Phillips, definitely," said Marsham, instantly asking himself why he hadn't just said *yes*.

"Awesome," said Gavin. "You'll be sitting at table 19 and, as you'll see, our canteen is a little different, but I'm sure you'll work things out. Make sure to get something to eat, but most importantly, have fun."

"Thank you," said Marsham, taking tentative steps into the room.

It didn't take him long to spot the first difference. Over by the serving hatch was a large blackboard displaying the menu. The prices of all the items were listed as complex mathematical problems. So a cheese sandwich was the fourth root of 81 in pounds plus the area of a circle with a radius of 3.5 . . . in pence.

This must be part of the selection process, thought Marsham, and it wasn't long before he spotted another difference: there was a series of questions printed on to the top of each table. He rushed over to table 19 to look at his.

There were nine questions in total:

What is a traditional, flat-bottomed Venetian rowing boat called?

Bees, birds and insects transfer what substance between flowering plants to help them reproduce?

In Shakespeare's *Macbeth*, the characters who say "Double, double toil and trouble; fire burn, and cauldron bubble" are commonly known as the what?

One billionth of a second is called what?

Which British football club has won more European trophies than any other?

Litecoin and Bitcoin are forms of what virtual asset?

What juggling toy consists of an hourglass-shaped object balanced and spun on a string stretched between two sticks?

Stainless steel objects like cutlery do not go rusty because they contain nickel and what other chemical element?

How many days does the Jewish festival Hanukkah last?

There was also a message which read, "Answer all the questions and follow the instructions."

"Yes!" said Marsham, pumping his fist. Just at first glance he knew the answer to question one, and was pretty sure about two as well. He felt a surge of confidence and decided to get something to eat before tackling the table-top quiz.

"Cheese sandwich, please," said Marsham to the man at the serving hatch.

"Certainly," said the man. "How would you like to pay?"

"I only have a five-pound note," said Marsham, handing it over.

"Thank you," said the man. "And how much are you expecting back?"

"One pound sixty-two, please," said Marsham, because he'd worked out that the cost of the sandwich was £3.38.

"That's correct," said the man. "Here's your sandwich. Have a lovely day."

Marsham returned to table 19 buzzing with excitement. *Maybe, just maybe, I can do this,* he thought.

He took a bite of his sandwich and started writing down the answers to the questions.

Gondola

Pollen

Witches

Hmm, a billionth of a second, mused Marsham. *I know we've talked about this in school. . . Of course, nanosecond!*

He wrote the answer down and continued with the quiz. Five minutes later he had a list of answers in front of him.

Gondola
Pollen
Witches
Nanosecond
Manchester United
Cryptocurrency
Diabolo
Chromium
8

Now he had to "follow the instructions", but his list of answers didn't seem to be telling him anything. He wrote them in different orders and turned his notebook upside down, but nothing jumped out at him. To make matters worse, he heard a squeal from a girl on a nearby table and glanced up to see her running out, looking very happy indeed.

"Ten minutes left for this sitting!" shouted the man in the serving hatch.

Suddenly, Marsham's heart began racing and he could feel his mouth getting dry. As quickly as he could, he went over his answers again.

Gondola, Pollen, Witches, Nanosecond, Manchester United... No, wait, that's not right, it's ... it's ... Liverpool. Yes, that's it.

He wrote the new answer in, but he still couldn't decipher any instructions.

A cry of *yes!* rang out as another child jumped up and left. With time fast running out, Marsham stared and stared at his answers.

"Come on, show yourself," he muttered, in mental anguish.

Another minute went by and then, suddenly, the dark clouds in Marsham's mind parted and a ray of light poked through.

"What if I take the first letter of the first answer, the second of the second? Yes! That gives me G and O. Then the third letter of the third answer is T. . ."

With his heart pounding, he carried on until in front of him he had. . .

G O T O R O O M 8.

"Go to room 8. That's it," he whispered.

"One minute left," said the serving hatch man.

Marsham looked at the others who hadn't worked things out yet. He felt sorry for them, but he wasn't about to stick around. He grabbed his bag and shot off to find out what awaited him in room 8.

CHAPTER 9

Out in the corridor, Marsham saw a sign on the wall for "Interview Rooms", with an arrow pointing to the left. He charged off in that direction and found himself at the bottom of some stairs. He raced up them.

At the top were some lifts, and to the right of them a set of double doors. Marsham went through the doors and found himself in another corridor with five doors on one side and five on the other. The doors each had a number, but no door had a number 8. Instead, they were numbered 1, 2, 3, 4, 10, 11, 12, 13, 14, 20.

"Is this a code?" mulled Marsham. "Maybe I go into rooms 1, 3 and 4 to make 8?"

That didn't seem right, so Marsham sat down and wrote the numbers out in his notebook. He began to focus on them when something he'd overheard earlier came back to him.

"Is there somewhere Bertie can go to meditate? He can't do anything unless he has meditated for forty-five minutes."

Remembering those words, Marsham shut his eyes and let his mind relax and drift. It was a very pleasant feeling. He felt floaty, he felt dreamy, he felt. . .

"They're not in base 10! The numbers are not in base 10!"

It had just come to him, but, looking at the numbers again, he knew he was right.

"They seem normal up to four, so that must mean they're in base 5, which means" – Marsham did a quick calculation in his head – "room 8 is room 13!"

Praying he was right, Marsham went to room 13 and knocked.

"Come in," said a voice from inside.

Marsham checked his wig and entered. Sitting at a table were two women and a man. They all seemed quite teacher-y, and Marsham instantly felt as if he must have done something wrong.

"Welcome," said the woman in the middle, who had ruddy cheeks and curly, fair hair. "What room were you instructed to go to?"

"Room 8, miss," said Marsham.

"Excellent," said the woman. "You're in the right place. So, tell us your name and a little about yourself."

"Well, I'm Daniel Phillips. I'm twelve and I live with my mum, dad, and gran. Mum and Dad are, erm, explorers, who, erm, explore, they're in—"

"What is the capital of Bangladesh?"

Marsham stopped. The other woman at the table had just interrupted him with a question. She had long, straight, brown hair and a stern-looking face. He was thrown for a moment, but then said, "Dhaka."

The woman didn't say anything, so he carried on.

"My parents are in Ecuador. I also have a cat called Piffle. I'm homeschooled, and I would say my favourite subjects are—"

"What is the densest metal on Earth?" It was the man this time. He looked quite old and fusty, like a retired professor.

"It's ... it's ... osmium," said Marsham. The man made a note and stared at him.

OK, so they're going to fire questions at me randomly as I talk. Fine, thought Marsham defiantly. *Hit me with your best shots.*

And they did: thirteen more times as Marsham was speaking. Sometimes two questions came in quick succession, sometimes there wasn't one for a while. Eventually the woman in the middle said, "Thank you, Daniel. You can stop now and relax for a while."

Marsham looked at his interviewers. There had been fifteen questions, and by his reckoning he'd definitely got twelve right. Two he wasn't sure about, and one had been a complete guess – who was the youngest British prime minister? Marsham had said Tony Blair. (He looked it up later and the answer was, in fact, William Pitt the Younger; there was a clue in the name.)

"Thank you," he said. He left the room and walked back to the lifts. He was exhausted and quite hot. He was worried about his disguise and wished he'd taken one of Ethel's fans, but he could just about make out his reflection in the lift doors and everything seemed fine.

Something else was bothering him, though. The ominous way the woman had said he could relax "for a while". There was no point trying to work it out, though, so he retraced his steps back to find Gran amongst the anxious parents, holding forth to a small crowd of them:

"Of course, parachuting is very difficult; you have to know where you're going to land. But I've got a nose for these sorts of things, which stood me in good stead when I joined the circus and was fired out of a cannon."

"Hi, Gran," said Marsham, coughing loudly to attract her attention. He wasn't sure what she was doing and felt a little uneasy about it.

"Is that your grandson?" said a woman with pointy glasses and far-too-perfect teeth. "The one who has swum the English Channel with an otter on his back?"

"Yes, that's him," said Gran, standing up. "Anyway, lovely talking to you, see you again soon, bye."

Gran took Marsham by the arm and led him back to where Ethel was sitting quietly.

"I'm not sure it's such a good idea to tell people I swam the Channel, Gran," said Marsham. "Especially with an otter on my back. And you've never told me about any parachuting, or your time in the circus."

"Oh, I just thought if *you* can be someone else, so can I," said Gran, chuckling. "I had to amuse myself somehow."

Marsham looked at his grandmother and smiled. "Ah, what's another couple of made-up stories in the life of Daniel Phillips?" he said. "But maybe not *too* many, Gran. I don't want to draw attention to myself."

"Fair enough. So, tell us everything," said Gran.

Gran and Ethel listened intently as Marsham told them about the canteen and the interview room. Ethel then discreetly checked his disguise and sent him off to the toilet with a fan, to try and get rid of any moisture build-up.

After Marsham had returned, they spent the next ten minutes giving the screechy parents funny names (such as Mrs Squawker and Mr Yelly Yellstone), another five minutes staring into space, and then Marsham looked at his phone for half an hour while Gran and Ethel had a snooze.

"Gran, Ethel, wake up," whispered Marsham.

Ethel opened her eyes and came round, but Gran said, "Leave my bread pudding alone and lend me your soap!"

Marsham gave her a nudge.

"Hey, what? Hello," she said, waking up. "Ooh, lummee, I was having a very strange dream."

"Tell me later; look who's back at last," said Marsham.

Gran glanced up and saw Khalid, the executive producer, in the middle of the room again. He'd clearly learnt from last time and boomed out, "COULD I HAVE EVERYONE'S ATTENTION, PLEASE?"

The room settled down, apart from Mr Yelly Yellstone, who muttered, "There's no need to shout," which was rich coming from him.

"Thank you for your patience. I know it's been a

long day, but we have now made our decision on this year's final twelve."

The room was dead silent. Marsham looked at Gran. This was it.

CHAPTER 10

"Yes!" squealed the eighth person Khalid read out, a boy called Howard Granville.

There were only four places left, and Marsham reckoned there were at least eighty children hoping for one of them. The odds were not in his favour. He looked nervously at Gran and Ethel. They smiled back reassuringly.

"So," continued Khalid. "The next child through to the final twelve is. . ."

Marsham shut his eyes.

"Liselle Billington!"

Yelps of joy emanated from Liselle and her family as a deflated Marsham sank back into his chair.

"Don't worry," whispered Gran. "Whatever happens, I know you did your best."

Marsham didn't find that particularly helpful, and

then made matters worse by scratching at an itch on his nose. Thankfully, the nose stayed put.

"Just three places left now," said Khalid. "And our next finalist is . . . Daniel Phillips!"

It took Marsham a moment to realize what had happened. Part of him had been waiting to hear his real name, so he wasn't entirely certain Khalid had said Daniel. Marsham thought so, but perhaps he'd misheard.

"Sorry, Khalid, was that me?" he asked.

A couple of people sniggered.

"Are you Daniel Phillips?" asked Khalid.

"Yes, yes I am," said Marsham.

"Then it was you," said Khalid. "Congratulations."

Marsham sat back and puffed out a huge amount of air, as if he was expelling a cloud he'd swallowed. He had thought he might jump for joy or punch the air if he'd heard Daniel's name, but the main thing he felt was relief. It made him realize how much this really meant to him.

"Congratulations to our final twelve, and well done to everyone else," said Khalid after he'd read out the last two names. "I'm afraid our decision is final and we won't be answering any questions about it. If your name wasn't read out, please could you make your way to the exit."

The children who hadn't made it trooped out with their dejected parents still moaning – *this building really*

*isn't ventilated properly some of the questions were very
badly worded I should never have told Khalid my recipe for
olive and banana soup* – but the fight had gone out of
them, and it was more of a defeated grumble than a
full-throated call to arms.

"Congratulations again," said Khalid once the last
of them had left. "You should all be very proud of
yourselves, that wasn't an easy challenge. But. . ."

Khalid paused and the atmosphere in the room
shifted. Something was up, and the ominous words of
the woman in the interview room came rushing back
to Marsham.

"As I'm sure you're all aware," continued Khalid,
"we promised that this series would be full of surprises,
and you're about to get the first one."

"Well, really, this is most irregular," said someone's
mum, despite not knowing what the surprise was.

"*Britain's Smartest Kid* is about testing intelligence, but
intelligence is not just one thing; it has many different
components," said Khalid. "Which is why this year we
are determined to test as many of those components
as we can. So, as well as what might be termed *mental*
intelligence, we will also be testing *physical* intelligence."

Murmurs of surprise, disbelief and discomfort
scurried round the room.

"What on earth is he talking about?" said a voice, rising above the others.

"Consequently, we have decided," said Khalid, shooting a glance at the other staff members in the room, as if he was telling them to brace themselves, "that in each week's episode, one of the rounds will take place. . ." There was that pause again. "On ice."

Suddenly, there was pandemonium. It didn't matter that the majority of the crowd had left; those who remained more than made up for them.

"Did he say, on ice?" said Gran as loudly as she could.

"Yes!" shouted Marsham. "I think so."

"Wonderful," said Gran, who clearly loved the idea.

Marsham wasn't so sure, and looked at Ethel, who said, "Don't worry, it'll be fine." Her face wasn't giving anything away, but Marsham remembered her words from earlier: *It's a quiz show, so I can't imagine you'll be moving about all that much.* His stomach lurched and he felt a little sick.

"THANK YOU," boomed Khalid over the throng. "PLEASE, CAN EVERYONE CALM DOWN!"

The pandemonium turned into an uproar, then into an outcry, then into a hubbub and finally into a gentle undercurrent of discontent, which was good enough for Khalid.

"One last thing," said Khalid, looking as if he was holding the lid down on a very bubbly pot. "We only need six children for the actual show, and that is going to be decided by a speed skating race that will take place . . . *now!*"

Silence. Complete and utter silence.

Then. . .

Mayhem.

It took Khalid half an hour to quell the uproar, which Gran, Ethel and Marsham watched as if they were spectators at some new sport – Shoutbawl, perhaps, or Angery.

It was a spectacle, but Marsham's thoughts raced: he'd only been ice skating three times before. On two of the occasions, he'd fallen over and hurt an arm, and the third time he'd bumped into someone, sending them into a sidewall, where they broke their nose. And on none of those occasions had he been in disguise pretending to be someone else! His stomach was going into full-on panic mode now, and adrenalin coursed round his body. Marsham knew he was in what was known as fight-or-flight mode, and as far as he was concerned, the best option was flight.

Eventually, Khalid calmed things down enough

to explain things further.

"I understand that this might come as something of a shock," he said. "But, just as you didn't know exactly what to expect with the other tests and so couldn't specifically prepare for them, we decided the physical test should also be something that you are unprepared for. That way we can test your natural ability."

"What about my daughter?" said a defiant voice.

Everyone turned to see a woman standing next to a girl in a wheelchair. The girl peered out over her small, round glasses. She had braided hair in beads and braces on her teeth that glinted as she moved her head. She seemed to be enjoying the attention.

"She can use her own wheelchair on the ice," Khalid smoothly replied. "We can adapt it, or we have an ice sledge she can use. . ."

"I'll use my own chair," interrupted the girl in a very definite tone that startled everyone, including her mother.

"Wonderful," said Khalid. "Now, if you could all follow me, the rink is located across the car park."

"Come on," said Gran.

"OK," said Marsham, standing up. "But I'm worried. With my track record on skates. . ."

"Oh, you'll be fine," said Gran. "I used to ice skate

78

on a frozen lake near our house when I was your age. It was when I was living with an Inuit family and—"

"Gran, it's me," said Marsham. "You don't have to make things up with me."

"OK, OK," said Gran as they followed the others out of the room. "But I *did* skate on a frozen lake and I loved it."

"I'm sure you did," said Marsham. "But you weren't in a competition to get on a TV show. What if some of the others have been having skating lessons for years?"

"I'm sure some of the others have been having private tutors for years as well," said Gran. "But you still beat most of them in the other rounds. Just relax and try and enjoy it."

Marsham sighed and shook his head. He'd been so relieved to have made the final twelve, but now he might not get on the show after all. The tension was creeping back into his body as if he were an inflatable child being blown up.

"Ethel," said Marsham as they approached reception. "What do you think? Is everything going to stay on?"

"Hmm," she said. "The honest truth is I don't know. The wig should be fine, and as it's not exactly going to be hot in an ice rink, the nose should be as well. But it won't be able to withstand too much impact. If we had more time I could put extra adhesive on it, but, for now, all I can suggest is: try not to fall over."

"Thanks," said Marsham grumpily. As well as feeling tense and nervous, he was now a little angry too, though he accepted that there wasn't much Ethel could do.

They left the main studio building and walked to a similar-sized building opposite. It housed the rink that was used for ice dancing shows on television and, when they arrived, Marsham was whisked away to the boot room to be fitted for skates.

The atmosphere was strange and subdued. Most of these children had been confident and self-assured earlier, but now they seemed as unsure as Marsham.

"Bit unexpected, this, isn't it?" Marsham said to the girl whose father was the famous actor. She'd got through and was putting on her skates with a stern look on her face, as if she was somehow hoping to infuse them with her brainpower. She ignored Marsham, which made him feel even worse.

"If everyone's ready, could you all please follow me out to the rink," said Gavin, the chirpy man with a nose ring from the canteen.

Everyone got up and, because they were now on ice skates, made their way unsteadily out of the room.

They looked like a group of dizzy ducklings.

"Thank you, Gavin," said Khalid when they got out to the rink. "As you'll see, we've marked out the rink with twelve straight lanes running from one end to the other. Once you have been assigned a lane, you must stay in it. Any crossing of lanes and you will be disqualified. You'll be racing to the far end, where you must touch the wall, turn round and then return to the other end. The first six children will earn a place in the show and the seventh will be our reserve. All clear?"

For once no one said anything; but, really, there was nothing much to say. It was all very straightforward.

"And, of course, grown-ups," continued Khalid, "this is when we actually want you to shout and scream, so feel free to let rip and show your support."

The grown-ups had all been seated together on the far side of the rink, and if that was meant to be a pep talk, it fell on deaf ears – apart from one set of ears.

"Yay, come on, Mar ... Mar ... *mar*vellous Daniel, you can do it!" shouted Gran in response. The other grown-ups looked at her as if she'd just farted loudly. Even Ethel blushed slightly. Marsham wanted to crawl away and hide in a cave.

A couple of minutes later, they were all lined up

and ready to start. Marsham was in lane five, and as he looked to his left and then to his right, a change came over him.

They all look pretty nervous as well, he thought. *So what have I got to lose? I might as well just go for it.*

With what he hoped was a determined look on his face, he turned to face the front, and waited for the race to begin.

CHAPTER 11

"On your marks..."

"Get set..."

"Go!"

Boom!

Marsham was off as if he'd been shot out of the cannon Gran had made up earlier.

Then, half a second later, he was flat on his back and heading for lane six and instant disqualification.

With all his might, he managed to heave his body to the right, just about avoiding crossing over into the other lane, or flattening his nose.

It was a bad start, but thankfully he wasn't alone. Looking up, he saw that three other contestants had fallen over as well. Unfortunately, he also saw three kids way out in front.

He got up and, gingerly now, began to make his way

forward. His determination was still there, but it was time to be more tortoise than hare.

Slowly, he made his way forward. It wasn't quite speed skating, more baby-steps skating, but at least he was upright and heading in the right direction.

When he got halfway to the far wall, the three children who had been out in front passed him going the other way. They were definitely going to make it on to the show.

Marsham decided to risk going a little faster, and, despite a couple of wobbles, he didn't fall over. He made it to the wall and turned round, clinging on to it and catching his breath.

The three kids in the lead had already finished and were celebrating. Two others were already making their way back to the start ahead of him, and two kids were next to him, also holding on to the wall. The other four were still making their way towards it.

Marsham shot a look at the two other children by the wall. He recognized one of them as the daughter of the famous actor. She was small and compact, almost gnome-like, with expensive designer clothes. She had braces on her teeth and a face that raged with determination. She snarled at him and set off, taking small steps forward. The other was that boy, Howard Granville, and he looked pretty exhausted.

Marsham pushed himself away from the wall. Immediately, he realized he'd pushed too hard. He was zigzagging from side to side and desperately flapping his arms in circles to keep his balance.

Thankfully, he didn't topple over and managed to steady himself, but now he was only plodding slowly forward and the girl was still ahead of him.

With fifteen metres to go, Marsham was seventh. It was now or never.

Throwing caution to the wind, he dug his right skate into the ice and really pushed.

"Whhhoooooooaaaaa," he cried as his left foot came off the ice, followed closely by his right foot.

SPLAT!

Marsham had lost his balance! He was now flat on his front, desperately holding his nose above the ice heading . . . *somewhere, very quickly*. He had no idea if he was going backwards, forwards or round and round. All he knew was that a few moments later he came to a stop on the ice.

"Tell them, Daddy, tell them! I came sixth, didn't I, Daddy? Tell them. It's not fair!"

A somewhat dazed Marsham looked to his left and saw the girl shouting at her famous father. He was tall and rugged-looking, but in a manufactured, expensive way.

"Yes, I will, Vera darling. I certainly will," said the man.

"Hello," said another voice that Marsham recognized as Gran's.

"Hello, Gran," said Marsham, looking up. "What happened?"

"Well," said Gran, "you were seventh but then you fell over and sailed along the ice on your front."

"Did I?" said Marsham. "Which direction did I sail?"

"You sailed past the girl in front of you and all the way to the finish line," said Gran.

"Really?" said Marsham. "So that means. . ."

"Yes," said Gran. "You did it!"

"First things first," said Khalid. "I promise you, there will be no more surprises today."

"Well, that's a relief," said Marc, the boy from *The Q&A Kids*.

Marsham and the five other successful candidates, along with Vera, the reserve contestant, were in a room back in the main building. They were seated around a table with Khalid at the head. No family members had been allowed in with them.

Despite Vera being very angry and having a famous dad, Khalid had told her that it didn't matter that Daniel was flat on his stomach and knew nothing about it when he crossed the finish line. He'd stayed in his lane, so he got sixth place. The scowl on her face was still there.

"I have a number of things to tell you," continued Khalid. "But first, could we all introduce ourselves? I'll start. I'm Khalid Mahmaby, I'm the executive producer of the show. This is my fourth series, and in my spare time I play the trombone and fly kites."

Khalid turned to the girl on his left. Going that way meant it would be Marsham's turn next. He gulped quietly and shifted slightly in his seat. He didn't like this sort of thing at the best of times, but being in disguise made it a whole lot worse.

"Hello, everyone," said the girl, smiling sweetly. She was expensively dressed and her shoulder-length brown hair had been expertly fashioned into a bob. Her brown eyes appeared to be taking everything in eagerly. She seemed shy, but confident. "My name is Dionna Witton. When I was five I invented an X-ray saucepan that allows you to see when an egg is perfectly boiled. I now have my own multimillion-pound business."

"Thank you, Dionna," said Khalid. All eyes turned to Marsham.

"Erm, hello," he said. "My name is Daniel Phillips. I haven't invented anything yet, but I love doing quizzes, I have a cat called Piffle, I play computer games a lot, and, er, I'm into calligraphy."

"Thank you very much, Daniel," said Khalid. Everyone now focused on the girl next to Marsham, which made him feel as if their eyes had lifted a big weight from his head.

"Hi, I'm Liselle Billington," said the girl. She was wearing a long floral dress and a cardigan, and was twiddling her curly ginger hair. She seemed quite vacant and spaced out. "I'm the youngest person ever to study Molecular Biology and Extreme Maths at university. I'm also a member of Mensa and have an IQ of 140."

Not quite so vacant, thought Marsham.

Next up was a boy everyone knew. His blonde hair was slickly gelled and he had green eyes that oozed liquid-emerald sparkle. He was cool and relaxed.

"I'm Marc Elton," he said. "I host the online show *The Q&A Kids* with my older brother, Paul. I'm also the UK's top under-fourteen Scrabble player, and I like computer games as well."

"Thank you, Marc," said Khalid.

Vera was next. "Yeah, I'm Vera Lanston," she said quite aggressively. "I started reading when I was one and a half. I've never got less than an A for anything, and I'm going to take seventeen GCSEs and eight A levels. Oh, and my dad is an actor."

And you're very angry, thought Marsham, though no one else seemed remotely bothered by her manner.

"Hi, everyone, I'm Naomi Inwald," said the girl using the wheelchair, without waiting for Khalid to say thank you to Vera. "I've written two books that have been published, both of which got five-star reviews, and I like horses, making and eating ice cream, and origami."

"Well, thank you, Naomi," said Khalid as he and

everyone else turned to the last person, a boy with messy, curly black hair. He was wearing a shirt and tie, and had a wide-mouthed, nervous grin on his face.

"Hello," he said. "I'm, erm, Medhansh Gupta. Medhansh means wisdom. My father is an antiques dealer and my mother is a doctor, which is what I want to be, I think. Erm, I like collecting stamps."

"Wonderful," said Khalid. "So, I won't keep you long, I know it's been a tiring day, but I just wanted to give you some information about this year's show. There will be three episodes, so effectively a first round, a semi-final and a final. The show is not live, so we will be recording them over three weekends and they will go out on television the following Monday evening. Aaaaand, maybe most importantly, this year you will be competing for one hundred thousand pounds, and the winner will also get to go to the Nobel Prize ceremony in Stockholm, Sweden."

"Wow!" said Liselle, as a current of excitement fizzed around the room.

"Yes, I'm pretty jealous myself," said Khalid. "Now, I also wanted to have a word about being on the show. It's a big show, and as I'm sure you know, that means our contestants – you – are suddenly in the public eye a lot. From our point of view, we'll organize all your official show publicity, photographs, interviews, film shoots, that sort of thing, but newspapers and other TV shows will be interested in you as well, so you just have to be a little careful about what you do and say. If you are asked any questions you don't like the sound of, or asked to do anything that our publicity department hasn't arranged, always refer them to me."

"Or Marc," said Naomi. "He knows about being famous already."

Marc turned a deep shade of red.

"Thank you, Naomi," said Khalid, a little thrown. "But if it's OK with all of you, I'd rather you spoke to me first."

"Of course, Khalid," said Naomi, whom Marsham had already pegged as something of a well-meaning busybody.

"Most importantly, though," continued Khalid, "I want you all to have the most amazing time. It's going to be great!"

"Yay!" cheered Naomi.

"Yeah, right," huffed Vera.

PART 3

ROUND 1

CHAPTER 12

That night Marsham's eyes closed *before* his head had even hit the pillow. "Exhausted" didn't come close to describing how exhausted he was. He'd been desperate to get home after the selection interview, but they'd had to go back to Ethel's so she could remove his disguise, which had taken half an hour.

It was eleven a.m. before he woke up, having slept so deeply it felt as if he'd been lying underneath a mattress with a herd of elephants and a steamroller on top of it.

He was groggy, but a couple of huge yawns and a splash of cold water later, Marsham was reasonably awake and sitting at his desk, waiting for his computer to boot up.

He got the emails for Daniel Phillips up and immediately saw one entitled *"Britain's Smartest Kid . . . on Ice!"* A burst of excitement jolted him fully awake.

Dear Daniel,

CONGRATULATIONS!!!

You did it. You are officially a contestant on the new series of *BSKOI*.

The recording of the first episode will take place on Saturday 18th November at the studio building. There will be a general knowledge round, and then a memory challenge which will take place on ice.

Your memory challenge is to learn the words to the football song "Three Lions" backwards.

Before then we would like to come to your house and shoot a short film with you. Please could you respond and let us know when would be convenient.

We look forward to welcoming you at 9 a.m. on the morning of the 18th.

Khalid and the team.

Marsham sat back in his chair, a bubbling mish-mash of emotions swirling around inside him. It felt fantastic to "officially" be a contestant. This was unquestionably the most exciting thing that had ever happened to him.

He wanted to tell the world, but he couldn't tell anyone. Or could he? A delicious thought occurred to him.

Maybe being famous for being clever would change things at school! Then I could start getting good results again and Mum and Dad wouldn't ask me difficult questions. . .

On top of that, yesterday had been tough, and now they wanted to film at "his house". The enormity of being in disguise really hit him, but was it too late? If he told the show he'd made up Daniel Phillips, would they still let him take part? It was definitely risky. He'd have to think some more about it and speak to Gran.

Still mulling it all over, he headed downstairs. Mum, Dad and Gran were in the living room watching television.

"Morning, sleepychops," said Dad.

"That beekeepers' conference must have been exciting," said Mum. "You haven't woken up this late for ages."

"We kept him very busy," said Gran, saving Marsham from having to make anything up himself. "He moved some very large jars of honey."

"Did he now?" said Mum, slightly suspiciously.

"Yes, I did," sparked up Marsham. "Huge, some of them were, and. . ."

Marsham stopped. His attention had been diverted

by Selina Constantin, who had popped up on the TV screen.

"The new series of *Britain's Smartest Kid* is starting soon," she was saying, "and this year it's going to be full of surprises. In fact, I can now tell you one of them. It's now called *Britain's Smartest Kid ... on Ice!* That's because some of the rounds will be taking place – you guessed it – on ice. So get your skates on and make sure you tune in when the new series starts very soon!"

"Well, that's certainly going to be different," said Mum. "Maybe the ratings have been dropping. What do you think, Marsham?"

Marsham had been planning his response during the trailer. He didn't want Mum and Dad to focus on the show too much, but they knew it was his favourite programme, so he couldn't ignore it. He'd decided to be enthusiastic – but hungry, which was often the perfect diversion.

"Sounds brilliant!" said Marsham. "I think it's a great twist, and I can't wait to watch it. Hey, is there any bread, Mum? I'm starving."

"There's some in the freezer," said Mum. "You can toast it."

Marsham started heading out, feeling pleased with how he'd reacted, when Gran said, "I'm looking forward to that show. I hear they've got some amazing contestants this year."

"Wherever did you hear that from?" said Dad. Marsham threw her a "what on earth are you doing?" look. She grinned mischievously.

"It's the word on the street," said Gran. "A little dicky bird told me. Or maybe it was a dream. I don't know."

Mum and Dad laughed, and a relieved Marsham went to the kitchen. A couple of minutes later Gran wandered in.

"What did you say that for?" said Marsham.

"Got to keep you on your toes, Marsham," she said. "This is not going to be easy."

"I know," said Marsham. "I got an email this morning. The show want to film me. And probably you as well. We'll have to do it at Ethel's house."

"Ooh, exciting," said Gran.

"Erm, Gran," said Marsham. "I've been thinking. Ethel's worked with lots of famous people, and you, erm, you are very wise and experienced in life, so with you two around, maybe being famous might be not so difficult, so what do you think the show would do if I told them who I really was?"

"Really?" said Gran.

"Yes. No. I don't know," said Marsham.

"It'd be a shame," said Gran. "I was just getting to like Daniel."

"Gran, I'm serious," said Marsham, feeling irritated by Gran's flippancy.

"Hmm," mused Gran. "I think the thing to do is . . . sleep on it. You don't need to decide anything right now."

Marsham smiled. "Very wise, Gran," he said. "Just like I said you were."

The rest of that day vanished, as Sundays sometimes do, and before Marsham knew it, it was Monday and he was back at school. It seemed strange being there. It felt as if his life had changed after the events of the weekend, and it had. For Daniel. Marsham was still the same person who had to go to school and make sure he didn't get top marks.

He struggled to concentrate all morning as the previous day's dilemma came back to him.

Marc from The Q&A Kids *is famous for being clever,* he thought. *So maybe I could be as well and it would be OK at school.*

Once again he began to question what he'd done, but at lunchtime the questions abruptly stopped.

"You OK today?" asked Nainan, as the two of them

sat at a table eating their sandwiches. Adrian was at football training.

"Yeah, fine," said Marsham, in a way that most people would interpret as meaning, "no, I'm not".

Nainan pushed his glasses up his nose and took a bite out of his cheese-and-tomato sandwich.

"Tell him! Tell him!" screamed a voice in Marsham's head.

"Actually, Nain," said Marsham. He was going to tell him something. He didn't quite know what exactly, but Nainan was one of his best friends; surely he could confide in him. He was about to continue when a group of older kids sat down behind them.

"Yeah, I saw the trailer," said a loud, mean-sounding voice that Marsham recognized instantly. It was the boy with slicked-back hair who'd called him a slug. "It's a stupid show for losers."

The others all agreed.

"But I'll be watching it," said the boy. "It's going to be hilarious watching them go flying on the ice and fall flat on their nerdy faces."

Laughter rang out from the group.

It was like a punch to the stomach. The voice in Marsham's head was quiet now, and a wave of dejection came over him.

"Come on, let's go," he said, standing up. Nainan nodded, and the two of them sloped out quietly.

That evening Marsham was trying to do his French comprehension homework, but he couldn't stop thinking about what he'd heard at lunchtime. All they wanted was to see kids like him fail – or, better yet, get hurt. What was so wrong with being clever? He wished he could make all the mean kids vanish and replace them with new ones who appreciated the fact that he was clever. Now that would be a great school to go to.

Marsham felt angry and sad, but above all he was now certain that he'd made the right decision pretending to be Daniel.

He tried to focus back on his homework when he heard the familiar "ping" of an email arriving.

It was from the show again, and this one was marked *Top Secret*.

CHAPTER 13

Dear Daniel,

As you know, this year on *Britain's Smartest Kid* we are testing all aspects of intelligence. One of the aspects we would like to test in the first show is cunning.

Cunning, or devious intelligence, requires flexibility of thought, ingenuity, planning and confidence. So, in the general knowledge round we would like you to cheat as cleverly as possible so that no one knows you are doing it.

For now, only I and two other producers are aware of this challenge and you MUST NOT TELL ANYONE ELSE, or even try to discuss it with us. You will lose points if other people discover that you are cheating, but if you are successful you will earn extra points.

Good luck!

Khalid.

Marsham read the email three times. He was both excited and concerned by it. Cheating did appeal to a part of him. It was something that loads of people probably think about doing in certain situations, but never go through with it in case they get caught. Now he was actually being *asked* to do it.

The real problem, though, was that, as well as revising for the general knowledge round, learning the song – backwards – and practising skating, Marsham now had even more to think about. And that didn't take into account his schoolwork. It was going to be a very busy few weeks.

The following morning, Marsham was ready to leave the house an hour earlier than usual.

"See you later!" he called up the stairs.

"Marsham? Is that you?" shouted Dad back down. "It's only seven thirty. Mum's in the shower and I haven't even had a cup of coffee yet. Why are you leaving so early?"

"There's a new breakfast revision club," said Marsham. "My friends are all doing it. See you."

Before Dad could reply, Marsham was out and heading for the bus stop, which was odd, because usually he walked to school. This morning, though, he had another destination in mind.

"One child ticket, please," he said ten minutes later to the woman at the ticket office of the local ice rink.

"Bit keen, aren't you?" she said, looking him up and down.

"Yes, I am," said Marsham.

"Three pounds fifty," she said.

Marsham paid and rushed inside. A quick look around confirmed what he'd hoped: the ice rink wasn't busy that early in the morning, so he could do some skating practice in peace. He'd taken it pretty slowly on the interview day, and had still fallen over twice, so he knew he needed to improve.

He headed to the boot room and tried on four pairs of skates before finding some that only hurt a little bit. He then made his way out to the ice.

There were only three other people on the rink, but Marsham wasn't going to rush things. He spent the first ten minutes holding on to the wall and walking round and then, slowly, he began to get a little more adventurous.

Another ten minutes and three very big wobbles later, he'd pretty much made it once round the rink without holding on to the side.

I can do this, he thought to himself, pushing off again.

"Oi, I know you, don't I?" said a voice. "It's Martin, isn't it?"

Marsham looked up and just about recognized the face he saw before the world turned upside down, and he was heading towards the other side of the rink a lot faster than intended.

"Oooh, my arm," he moaned, lying on the ice.

"Don't worry, it'll be fine, I used to fall over loads."

It was that voice again. Marsham had wondered whether he was in fact still asleep in bed and had dreamt it, but there was no doubting it now.

"H . . . hello, erm. . ." he said.

"Tabatha," said the voice, which belonged to a tall girl with small green eyes which were almost hidden under heavily made up eyebrows. Her blonde hair was tied up in a bun. "You go to my school, don't you, Martin?"

Marsham looked at Tabatha properly. Yes, he knew

her. She was one of the cool gang. He was pretty certain she'd laughed when he was called a slug. This could be tricky.

"Erm, yes, I do," said Marsham. "And it's Marsham."

"Oh yeah, that's it, *Martian*," said Tabatha, matter-of-factly. It was as if she'd just chanced upon something vaguely interesting. "What are you doing here? No, don't tell me: you saw that *Britain's Smartest Kid* thing on telly and it made you want to try skating."

"Yes, that's it," said Marsham, a little relieved. "I don't like all the other stuff, but I've always liked the idea of skating, so I thought I'd give it a go. What about you?"

Tabatha looked down and seemed a little embarrassed.

"I like skating," she said. "But my friends think it's a bit naff, so I come here early and do it on my own." She suddenly looked back up, panic flooding her eyes. "You won't tell anyone you've seen me here, will you?"

"No, I won't say anything, anything at all," Marsham reassured her.

Tabatha relaxed and gave him an appraising look. "You know, I could help you get better if you like."

"Erm, yes, that would be good," said Marsham. Tabatha held out an arm. "Up you get, then, and I'll show you how not to fall over."

"Great," said Marsham, grabbing Tabatha's arm and then nearly falling over again as he got up. "Sorry, not a good start."

But when it came to the skating, it was in fact an excellent start.

"Ethel says it's fine to use her house for the film about you," said Gran.

It was later that day and they were in his room.

"She said it'd be best to pretend the spare bedroom is yours, her bedroom can be Mum and Dad's, and then I'll say her film room is my room, but we'll keep it closed so they don't go in there."

"OK," said Marsham. "And she's OK with eleven this Saturday?"

"Ooh, yes," said Gran. "We'll pop over on Friday with some things to make the spare room look like your bedroom. I was also thinking about taking my hive. The bees would love to be on television . . . but they don't like to be moved, so I think maybe it's best not to."

"Yes, I think so," said a relieved Marsham. "Thanks, Gran."

Gran wandered off, leaving Marsham feeling that he'd made progress with some of the things on his "to do" list, but he had loads more still to worry about. Most pressingly of all, figuring out how to cheat.

He reckoned the questions must be on a database somewhere, probably on the show's computer system, so he thought about trying to hack into that, but he had no idea if they'd even been written yet. He'd heard about another show in which someone in the audience had coughed when the contestant came up with the right answer, but the audience had to turn their phones off and he wasn't sure Gran or Ethel were quite right for that job, so that was a non-starter.

Eventually, late on Thursday evening, in the middle of a huge yawn, inspiration came and clouted him over the head.

"Lulu!" he yelled, making Tonks charge out of his room as if she'd seen a ghost.

Lulu was the virtual assistant they had in their house. Last year, Marsham and Adrian had taken it apart. It was risky, but they were confident they'd be able to put it back together again, which they had done. The working parts inside the casing were only a flat printed circuit board and a flat microphone board. They'd also discovered that you could change the wake or trigger name to anything and had a lot of fun renaming it, "bumface", "Mr. Wee Wee", and, "Her

Majesty Queen Snotfeatures the third". If Marsham could charge the boards up and fit them under his wig, one by each ear, he felt sure they would hear Selina ask a question and then provide an answer. He'd have to play around with the volume, and change the trigger word to "question", but he didn't think that would be too much of a problem.

Feeling excited, he snuck downstairs to the kitchen/dining room. Lulu was on a shelf near the fridge. Very occasionally his parents would ask it something, usually to check the weather if they were going out, but otherwise, he was the only one who talked to it, mainly to put music on.

It was nine thirty and Gran had already gone to bed. Mum and Dad were in the living room watching television. Marsham quietly unplugged Lulu and took it upstairs. He changed the trigger word, then got a set of screwdrivers out of a drawer and five minutes later he had the two boards. He held one on each side of his head, just above his ears, and said,

"Question one: what is the capital of Tonga?" A moment later, he heard, "The capital of Tonga is Nuku'alofa."

It worked! There was still the issue of getting the electronics under his wig, but Marsham felt a wave of pressure leave his body. For a moment he thought about not revising for the general knowledge round any more; but he knew if anything went wrong, he'd be on his own again.

CHAPTER 14

"Hey, I was reading about military history last night," said Marsham. It was morning break at school the next day and he was with Adrian and Nainan. "It was really interesting. I'd like to know more. Can I borrow some of your books, Ade?"

"Yeah, I . . . er . . . I guess so," said Adrian, sounding a little bemused. "I can bring some round this weekend."

"Oh, I can't this weekend, I'm really busy," said Marsham. "Can I come and get them after school? And actually, Nainan, I'd like to read some graphic novels as well. I think we should be more interested in each other's hobbies."

Adrian and Nainan glanced at each other. Marsham could tell they thought he was being odd, and he *had* left it late to ask them, but having told the show he was into military history and graphic novels, he'd need to know *something* about it and have some stuff to put in his "bedroom" at Ethel's.

"Yeah, I know it's a bit weird," said Marsham, hurriedly. "But when you really, really want to do something you just can't wait, can you?"

Marsham had reckoned *admitting* he was being weird would be a master stroke, a bit like saying, "yeah I know what you're thinking, and I would be thinking the same thing too if the situation was reversed, but it's OK because I know I'm being like this and there's a reason for it", but if anything he saw that it only made Adrian and Nainan think he was being weirder. Nonetheless, they agreed that he could pick up some books after school.

As it turned out, he borrowed four books and two model tanks from Adrian, and three books from Nainan. Marsham said he wanted to see how they would look in his room. He knew his friends still thought he was being strange, but he hoped they wouldn't dwell on it too much.

The next part of the plan involved Gran booking a cab for Friday evening, which they had to fill with Marsham's duvet – the one in Ethel's spare room wasn't exactly right for a young boy – some of his clothes, more books, magazines and some of the stuff from

Adrian and Nainan. Finally, Marsham had to unplug his computer and put it in the cab.

It was a difficult operation which involved Gran keeping Mum and Dad talking in the living room – she gave them what amounted to a lecture about bees which might not have been entirely accurate – while Marsham tiptoed out to the cab with as much as he could carry.

He had to make three journeys, and apart from nearly dropping his computer on the stairs, all went well, though afterwards Gran told him that things had got tricky when Dad needed the toilet. She had to tell him that feeling like you need the toilet was all in the mind and that if he focused on what she was saying, the feeling would go away. Thankfully, Dad had stayed put, though when Marsham walked into the room – the signal that the coast was clear – and Gran stopped talking, he rushed out very quickly.

Gran then said that she was popping to Ethel's – "the poor soul's had terrible trouble with her back lately, I said I'd go and cheer her up" – and jumped in the cab. Marsham was a little concerned about the two of them setting up "his room" without him, but he felt it was less suspicious this way.

All told, things seemed to have gone well, but it was yet another reminder of how tough keeping up the pretence was going to be. Marsham went to sleep that night worrying about the filming the following morning, and also getting annoyed. If he was just himself, this would be a lot of fun. Instead, it had become a difficult ordeal.

"Morning!" said Gran chirpily the next day.

"Morning," said Mum and Dad a little less chirpily. They were sitting in the dining room, each holding a steaming cup of coffee.

"Me and Marsham are just off to Ethel's," said Gran. "When he heard about her back, he said he wanted to go round and cheer her up as well, so we're going to make her breakfast. He's such a good boy. See you later."

Before Mum and Dad could answer, Gran had breezed out and rendezvoused with Marsham by the front door.

"How'd it go?" he asked.

"Perfect," said Gran. "My acting was wonderful, if I say so myself. Come on, let's go, chop chop."

Twenty minutes later, Marsham was back in the chair by the mirror while Ethel told him about turning Raquel Welch into a three-headed alien. There was something calming about listening to Ethel chatter away, but he was still feeling nervous. As well as Daniel's upcoming film debut, he also had the Lulu boards in his pocket and was hoping to see if he could slide them under the wig when it had been fitted – he would have to do that privately in the toilet, of course.

At ten o'clock, Ethel stood back, surveyed her work and said, "Excellent. Hello, Daniel."

"Hello, Ethel," said Marsham, in Daniel's voice. It still felt odd and a little uncomfortable in all the make-up, but he was definitely getting more used to it now. "And thank you, Ethel. And also, can I use your toilet, please?"

"I don't know why you're asking me, dear," said Ethel. "This is your house!"

Gran and Ethel chuckled as Marsham got up and went to the loo.

He stood in front of the toilet mirror and felt around

the bottom of his wig with his hands. Ethel had fitted it well, but there was a little give in it. He had to be really careful, though, he didn't want to loosen it too much. He took one of the boards out and, after a little gentle manipulating, was able to slip it under the wig by his right ear. The left side seemed to be tighter, but eventually he got the other one in.

He looked at himself in the mirror. There was no obvious bulge on either side.

"OK, this is it," he said. "Question one, in what year did the Second World War end?"

"Coo ee, Marsham, everything all right in there?" came Gran's voice from outside.

"I'm fine, Gran," shouted Marsham, his heart suddenly racing. "Be out in a minute."

"Make sure you are," said Gran. "They'll be here soon."

Marsham calmed himself down and tried again.

"1945," said Lulu.

"Yes!" said Marsham, punching the air. He took the boards out and put them back in his pocket.

Five minutes later, he was downstairs rehearsing Daniel's life story with Gran and Ethel.

"Daniel sounds like a lovely boy," said Ethel. "Right, it's quarter to eleven. Time for me to skedaddle."

"OK, and sorry again, Ethel," said Marsham. "I just think the less of us around the better."

"Oh, don't you worry. Your loss is the ducks' gain," said Ethel. She held up a bag of mouldy bread. "Good luck."

The next few minutes passed in torturous agony for Marsham. Gran kept fussing and moving ornaments a few millimetres. *He* kept sitting down, then standing up, then sitting down again, and he also had an itch on his scalp that he just couldn't quite reach through the wig.

Eventually, on the dot of eleven, the doorbell rang and two people from the show arrived, one hauling a camera.

"Hi, Daniel," said a man loudly and cheerily. He was a smiley person, with short dark hair and a goatee beard and moustache. "I'm Damian, an assistant producer for the show. Ready for this?"

"You bet!" said Marsham, hoping he sounded excited and confident.

"Great," said Damian. "This is Jill, she's the camera operator. Mind if we do a quick recce to see where the best place to set up is?"

"Course you can, dearie," said Gran, joining the conversation. "I'm Elsie, by the way. Daniel's grandmother. His parents aren't here."

"We know," said Damian. "They're in Ecuador. We were told. No worries, though, you'll look great on film."

Gran simpered a little and stood back as Damian and Jill entered the house. They nosed around downstairs and then asked if they could go upstairs.

"Of course," said Marsham. "We'll show you around."

"Yes, come on," said Gran.

Damian and Jill followed Gran and Marsham upstairs and after a brief look in "Mum and Dad's room" and "Daniel's room", they stopped outside "Gran's room".

"Mind if we have a peek in here?" said Jill, who was quite short, with dyed purple hair and arms full of tattoos.

"Oh, it's terribly messy, dear," said Gran. "I haven't had a chance to tidy up this morning."

"Don't worry, we aren't easily shocked," said Damian. His hand was practically on the door handle.

"Oh, but it's actually very bad luck to go into a messy bedroom, isn't it, Gran?" said Marsham, speaking quickly.

"Oh goodness, *yes*," said Gran. "Worse than walking

under a ladder, in fact. Terrible things will happen if you go in, and I wouldn't like to be responsible for that."

Damian stopped and a quick look passed between him and Jill.

"No problem," said Damian. "I think Daniel's room is best anyway, don't you, Jill?"

"Yeah, just what I was thinking," said Jill. "I'll set the camera up in there."

A short while later, "Daniel" was being filmed sitting on the bed with some of "his" graphic novels around him, introducing himself and talking about his life.

It was all going well when Damian asked about the cat, Piffle. Marsham chatted away happily about him without thinking anything of it. Then, when he'd finished, Damian said, "That's great, Daniel. I'd love to get some shots of you and Piffle together. Do you think you can get him to sit next to you on the bed?"

Marsham immediately tensed up and felt himself get quite hot. He looked at Gran, who was standing behind the camera.

"Yes, yes, of course," he said. "Gran, can you call Piffle in?"

"What?" said Gran, who had been quite engrossed

in the filming.

"The cat," said Marsham. "Can you get him to come in?"

"But he's at home," said Gran.

Marsham's heart missed a beat.

"Ha ha," he said. "We call his special place in the garden his home. I'll go get him."

Marsham left the room, hoping and praying that Gran didn't put her foot in it while he was gone. He went to the back door and shouted loudly for Piffle three times. He then found a cereal packet and shook it at the door – Tonks always came when he shook a packet of cat treats. He shouted "Piffle!" loudly once more and then returned upstairs.

"I'm really sorry," he said. "He's not coming in. I don't know why, but cats can be like that, they're very temperamental. He might have seen you arrive with all your equipment and got scared. He's probably hiding in next door's garden."

"That's a shame," said Damian. "Ah well, can't be helped. Let's just continue here, then."

"Yes, good idea," said Gran. "Shall I make us all a lovely cup of tea?"

No one wanted tea, but Gran went and made one for herself anyway. Marsham sat back on the bed, cursing himself for forgetting to bring Tonks. They could have put him in a cat box and brought him with them. It was a silly mistake. He was relieved to have got out of it, though, and the rest of the interview went well.

"That's terrific. Thanks, Daniel," said Damian. "All we need now are some shots of your gran, maybe in the kitchen?"

"Ooh, am I going to be a star?" said Gran excitedly.

Damian smiled and they all started making their way downstairs.

"Oh no," shouted Marsham when they'd got to the bottom.

The other three all turned to look at him.

"Gran, you must have forgotten," said Marsham. "Remember we met that woman who told us that it is really, really bad luck for an older woman to be filmed, erm, on a Saturday? I really wouldn't risk it."

The three of them were still looking at him, though now they were perplexed.

"Remember, Gran," continued Marsham. "She said that if people, LOTS OF PEOPLE, SEE YOUR FACE on a film that was shot on a Saturday, it will spell disaster?"

The penny finally dropped for Gran.

"Goodness me, yes," she said. "I'm sorry, I can't possibly be filmed today."

"Sorry, but she's very superstitious, as you already know," said Marsham.

Damian sighed.

"We haven't got time to come back another day," he said. "So would it be OK if we just filmed you from behind? It might not be usable, but at least we'll have something."

"Yes, I should think so," said Gran, looking at Marsham, who nodded.

Jill then set up her camera in the kitchen and took some footage of predominantly Gran's back while she was talking about Daniel.

"And cut," said Damian. "That'll have to do, I guess. Right, one more thing."

Marsham felt apprehensive. What could Damian want now?

"Your parents," he said. "I didn't see any photos of them or anything. You must have some around, you know, with you when you were younger, Daniel, that sort of thing? It would be good to cut to one when you're talking about them."

Marsham felt a wave of exhaustion seep over him, a realization that this was going to be endless, a constant stream of backtracking, thinking quickly and, essentially, lying. For a moment he felt like giving up there and then, and telling the truth. Thankfully, Gran's cup of tea must have pepped her up because she said, "Oh, would you believe it, I just took all the framed photos to the cleaners."

"The cleaners?" said Damian.

"Yes," said Gran. "I want them to look all sparkly and new for when Daniel's parents return; it's our welcome home present."

Marsham could see about a million questions shooting around inside Damian's head, but before any of them could get out he said, "But don't worry, I'll email you some pictures of my parents, I've got loads on my phone."

Damian looked at Marsham and Gran. He seemed worn down and defeated. Ten minutes later he and Jill had packed up and left.

"Job done," said Gran as if it had been the easiest thing in the world.

Yeah, and so very nearly was I, thought Marsham.

CHAPTER 15

The next couple of weeks passed in a frenzy of schoolwork, prepping for the show, and skating practice. Marsham also photoshopped some pictures of his parents and sent them to Damian. They now had different-coloured eyes and hair, a few more spots and freckles, and in Dad's case, glasses, along with new names: Bill and Ruth. Marsham doubted they would be shown on the film for very long, so it was unlikely anyone would study the images too much.

There was also some publicity for the show that needed to be done. Marsham, as Daniel, had his picture taken and was then interviewed by some journalists. The articles were due to go out the weekend before the first episode was aired.

Marsham felt it had all gone well, but the following day got tricky. Marsham was contacted by an

Ecuadorian newspaper asking awkward questions about the exact location of his parents. Once again Marsham's brain went into overdrive and he told them the location was top secret, as a team of rival explorers were hunting for the same toadstool. It seemed to work.

Finally, the big day arrived and Marsham, Gran and Ethel found themselves back in the studio building for the recording of round 1.

They were standing around in what had been the registration room with the other contestants and their families. Marsham was nervous, but he also felt a sense of relief. Finally, it was time to properly start. He checked out his fellow contestants:

Medhansh was with his parents and looked as if he was standing to attention.

Marc was with Paul again, and their parents, who were fussing over him, which made him seem less cool than previously.

Dionna was with her mother, who looked proud and fearsome. The two of them looked like a formidable pair.

Naomi and her parents were there, along with some other members of her family. She had a notebook and was jotting things down intermittently. She seemed quite relaxed – unlike her mother, who was holding tightly on to one of the arms of her wheelchair and looking around like an anxious meerkat.

Liselle was with her parents and two older siblings. She was twiddling her hair and blinking a lot. She seemed oddly nervous to Marsham, who'd thought she was unaffected by this sort of thing and had seemed quite detached when they'd all been introducing themselves.

Vera was also there doing a terrible job of trying not to look miffed. Her famous father, Mikey Lanston, was with her and doing a terrible job of trying not to look famous.

After a few minutes of uncertainty and muted chatter, the doors opened and in walked Khalid and Selina. The room fell silent, apart from Ethel, who gasped and said, "Oh my!"

"Hello again, everyone," said Khalid when they'd reached the centre of the room. "Wonderful to see you all again, and thank you for the films you've made and interviews you've done. You all look great; you're stars already."

A small murmur of pleasure trickled round the room.

"We have an exciting day ahead. But first, I'd like to

introduce you to someone I'm sure you all know: the one and only Selina Constantin."

A ripple of applause broke out as Selina smiled warmly.

"Thank you, Khalid," she said. "And welcome, everyone. I am proud and humbled to call myself a self-made genius. That's right: self-made. I didn't go to a posh school, I didn't even go to university..." She paused to let the enormity of what she'd just said sink in. "But through hard work and my passion for learning, I showed that anyone, anyone at all, can be not just smart, but super-smart. And that means any one of you could be our winner this year."

"But it's going to be you, Daniel," whispered Gran, far too loudly.

"Now, as you know, *this* series, someone" – she pointedly looked over at Khalid – "decided that we need to expand our horizons. I'm not sure Plato would think it wise, as I'm sure you know he was of the opinion that 'each man is capable of doing one thing well. If he attempts several, he will fail to achieve distinction in any.'"

"Why is she talking about plates?" whispered Gran.

"But," continued Selina. "Such is the situation, so joining us this year as our ice-skating judges" – she practically spat the words out – "are Team GB Olympic skater Edgar Brookes-Jocelyn and ice dancer Julia Lockwood."

The doors opened and in came Edgar and Julia. Edgar had fair hair and a moustache that seemed to be out of control under his nose. He had a big, square chin that was saying, "I'm the boss of this face". Julia had striking blue eyes and hair dyed jet black. She was small, but rippled with toned, taut muscles. Edgar was the better known of the two of them. After winning bronze at the last Winter Olympics, he'd been involved in a car accident that had meant his left leg had had to be amputated below the knee. He now wore a prosthetic leg. The accident had ended his Olympic skating career, but he was now campaigning to have ice skating recognized as a Paralympic sport.

Khalid began to applaud, but Selina immediately continued speaking, so he stopped.

"So lovely to have them with us this year," she said dryly. "Well, that is it from me, but remember, as the

Chinese philosopher Sun Tzu said, it is best to win without fighting."

"What does she mean?" asked Ethel, which was probably what everyone else was thinking too.

A short while later, Marsham, Gran and Ethel were in a dressing room. Marsham's, or rather, Daniel's, dressing room. All the contestants had one: they were next to each other on the first floor; they were the rooms that had been numbered in base 5 on the selection day. Marsham's was fairly small, but there was a sofa, a table, a chair, a desk and a mirror in there. There was also a bowl of fruit on the table, and some magazines.

"Selina really doesn't like the ice-skating judges," said Ethel.

"Shh," said Gran, gesturing to Marsham. "He's revising for the general knowledge round."

Marsham smiled. What Gran said was partially true, but he was also thinking about the electronic Lulu boards and when to go to the toilet and put them into the wig.

He was chewing it over when there was a knock at the door.

"Come in!" all three of them shouted.

The door opened and in trotted a buzzy girl, probably seventeen or eighteen, with long blonde hair, blue eyes and a warm, welcoming smile. She was wearing jeans, a T-shirt and trainers. She had headphones on and a walkie-talkie unit clipped to her back pocket.

"Hello," said the girl. "I'm Gloria, your runner."

"Runner?" said Gran, a confused look on her face.

"It means I run around doing things for people," she said. "Like get them drinks and food. I also do other stuff, like photocopying, and generally help out."

"Do you always run?" said Gran.

"Not always," said Gloria, laughing. "But I like to be quick."

"Isn't that lovely?" said Gran. "I'll have a cup of tea, dear. Milky, please. Ethel?"

"Tea for me too, thank you, love," said Ethel.

"Daniel, can I get you anything?" said Gloria.

Marsham was about to politely say no when he had a sense that Gloria was looking at him oddly. Was his wig lopsided? His nose? Had a contact lens fallen out? A surge of adrenalin hit him and he felt himself go red. Thankfully, though, a moment later Gloria's walkie-talkie crackled. Marsham glanced at himself in the mirror. All looked well.

"Selina wants a coffee," said Gloria. "I'm *her* runner as well. It won't take long, though, I'll be back with your tea soon."

"Never mind, dear," said Gran. "I'll get it myself; I fancy a wander."

"OK," said Gloria. "See ya."

Gloria buzzed out as brightly as she'd buzzed in.

"Come on, Ethel," said Gran. "Let's go to the canteen and leave Marsham in peace."

"Actually, Gran," said Marsham, still feeling uneasy. "I think you and Ethel should always call me Daniel while we're here, even in this room. It's good practice, and you never know if someone can hear us, or maybe walk in on us."

"I second that, Daniel," said Ethel.

"And I third that, Marrrrrr ... Daniel," said Gran, smiling.

"Thanks," said Marsham. "And Gran, please don't tell anyone you're an astronaut or something."

"I wouldn't dream of it," said Gran, heading out with Ethel.

Marsham turned back to his computer and tried to focus, but he just couldn't. He'd been thrown by what he imagined Gloria had seen. It seemed like a tiny thing, but it had had a big effect on him and brought his fears and anxiety back in spades.

"Aaccch!" he exclaimed suddenly, his face scrunched up like an especially wrinkly pug. He sat staring into space until, a few minutes later, Ethel returned. She could tell straight away that something was up.

"What's the matter?" she said.

"Everything," said Marsham. "I've got so much to do. The general knowledge round, the skating, the song. *And* I'm in disguise. I'm sure Gloria could tell, she looked at me oddly."

"I don't think so," said Ethel. "You look fine."

"And then there's also the ... the..." Marsham stopped. The weight of carrying around the secret about cheating was like having a bag of wet sand with him all the time. Surely it couldn't hurt to tell one person? "The cheating."

"Sorry, dear, what did you say?" enquired Ethel.

Marsham sighed. He instantly felt some of that sand falling away, so he told her everything.

"Hmm," said Ethel. "I'm glad you told me. I can help you fit those board things into the wig, but are you sure you read the email correctly? It does seem unusual."

"Yes, I'll show you," he said, picking up his phone. He searched through his emails. "That's odd."

He got the emails up on his computer and searched again, but he couldn't find the one marked "Top Secret" anywhere!

"I don't understand it," he said, a queasy feeling beginning to slither its way around his body. "It was definitely there."

"Maybe it was a joke?" said Ethel.

Suddenly Marsham looked up. That queasy feeling had turned into a huge ball of dread. Something was definitely not right.

"The case of the missing email," said Gran, rubbing her chin and pacing back and forth. Marsham could tell she was imagining herself as a detective. "We should investigate!"

Gran had been in the loo, so Marsham had told her about the cheating when she returned. That ball of dread was growing and was now far worse than the bag of sand had been.

"I don't know," said Marsham. "There's probably a simple explanation, a computer glitch or something."

"Orrrrr," said Gran, still pacing. "It's a trap. Whoever sent it made it look like it was from the show to get you disqualified because they want to win at any cost. You should tell Khalid."

"I don't think that's a good idea," said Marsham, biting his thumbnail. "I'm in disguise, remember? I don't want any more attention on me. And what if it isn't a trap, what if it's a real challenge? The email specifically said not to discuss it with the producers."

"So what are you going to do?" asked Ethel.

"I'm not going to cheat," said Marsham, suddenly finding a decisive streak in himself. "It probably *is* a test the show are doing, but I can't be certain, and surely they wouldn't disqualify me for *not* cheating. . ."

"I agree. Something just doesn't feel right about it," said Ethel.

"There's definitely something funny going on," said Gran. "I'm going to keep an eye on the other contestants, and I suggest you do the same, Mar . . . er, Daniel."

"Yes, OK," said Marsham. "But be discreet about it."

Knock knock.

"Come in!" shouted all three of them. It was Gloria.

"All set, Daniel?" she asked. "They're ready to record the general knowledge round. Exciting!"

"Give us a second, dear," said Gran.

"Sure," said Gloria. "I'll be just outside the door."

"Are you ready, Daniel?" asked Gran.

"Well," said Marsham. "Now that we think someone is trying to get me kicked off the show, I'd say absolutely not."

"Great," said Gran. "Let's do this!"

CHAPTER 16

Suspicion is a strange thing. If you think someone's up to no good, then suddenly something normal, like blinking, becomes something completely different: a sign that maybe the person is *especially nervous* because they are *doing something they shouldn't be*.

For Marsham, being suspicious was playing havoc in his already very full mind.

He was in the actual studio of *Britain's Smartest Kid*. It was directly behind the reception area and felt like a gladiatorial arena. The audience were seated around a heavily lit central circle, which had a lectern in the middle of it. About three metres directly opposite the lectern was a desk with two chairs, and the same distance directly behind it were chairs for the contestants. That was where Marsham was sitting with the others. (Vera was in the audience with her arms folded, *still* looking huffy.) Selina was at the desk next to the show's adjudicator, a serious-looking man called Alexi.

Around the sides were cameras and camera operators, and behind them various other producers, runners and show staff who were lurking where the cameras wouldn't see them. There were also two big screens above the audience on opposite sides.

They weren't recording just yet. Khalid had come out and given a brief talk about health and safety, and now they were waiting for proceedings to properly start.

Marsham had been told he was going last, which allowed him to keep an eye on the other five. But it also meant his nerves might go haywire. Just being on the show, *and in disguise*, was scary enough, but now he was also looking out for someone who could be trying to get him disqualified – a person who would most likely be watching *him* as well.

He glanced up and saw Gran and Ethel in the audience. Gran saw him and pointed two fingers to her eyes to say, "I'm watching things closely." She probably thought she'd done it quite subtly, but to Marsham it seemed about as subtle as a bulldozer being driven by a rhinoceros.

A medium-sized woman with long, light brown hair walked out into the circle. She was the floor manager, the eyes and ears of the show's director, who was directing from a room called the gallery.

"Thank you for waiting, everyone," she said. "We are ready to start. You'll see the show's opening titles and music on the screens, and then we'll come straight to Selina. Here we go in three, two, one. . ."

The show's theme tune burst out around the studio and the screens filled with pictures of Selina and clips from the contestants' films. Marsham looked up and saw Daniel. It was odd, seeing himself in disguise on the screen, but he also had a sense of pride. He'd done it. He was here on the show. This was really happening.

The opening titles finished and all eyes turned to Selina.

"Hello, everyone, and welcome to *Britain's Smartest Kid . . . on Ice!*"

The floor manager started clapping, which was the cue for everyone else to break into rousing applause.

"Yes, that's correct," said Selina. "I did say *on ice*, because in this series we will be testing many different types of intelligence and subjecting our contestants to all manner of different challenges . . . how exciting. It promises to be quite a contest, and we have six wonderful contestants ready to show us just how smart they are in the hope of becoming Britain's Smartest Kid, a title that comes with one hundred thousand pounds and a trip to the Nobel Prize ceremony in Stockholm, Sweden. Thankfully, we are starting with something more traditional: a general knowledge round that is *not* on ice, and our first contestant is Medhansh Gupta. Let's find out a little more about him."

Medhansh's film then played out on the screens, after which Selina said, "Medhansh, could you come to the lectern, please?"

Medhansh jumped up, glanced nervously at his parents in the audience, and made his way to the lectern. When he got there he let out a nervous chuckle that to Marsham sounded like a kitten sneezing.

"Welcome, Medhansh," said Selina.

Medhansh managed a very grimace-y smile at her.

"You have fifteen questions and five seconds in which to answer each one. Are you ready?"

"Yes ... yes ... I am," said Medhansh, blinking as if someone were shining a torch in his eyes.

Clearly, thought Marsham, *I'm not the only one who is nervous.* But was there another reason for Medhansh's nerves?

"Good luck, though I don't think luck will have much to do with it," said Selina. "Question one: the spice saffron is derived from which flower?"

Still blinking furiously, Medhansh said, "Crocus."

"Correct," said Selina.

Having got the first question right, Medhansh seemed to relax a tiny bit. His shoulders dropped and his breathing became a little slower.

By the end of the round, he'd got thirteen correct answers and seemed much happier. Had he cheated, though? Marsham didn't think so, but Medhansh had glanced at his parents a lot during the round. Did they have some sort of code?

YouTuber Marc was up next, and in contrast to how

he'd been earlier, he also seemed nervous. He slipped on the way to the lectern and had to have a sip of water to help calm himself down. Was *that* part of his plan to cheat? Was he the one who had sent the email? He finished the round with twelve correct answers.

The third contestant was Dionna. She brushed her brown hair out of her eyes as she walked to the lectern. She was immaculately dressed again in a smart top and jeans, and seemed confident, but Marsham knew that sometimes people who are nervous and shy pretend to be like that to hide how they're really feeling.

She had a great round, though, and if she hadn't given an incorrect answer to a question that Marsham thought was easy (What is the capital of Nicaragua?), she would have got a perfect score and received an extra point for doing so. Instead, she finished with an impressive fourteen correct answers, though Marsham did notice that someone sneezed loudly twice during her round. Was that a signal?

Naomi and then Liselle followed. Naomi kept tapping the sides of her wheelchair, which she'd manoeuvred next to the lectern, and rubbing her hands along the wheels. She also asked for a question to be repeated because someone coughed quite loudly in the middle of Selina asking it. During Liselle's round, Liselle was constantly touching her glasses and her left foot was bouncing up and down like there was a spring underneath it. They had both finished with eleven correct answers.

Marsham was next. As Liselle headed back to her seat, he felt a huge surge of adrenalin. He also felt a knot of anger and frustration inside his belly. The other five had all seemed nervous in different ways, and they had all done some slightly unusual things.

Or had they?

The suspicion was driving him round the bend.

They couldn't *all* be cheating?!

"Can I have our sixth and final contestant, Daniel, please?" said Selina.

Marsham smiled weakly, gulped and stood up.

CHAPTER 17

"Hello, Daniel," said Selina after his film had played – Gran's back had featured for a moment. Selina's voice was calm and silky. "Are you ready?"

"Yes," said Daniel, far too loudly. He'd wanted to come across as confident, but had just sounded weird.

"Good," said Selina, completely unfazed. "Question one: what is the smallest state in America?"

Part of Marsham's brain knew he knew the answer, but another part told him to wait to hear it from the electronic boards in his wig. Then another part reminded him that he no longer had the boards in his wig, after which yet another part told him to relax in case someone was watching him closely – which about two hundred people actually were doing.

The part that knew he knew the answer then took control and told him to just say the answer,

which he was about to do when Selina said, "Sorry, you're out of time. The answer is Rhode Island. Question two: which English city was once known as Duroliponte?"

This time Marsham wasn't a hundred per cent certain. There were two options in his head, so he settled on one.

"Oxford," he said.

"No, that's incorrect," said Selina. "The answer is Cambridge."

Marsham groaned inwardly. The nerves, the suspicion, the pressure, the disguise, being in front of an audience – it was all getting to him and scrambling his mind. He couldn't think straight.

He felt the panic start to bubble up. He pushed it back down, but suddenly realized he should have been listening to Selina!

". . . planet in our solar system."

"Erm, I didn't hear, I think . . . is it . . . Jupiter?" he spluttered.

"No," said Selina. "That's the largest. The smallest is Mercury."

Now there was a feeling of collective embarrassment coming from the audience. People shifted in their seats, and there were some nervous coughs. If Marsham didn't pull himself together soon, Daniel would be a laughing stock. He forced himself to concentrate.

"Question four: where is the British Formula One Grand Prix held?" asked Selina.

Marsham looked at Gran and Ethel. They were sitting forward in their seats, chewing their top lips and gripping their hands tightly together. Marsham took a deep breath.

"Silverstone," he said.

"Correct," said Selina, as the whole audience relaxed a little and Gran let out a yelp.

Having finally got a question right, Marsham managed to calm down for the rest of the round. He didn't exactly sail through it, but he didn't do too badly. He got eight more questions right, so finished with nine correct answers. It meant that he was bottom with just one point on the leader board. The person who came first in each round got six points, the second person got five points and so on. Naomi had answered her questions more quickly than Liselle, so even though they both had eleven correct answers, she had three points, and Liselle had two.

"Thank you, Daniel," said Selina.

Marsham got up to a small round of applause and

two loud whoops, and made his way back to the other contestants.

"Really well done," said Medhansh as Marsham sat down.

"That was great," said Dionna.

"Terrific, Daniel," said Naomi.

"You did good, bro," said Marc, now back to his slick, cool self.

"Excellent round," said Liselle.

Marsham smiled, but couldn't help thinking they were all putting it on for the cameras.

"That is the end of the general knowledge round," said Selina. "And if we look at the scores. . ."

Selina stopped. Khalid had come out and was walking towards her. He looked very serious, almost as if he was going to tell her off. He didn't; instead, he whispered something in her ear.

For the first time that day, Selina looked unsettled, a veil of disbelief falling over her face. A moment later, though, she had composed herself again. Khalid nodded and left.

"Well, it seems that we have *not* come to the end of the general knowledge round after all," said Selina.

Her tone was stern and serious, and a sense of unease and confusion permeated through the audience.

"This has never happened before, but. . ." Selina took a deep breath. "I regret to inform you that someone, and I can't believe I'm about to say this, someone . . . has *cheated*."

CHAPTER 18

The collective intake of breath was huge. All eyes were on Selina.

"No, that's not right, I mean . . . it is . . . but I was told to, *you* told me to, it was part of the show. . ."

Like a giant audience creature, everyone moved their head to look at the person who had just spoken: Liselle.

"Well, at least you're not denying it," said Selina. "But really, a receiver in your glasses? Did you honestly think we wouldn't detect that?"

"Yes, I hoped . . . but I got an email . . . from the show," spluttered Liselle, her face almost the colour of her ginger hair. "You told me to cheat, you called it devious intelligence, you know you did!"

"I know nothing of the sort," said Selina. "You may have fallen foul of a prank. Or perhaps you're lying.

Either way, I'm sorry, but you have been disqualified."

Liselle stared at Selina for a moment and then burst into tears. Marsham watched as her mother and father rushed out to console her, followed closely by Khalid and another member of staff who ushered them all out. He was feeling extremely concerned by this turn of events and was wondering whether he should say anything about the email *he'd* received. A moment later, he had his answer.

"Could it be true about an email?" said Dionna, wide-eyed with disbelief.

"Maybe," said Marc. "But I'd never be caught out like that."

The rest agreed with Marc, nodding their heads.

"Yeah, me neither," said Marsham, who was feeling both very stupid and very lucky. He wondered if any of the others had in fact received an email and were just bluffing, as he was.

"But if there was an email," said Naomi. "Who sent it? Who stands to benefit from this?"

As if in answer, Selina continued, "In the circumstances, we shall call upon our reserve contestant, Vera. She is now our sixth finalist and will join the competition."

Vera positively bounded out from the audience and

stood at the lectern with a huge grin on her small, ferret-like face. Marsham and the other contestants eyed her suspiciously.

Three minutes later she was sitting in Liselle's seat having answered ten questions correctly. Marsham was still last.

"Hello, everyone," chirped Vera.

The others said nothing, but then Dionna seemed to suddenly remember they were still being filmed and said, "Hello, Vera, really well done," at which point the others, including Marsham, all congratulated her.

"Well, that was quite a round!" said Selina. "After which the leader board looks like this."

Dionna	6
Medhansh	5
Marc	4
Naomi	3
Vera	2
Daniel	1

"Next for our finalists, it's the memory test, which of course this year will be taking place on ice." Selina could hardly have looked more disdainful; she may as well have vomited the words out.

Marsham took a deep breath and was about to stand up when Khalid came out and said, "Sorry, everyone! Could you please remain in your seats? We have a few pick-ups and retakes to do. Thank you, we won't take long."

Five minutes later, after Selina had been recorded saying some of the questions again, Marsham was back in his dressing room with Gran and Ethel.

"I don't understand," said Gran. "Why does Selina say the questions again? That will look silly on telly."

"You won't hear her saying the questions again on telly," explained Marsham patiently. "The show is not live, it's pre-recorded, so sometimes they do bits again in case they weren't so good the first time, or if there was a technical problem."

"Still seems strange to me," said Gran.

"Look, it's very simple," said Marsham, about to explain it again ... before deciding it wasn't worth it. "Forget it. We need to talk about what happened with Liselle!"

"I had a feeling she was cheating," said Ethel. "She was touching her hair the whole time, and her eyes were looking everywhere."

"I spotted some things as well," said Gran. "Naomi was fiddling with her wheels a lot, and Marc took far too many sips of water."

"And Dionna was smiling weirdly," said Ethel. "And someone kept sneezing near us, and one of the camera operators definitely looked at his phone once."

"OK, OK," said Marsham. "Great work, but the most important thing is that we now know for certain that someone – or maybe more than one person – is up to something. And who knows what they'll do next."

CHAPTER 19

"This is the production office," said Gloria. "It's pretty busy."

Marsham, Ethel and Gran peered into the office. It was indeed teeming with people.

"Who are they all?" asked Gran.

"Oh, there are all sorts in here," said Gloria. "Other runners, researchers, production secretaries, production managers, assistant producers, series producers. It takes a lot of people to make a show like this."

They were on a break. It was mainly for lunch, but a camera crew had come into Marsham's dressing room. They were filming all the contestants and asking them how they'd found the first round and the show in general. Marsham kept his answers pretty generic.

Once the camera crew had gone, Marsham asked Gloria to show them round the studio building. (With a mystery to solve, he thought they should find out more about the show and who everyone was.) Gloria was happy to oblige.

The actual building was like a maze. They'd walked past the registration room and turned left through some doors at the end of that corridor into another corridor where they found the production office. Opposite it was a door marked "Production Gallery".

"This is where the director and her team direct the show from," said Gloria, opening the door a little. The gallery was quite dark, but Marsham could see lots of people sitting facing a bank of TV screens.

"Why doesn't someone put a light on?" said Gran. "I can hardly see anything."

"Come on," said Gloria, chuckling, "Selina will probably want another coffee soon, so we'd better get a move on."

"Where does Selina live?" said Ethel.

"Erm, I don't know," said Gloria. "She probably has a big house somewhere."

"Oh, no, sorry, dear, forgive me," said Ethel. "I meant, where does she live here, in this building?"

"Ohhh, I see," said Gloria. "She has a dressing room on the second floor. The ice-skating judges are up there as well."

They walked further along the corridor past a medical room, a room where people were doing make-up, and a wardrobe room full of clothes on rails.

"What's in here?" asked Gran. They had come to a door marked "QS", nestled at the far end of the corridor.

"Oh, don't go in there," said Gloria quickly. "That's where the question setters work."

"The question setters?" said Ethel.

"They're the people who write the questions for the show," said Gloria. "And double-check the answers. What goes on in that room is top secret. Khalid is the only other person allowed in there. He goes through the questions and then takes them to Selina so she can rehearse them for pronunciation and things like that."

"Oooh," oooh-ed Gran and Ethel.

Marsham, on the other hand, had jolted when he'd heard the words *top secret*. Someone desperate to win the show would be very keen to get into that room.

"OK, tour's over," breezed Gloria. "I'll take you back to your dressing room."

They headed back, but just as they came out of the lift and approached Marsham's room, someone let out a terrifying scream: "Aaaaaaaaaaaaaaaaaaah!"

The four of them stopped in their tracks. Then, a moment later, they rushed through the double doors to see a very distraught Dionna lying on the floor. The other finalists had all come out of their rooms to see what was going on.

"Medical attention needed in the finalists' dressing room area!" said Gloria into her walkie-talkie.

"Owww," moaned Dionna, holding her ankle. Despite being on the floor in pain, she didn't have a hair out of place – though her dimpled cheeks were flushed red.

"What happened?" asked Vera.

"There was a spider in my room, a big one," Dionna said through clenched teeth. "I hate spiders, so I ran out quickly, but I've done something to my ankle, it really hurts."

"Perhaps your next invention should be a spider-catching machine," said Naomi, unhelpfully. "I'm sure that would be a big seller."

"Stand clear, please," said Khalid, hurrying through with Selina and the ice-skating judges, Edgar and Julia, following closely behind.

Khalid knelt down and held Dionna's ankle gently. He moved it slowly to the right and the

left. Dionna grimaced and yelped in pain.

"It looks as if you've twisted your ankle," said Khalid. "I'll fetch one of the medics to look you over."

"Dionna! Dionna! What's going on?"

Everyone turned to see Dionna's mother barging through the crowd.

"There was a spider in my room, Mother," wailed Dionna. "Someone put it there, I know they did! The interview I did last week reported that I hate spiders. Someone did this on purpose!"

A stunned silence followed Dionna's outburst. *This is very strange,* thought Marsham. *Could it be that whoever sent the email also put the spider in Dionna's room? And if so, was the email just the beginning, and now things are starting to ramp up and get dangerous?*

CHAPTER 20

"She won't be able to skate," said the medic after examining Dionna's ankle.

"I should think not," said Dionna's mother in a way that made it clear that if anyone dared to think otherwise they would have her to deal with. Marsham was just impressed that she was managing to stay upright on the sharpest stiletto heels he'd ever seen.

"Oh dear," said Selina. "Now we won't be able to test Dionna's physical intelligence."

The skating judges glared at her. She was being sarcastic and they knew it. Could their dislike of her, or her dislike of them, have something to do with the email and the spider?

"Oh, that is a shame, isn't it, Selina?" said a voice.

Everyone turned to see Vera's father, Mikey Lanston, who towered over everyone else. "Good to see you again, by the way," he said to her. "Loved doing that celebrity quiz show with you."

"Erm, yes, of course," said Selina, clearly a little unsure as to what Mikey was referring to.

"Soooo handsome," simpered Ethel.

"What's going on?" said another voice.

Everyone turned again to see that two more people had joined them: a tall, middle-aged man wearing a jacket with elbow pads and a woman with dark hair, glasses and big hoop earrings.

"Those are two of the question setters," Gloria whispered to Gran.

"It's fine," said Khalid. "Although Dionna has had a small accident and won't be able to skate."

"An accident!" shrieked Dionna's mother. "Didn't you hear what she said? Someone did this on purpose. What are you going to do about it?"

"I don't really believe..." Khalid started to say, but then seemed to think better of it. "I think the best thing is for Dionna to rest up now and let us figure out what to do about the skating round."

"Maybe we should cancel it," said Selina, quietly but loud enough for everyone to hear.

"Good one," chuckled Mikey. "Like it, Selina."

"Let's get you up," said the medic to Dionna. "But

don't put any weight on your bad ankle." He carefully helped Dionna up and back to her room.

"Ow, oo, ow," she cried with each step.

"Come on," said Marsham. "Let's go. Ethel?"

Ethel was watching Dionna. She seemed to be deep in thought.

"Sorry, dear," she said. "Coming now."

"Would you like me to bring you some lunch?" asked Gloria as they headed off.

"Yes, please, love," said Gran.

Back in the room, after they'd eaten the food Gloria had brought – lasagne and salad, with strawberry mousse for pud – Gran and Ethel were sitting quietly on the sofa while Marsham was at the desk writing his song out backwards. He was still finding it difficult to focus and kept tutting and shaking his head.

"Why don't I give you the once-over?" said Ethel. "Everything needs to be nice and secure for the ice skating." This time she hadn't brought the huge suitcase with her. Instead, she had stuffed various items into her already very full handbag.

Marsham agreed and moved his chair so that he was sitting in front of the mirror.

Ethel tinkered away on his face for a few minutes

and then said, "You know, when that girl was hobbling away, something about it didn't feel right."

"What do you mean?" said Marsham.

"Well, it's partly intuition," said Ethel. "But also, I've worked with a lot of actors in my time, some of whom were ... well, let's just say, *not the best*. So I know bad acting when I see it, and to me, that was bad acting."

"Really?" said Marsham. "Gran, what did you think?"

"Sorry, dear," said Gran. She'd been looking at something on her phone. "What did you say?"

"Did you think Dionna was acting oddly?" asked Marsham.

"Not really, dear," said Gran. "But I think I might know who the cheat is. Look!"

Gran handed Marsham her phone. There was a paused *The Q&A Kids* clip on it. Marc and Paul were sitting next to each other looking straight into the camera. They were both wearing white T-shirts with "The Q&A Kids" emblazoned across them. Paul was clearly older, he had designer stubble on his face, but otherwise he had the same blonde hair and green eyes that Marc had, making them look a lot like twins.

Marsham unpaused it.

"My brother is on *Britain's Smartest Kid!*" shouted

Paul, from the screen. "And he's going to win, aren't you, Marc?"

"You bet!" cried Marc. "Nothing and no one is going to stop me. I will destroy my opponents!"

"Failure is not an option," yelled Paul. "Whatever it takes."

"Whatever it takes!" shouted Marc as the two of them high-fived.

Marsham paused the clip.

"I don't understand," he said.

"Didn't you hear him?" Gran said. "He said he was going to destroy his opponents, WHATEVER it takes. So he must have sent the email."

"It's just hype, Gran," said Marsham. "Fighting talk. He doesn't mean it."

"Oh, I think he does, dear," replied Gran.

"Could I have a look?" asked Ethel.

Marsham handed the phone to Ethel when suddenly they heard someone screaming at the top of their voice.

"No! No! No! That's not right!"

The three of them looked at each other. It was coming from Medhansh's dressing room next door. It sounded like a woman's voice, so Marsham guessed it was his mother. She was being very loud and unpleasant.

"You have to do better!" she shrieked again. "No

one cares about who comes second! Start again, and concentrate this time!"

"She's being especially hard on him," said Ethel. "I'm not sure someone screaming at me like that would help me do well."

Things went silent for a few moments, then the short interlude of peace was shattered by:

"Wrong! Wrong! Wrong!"

Marsham shook his head and was about to get back to working on the song when there was a knock at the door.

"Oh, for goodness' sake," he snapped. "What now?"

"Come in," shouted Gran.

Gloria trotted in, as gleefully as ever.

"Hiiii," she said. "Got some news. Obviously Dionna can't skate, so it's been decided that she'll do another physical task during the memory test. But, because she won't have had the same amount of time to prepare, it'll be quite a simple one involving catching balls. Are you OK with that, Daniel?"

"No problem," said Marsham.

"Cool," said Gloria. "Catch you later."

"Bye," said Gran and Ethel, waving.

"THAT IS INCORRECT!!" came a humungous shriek from next door.

"Right, that's it, if you've finished, Ethel, I'm going for a walk," said Marsham. "This is a terrible place to concentrate."

"Yes, all done," said Ethel. "Nothing is going to shift that nose, apart from maybe if you fell on it at great speed on ice." She smiled broadly.

Marsham shook his head and smiled. Sometimes you just had to laugh. "See you later," he said.

"See you later . . . *Daniel*," said Gran.

Marsham walked down the stairs and was heading for the exit, but then decided to take a detour towards the question setters' room. He walked past the registration room and into the corridor where the production office was. A few people were milling about, and a couple of runners said hello to him, but the coast was clear. He was almost there when up ahead he saw Naomi. Luckily her wheelchair was positioned with its back to Marsham, so he stopped by the wardrobe room with all the clothes rails and watched.

Naomi was writing in her notebook and intermittently glancing up to look at the room. She suddenly took out her phone and quickly took a photo of the door and the surrounding area.

Marsham was intrigued. Was Naomi trying to figure out how to get inside unnoticed?

Suddenly, the door of the room opened and out came Khalid holding a folder. Marsham shrank back further; he was almost in the wardrobe room now, though thankfully it was empty, the people who worked there must all have been in the canteen having lunch. He could just about hear what was going on.

"Hello, Naomi," Khalid said. "What are you doing here?"

"Oh, I was looking for the disabled toilet," she said.

"I think you might be a little lost," Khalid said. "Come on, I'll show you where it is."

Marsham waited a few seconds before stepping out into the corridor. His head was buzzing with questions. Naomi was clearly up to something, but what? Was she trying to get into the room? Or was she somehow hoping to get a look at the folder Khalid was holding, which must contain the questions? Or, unlikely as it seemed, were they in this together?

It was hardly the best preparation for Marsham's memory round on ice. Incredibly, he'd almost forgotten about that. It was time to put everything else out of his mind. He had to focus on his song and try to mentally go through the skating lessons Tabatha had given him. He returned to his dressing room.

"Hi," he said as he entered.

"Ah, there you are, Daniel," said Gran. "We have interesting news. Sit down."

"But I really need to get on and—"

"It won't take a second," said Gran. "Tell him, Ethel."

"Well," said Ethel. "I was parched, so I went to get a drink and saw Vera on the phone to her mum. I worked that out because Vera kept saying 'mum' a lot."

"Erm, good work, Ethel," said Marsham. "Was there anything else?"

"Yes," said Ethel. "Vera kept assuring her mum that she was revising as much as possible and studying till really late – I think her mum was giving her quite a hard time – but then, at the end, she said she was going to get her dad to speak to Selina because celebrities always do favours for each other and she's sure Selina will help her win."

"Yes, that is interesting, but wait till you hear what I have to tell you," said Marsham, but they did have to wait, because the next moment there was a knock at the door.

"Time to get your skates on, Marsham!" shouted Gloria from outside.

CHAPTER 21

Push with both feet, don't look down, make sure your legs aren't too far apart.

Marsham, in skates, was sitting by the rink with the other finalists trying to remember what Tabatha had taught him. He'd decided not to be too ambitious in his first skating round, so he'd learnt a pretty basic routine. But he still had to do it in disguise, in front of cameras and a crowd of people while reciting a song backwards.

He glanced at the others. Marc seemed a little edgy, and Naomi was fiddling with the attachments to her wheelchair, but Medhansh was in a terrible state: he was blinking furiously and chewing his nails as if he hadn't eaten for a week. Vera, on the other hand, seemed smug and confident, and Dionna, who now had a bandage on her ankle, was quiet.

"Hope it doesn't hurt too much," said Naomi to her.

That was the cue for the others to all offer some sort of supportive comment to Dionna.

She responded ruefully with: "It is still quite sore. I'm gutted not to be able to skate. Good luck to all of you."

"Thank you, everyone," shouted the floor manager. "We're about to start recording, in three, two, one. . ."

"Welcome," said Selina, who was standing just off the ice at the opposite end of the rink to the contestants, "to our ice rink for our first test of" – she paused and the slightest smile meandered across her face – "physical intelligence. This will combine a memory test with ice skating. The memory test, of course, can be accurately scored. However, when it comes to ice skating, this is something of a more subjective skill, so we are welcoming two new faces to the show, Team GB Olympic skater Edgar Brookes-Jocelyn and ice dancer Julia Lockwood."

The audience applauded, and Edgar and Julia smiled from their judges' area tucked into the side of the rink.

"Edgar," Selina continued, "what will you be looking for today?"

The moment Edgar started talking, Selina made it quite obvious that she had no interest in listening to him by looking intently through her notes.

Marsham once again wondered if Selina's dislike of

the ice-skating part of the show could be connected to the mysterious goings-on. . .

He shook his head. This wasn't the time to be thinking about things like that.

"Thank you, Edgar," said Selina, suddenly looking up. She hadn't listened to a word. "Very informative. Now, unfortunately Dionna has sprained her ankle, so will be performing a different physical task, but otherwise I believe everyone else is fighting fit. So, let's begin. This time we're starting with Daniel."

There was another ripple of applause and Marsham carefully made his way to the centre of the rink.

He got there safely and came to a halt, thanks to Tabatha, by using a snow plough stop, where he bent his knees and pushed his skates into a V position.

There was a moment of silence that seemed to last for ages. In that time, Marsham's heart raced as if it was trying to prove to all the other organs that it was the fastest. He couldn't work out whether he was hot or cold or somewhere in between. He was bathed in a spotlight and couldn't see the audience at all. It was both a terrifying and magical experience, but a moment later he was yanked back to reality when Selina said, "Are you ready?"

Marsham nodded.

"Excellent," said Selina. "Best of luck."

Marsham took a deep breath and pushed off to his left.

"Shirt a on lions three. . ."

He glided forward, then put his right leg slightly in front of his left leg and eased himself left.

"Home coming. . ."

He felt himself wobbling and had to concentrate hard on not falling over. Ethel's jokey comment about his nose came rushing back to him. Thankfully he stayed upright, but now he had to think carefully about the next word in the song.

"Football's," he said suddenly, relieved. He stopped and very slowly moved backwards on the ice.

The next sixty seconds passed in a blur for Marsham. He didn't fall over, and he *thought* he'd remembered the words in the right order, but he couldn't be sure.

"Thank you, Daniel," said Selina. "You missed out two words and got one in the wrong place, so that makes three mistakes. Now let's hear from our ice-skating judges and their *opinion* as to how well you skated."

"Thank you so much, Selina," said Julia, smiling ever so sweetly. "Daniel, even though your routine was quite easy, you performed it well and showed a good grasp of basic skating techniques. Your focus was good, and when there were a couple of wobbles you readjusted and continued without too much difficulty. We have given you a score of 8.7."

"8.7, how precise," said Selina. "So, taking away your three memory mistakes, that gives you a total of 5.7. Well done, Daniel."

There was applause as Marsham skated back to his seat by the side of the rink. The others congratulated him, and then he carefully checked to see that everything was still in place. All seemed good.

"So, let's move on to our next finalist: Vera."

Vera stood up and smiled confidently. She skated towards the middle of the rink, but when she was halfway there, she turned and did a split jump in the air before landing, spinning round and stopping instantly.

It was frankly, gobsmacking.

CHAPTER 22

Vera started her routine, and it was immediately clear that she'd become a pretty good skater since the race, when she had been on par with Marsham. Her routine was full of jumps and tricks, and her recall wasn't too bad either. She finished with just one mistake in the memory test.

"Well," said Edgar, "that was rather impressive."

"I've been training intensively with a professional from *Dancing on Ice* that my dad knows," said Vera. "I pick up new skills very quickly."

"So it seems," said Edgar. "You threw in some quite difficult moves there, and you pulled them off well. A couple of your leg extensions could have been better, and you didn't land one of your jumps properly, but overall: excellent, 9.6."

Vera beamed – with one memory mistake her total

score was 8.6 – and gracefully floated back to her seat. The others congratulated her, but Marsham couldn't help wondering if it was fair that she'd had such a high level of coaching.

Naomi was next. Her wheelchair had been adapted for the ice, and her performance was good. Edgar was full of praise, and she scored 9.2. She also made three mistakes in her memory test, so her total was 6.2.

"Thank you, Naomi," said Selina. "Our next finalist is Dionna."

Dionna stood up and was helped to a chair by the side of the rink. She sat in it as a succession of tennis balls were thrown at her. Marsham couldn't help thinking that catching them was a lot easier than skating, a thought that was confirmed when she finished the round with no memory test mistakes and only one dropped ball. As ten was the maximum possible skating score, she lost one point for the dropped ball, so her final score was 9.

"Thank you, everyone," said the floor manager after Dionna had returned to her seat. "There'll now be a short break while we reset the lights and camera positions for the next contestant. Please stay in your seats."

Thankfully, the contestants could move around,

so Marsham stood up and did one of those awesome, blissful stretches that bring joy to every part of your body.

"I fancy a drink," he said to himself, as he crimpled back together.

He looked around and spotted Gloria by the entrance to the rink.

"Hey, Gloria," he said, wandering over. "Could I get a bottle of water? Gloria?"

For some reason Gloria wasn't responding.

"Gloria?"

She seemed to be miles away looking at. . .

Marsham followed her gaze. She was transfixed on Marc and his brother, Paul, who were standing together talking. Paul had been in the audience, so Marsham wondered if Gloria was caught in a trap of indecision – should she tell him to sit back down or not?

"Gloria?" said Marsham again, a little more loudly.

"What? Yes. Hello," said Gloria, snapping out of it.

"Sorry to bother you," said Marsham, "but could I get a bottle of water?"

"Of course," said Gloria. "I'll get it right away."

She headed off, still half-looking at Marc and Paul in a strange, dreamy way.

Once the break was over, Marc was in fact the next

finalist to skate. He was good on the ice – he'd finished first in the race on the selection day – and scored 9.1. He only made one mistake on the memory challenge, giving him a score of 8.1.

"And finally," said Selina, "Medhansh."

As soon as Selina said his name, Medhansh jumped up as if some wires attached to his head had been pulled very hard. He shot a glance at his mother and then made his way uncertainly to the middle of the rink.

"Whenever you are ready, Medhansh," said Selina.

Medhansh nodded about four times. The song he'd had to learn backwards was "Rolling in the Deep" by Adele, and as he pushed off he said, "Beat the ... whoooooaaah..."

He'd pushed off much too hard and was wobbling like a jellyfish on, well, ice. He just about managed to stay upright and came to a halt, but now sweat had started pouring down his face. He looked like a lost and very scared sparrow.

"Er, er ... yes, beat the..." he said, repeating the words he'd already said. Marsham could see he was really struggling.

"Ah, yes, I have to skate," he suddenly said, as if he'd just remembered where he was. He pushed off with his skates again.

"B, b, b, beat the to iiiiiiiiiiiittttttttttt!"

Medhansh was speeding towards the judges. Everyone knew what was about to happen.

He went flying into the side wall. . .

Thudddd!

Then the top half of his body went down over the wall while his legs went flying upwards.

"Ooooooohhhhhhhh!" he hollered.

A moment later he was lying spread-eagled across a shocked Edgar and Julia, moaning, "Have to do better, have to better, have to do better."

It was a complete and utter disaster.

CHAPTER 23

"What an interesting test of physical intelligence that was," said Selina. "So, if we look at the final totals, I can tell you that Dionna came first in that round, Vera second, Marc finished third, Naomi was fourth, Daniel fifth and Medhansh was sixth."

Everyone in the audience applauded, apart from Medhansh's mother. She looked like she might explode.

"Which means," continued Selina. "Combining the scores for these rounds, the leader board looks like this..."

Dionna	12
Marc	8
Vera	7
Naomi	6
Medhansh	6
Daniel	3

It didn't make great reading for Marsham, but as Selina was about to explain, there would be plenty of opportunities to catch up.

"So, that wraps things up for today," she said into the cameras. "But next week our finalists will be taking part in a spelling bee, a mental arithmetic round *and* we will be putting their *artistic* intelligence to the test by asking them to draw a picture whilst skating. I simply cannot wait for that. Goodnight."

The audience applauded and started to get up, but the floor manager came out and asked if everyone could remain seated for a few minutes as they had some more filming to do. A camera crew then positioned themselves by the side of the contestants, who each spoke about how the skating round had gone for them. Medhansh didn't say very much.

The moment the crew had finished and the floor manager had told everyone they could go, Marsham could see Medhansh's mother get up, the fury embedded in her face. She marched towards Khalid, who was standing behind one of the cameras just by the skating judges' area. Medhansh's father was trotting awkwardly behind her, looking intently at the floor.

"What are you playing at?!" she shrieked at Khalid,

her eyes glaring wildly. "Medhansh's memory task was much harder than anyone else's. It's completely unfair. I demand you give him another song to learn, right now!"

Khalid looked stunned. He was used to dealing with irate parents, but this was out of the ballpark. Unfortunately, Medhansh's mother's attack had opened the floodgates and a moment later Dionna's mother and three members of Naomi's family descended on him too, followed closely by the ice-skating judges complaining about Selina's attitude.

Marsham stood, looking for Gran and Ethel. He couldn't see them, but he did see Naomi. She was to the right of the contestants' area, chatting to the question setter with the big hooped earrings.

Whatever can they be talking about? thought Marsham. He was contemplating moving closer to try and hear when he spotted Gran and Ethel. They had joined the throng around Khalid – Gran was shouting at him about something. He caught Ethel's eye and she made a face which said, *I don't know what she's doing.* Then Ethel pointed over to the other side of the rink, where Selina stood with Vera's father. They seemed to be having a great laugh.

Marsham gave Ethel a thumbs up and started to

make his way towards the pair of them when he heard a heated discussion coming from the boot room to the left of the exit doors. He edged closer, but a moment later Marc burst out of the room and stormed past him, looking anything but cool. Marsham couldn't be sure if Marc had seen him, but a few seconds later, Dionna appeared and almost bumped into him.

"Hi," said Marsham. "Is everything OK?"

"Just peachy," said Dionna, smiling sweetly at him.

"Oh, good, because. . ." Marsham started to say, but Dionna had walked on. He shrugged and was about to head off himself when he felt a small tug at the back of his mind, as if he'd realized something but it hadn't quite made its way to the front of his mind yet. What was it? What was it?

Then it hit him.

Dionna hadn't been limping.

PART 4

THE SEMI-FINAL

CHAPTER 24

"I read the contestants' interviews," said Adrian. "Marc's going to win, no doubt about it."

"Vera's my winner," said Nainan. "She got lucky when that other contestant was disqualified, so it's all pointing to her."

It was Monday morning and Marsham was back at school. The show was due to be on television that evening, and the previous day's papers had been full of the Liselle cheating story. The show had leaked it and the publicity was doing them no harm at all.

For the last couple of years, as soon as the contestants were announced in the papers, Marsham and his friends had each picked the contestant they thought would win. Of course, having not actually seen them, this was based on very little; it was just a bit of fun.

"Nah," said Marsham. "Naomi all the way, she's super intelligent, I can tell."

"No chance," said Adrian. "Unless she's cheating *as well* and it hasn't been found out?"

"Yeah, she could have something in her wheelchair," said Nainan. "I mean, what was that other contestant thinking, putting a receiver in her glasses? She must be a complete idiot."

Marsham felt the pit of his stomach give a small flip. It could so easily have been him. He was also torn about the fact that neither of his mates thought Daniel could win. On one level he was pleased because it meant they wouldn't be focussing on him so much, but on another, he was miffed because they seemed to have written him off already. A moment later, he had other things to worry about.

"I quite like Daniel as well though," said Adrian. "Because he likes military history like me."

"Yeah, I saw that," said Nainan. "And he also likes graphic novels like me. Maybe I'll change to him instead of Vera."

"You can't," said Marsham, a bit too quickly. "Once you've chosen someone you can't change, that's the rule, isn't it?"

"Is it?" said Nainan and Adrian together.

"'Course it is," said Marsham. "Come on, we don't want to be late for Biology."

Marsham headed off, but he could sense his friends making a "I never knew that, is he right?" face to each other. Now that he'd actually recorded the first show, it was eating him up inside not being able to tell them. It was also eating him up having to lie to them. If he wasn't careful, he wouldn't have any insides left at all.

He knew they were trustworthy, but when you tell someone a big, big secret, then it becomes difficult for *them* to keep it. What if they accidentally said something to someone that gave the game away? Or what if the three of them were overheard talking about it?

No, it's too risky, thought Marsham. *Stay strong, stay strong.*

The show wasn't mentioned again till home time.

"When is it on tonight?" asked Adrian as they were leaving school.

"Seven thirty," said Nainan. "Hey, why don't we FaceTime each other and watch it together?"

"Great idea," said Adrian.

"Yeah, brilliant," said Marsham. 'I just hope the reception holds up at my house, it's been rubbish lately."

"It was OK when I was last round," said Adrian.

"Yeah, but my parents have changed provider since then, and it's been pretty bad," said Marsham. "Hopefully it'll be OK, though, see you later."

Marsham headed home and was relieved that Mum and Dad were working in their offices when he got in. He knew it was going to be tricky watching the show with them later; at least he could now relax in his room a little without having to deal with more difficult questions.

He went in to the kitchen to grab some orange juice and found Gran sitting at the table reading a book called *To Bee or Not to Bee?*

"Hello, dear," she said. "Looking forward to tonight?"

"Yes," said Marsham. "And no. It'll be weird."

"Don't you worry," said Gran. "I won't put my foot in it."

"Oh, no, I didn't mean that, Gran," said Marsham, instantly feeling bad that that was what Gran thought he was worrying about.

"Well, then," she said, "we'll just sit back and relax, watch the show all together, like we normally do."

"Yes," said Marsham. "Though, actually, Gran, let's keep an eye out for anything we missed when we were there. You never know, we might spot something."

"Right you are," said Gran. "I'll let Ethel know."

"Great," said Marsham. "Meet in my room after for a debrief."

Marsham headed upstairs and lay on his bed with Tonks nestled by his feet. His mind felt very full and he tried to empty it, but it kept filling up with thoughts again. It would be so much easier just to tell Mum and Dad the truth, but then, it *also* felt like it would be so much more *difficult* to tell them the truth. They might be disappointed in him for pretending to be average, they could get angry and upset, worst of all they could go to the school. The mean kid and his gang would have a field day if they found out; Marsham could already guess the sort of things they'd be saying: *"Ooh, Mummy Slug and Daddy Slug have come to school to tell teacher... Ooh, do you need them to hold your hand when you cross the road?"*

The thoughts kept on coming, along with nerves and excitement about seeing the show on television, until, incredibly, exhaustion won the day and Marsham fell asleep.

"Marsham! Marsham! It's nearly seven thirty. The show's about to start."

Marsham jolted awake. He felt groggy, he felt sleepy, he ... could hear something buzzing.

"My phone," he said.

He grabbed it and could see an incoming FaceTime call from Nainan. He declined it.

"Sorry, guys," he said to himself. "Coming, Mum!"

He rubbed the sleep out of his eyes and headed downstairs. He could feel the nerves reawakening, sending shards of anxiety coursing round his body. He'd already had plenty of tests, but this felt as if it was going to be a big one.

CHAPTER 25

"Ooh, look, Gran," said Mum. "She's got the same cardigan as you!"

Marsham froze. They were all watching the show, Selina had called Daniel to the lectern, and now his film was playing. Gran, with her back to the camera, was in Ethel's kitchen, talking about Daniel. Her voice sounded a little different coming out of the TV, but there was no getting away from that cardigan. Marsham felt the same anger and stupidity he'd felt about forgetting to take Tonks to Ethel's. It was such a silly mistake to make.

"Oh, yes, dear," said Gran. "That lady obviously has very good taste."

Gran chuckled and Marsham relaxed a little.

It was weird watching the show back, and not just because Mum and Dad were there. Seeing himself as

Daniel, and hearing Daniel speak, made him cringe. He could sense the nerves and awkwardness, and of course he knew what was coming, which didn't help. He also couldn't stop thinking that Mum and Dad and everyone watching must surely know it was him, but that was only because *he* knew. The truth was that Ethel had done a brilliant job.

It was also odd seeing the edited version of the show. It was sort of the same, but also different. It seemed much slicker than when they'd done it for real. There was also the perspective. When Marsham had been there, he'd only seen events unfold from where he was sitting, but now he could see things such as the look on Medhansh's face at the start of his round, or Marc smiling at his brother Paul in the audience at the end of his.

The film played out – thankfully the photoshopped picture of Mum and Dad passed without comment –

and Daniel's round started. Watching the first two questions, Marsham felt himself reliving all the confusion and anxiety he'd felt at the time, and, oddly, he found himself feeling sorry for Daniel. Then they came to question three.

"Erm, I didn't hear, I think, is it . . . Jupiter?" said Daniel on the screen.

"No, that's the largest. The smallest is Mercury," said Selina.

"Oh dear," said Mum. "He's not doing well, is he?"

"Seems quite nervous," said Dad.

"Where is the British Formula One Grand Prix held?" said Selina.

"Silverstone," said Daniel.

"Correct," said Selina.

"Oh good, he's got one right," said Mum.

"I had a feeling he'd know that one," said Gran, mischievously.

"You're very quiet, Marsham," said Dad. "Did you know the answer to that one?"

"What?" said Marsham. "Yeah, I knew it, the questions have been quite easy so far."

Once again, Marsham mentally kicked himself. Normally, he'd be answering all the questions, but it was so hard to be "normal" now.

"He's doing quite well now," said Mum as they watched the rest of the round. "I'm pleased; I think he's my favourite, though I also like Naomi."

Marsham and Gran looked at each other, but the moment passed and before long Mum and Dad were engrossed in the ice-skating round.

"Oh dear," said Mum, after watching Medhansh's performance. "Such a shame, he does seem very nervous."

"Well, it can't be easy for him having to skate and recite a song backwards," said Dad.

"Daniel did it," said Gran. Then, quickly: "And the others."

Marsham shot her a look and she smiled meekly at him.

"That was exciting," said Mum when the show had finished. "I can't quite believe that girl tried to cheat."

"I know," said Dad. "As if anyone could fool a show like that."

That did it for Marsham. He felt as if he'd mentally run a marathon. He did a yawn that was so fake even Gran gave him a weird look, and then said, "That was great, can't wait for the next show. See you cats later."

He retreated to his room, wondering why he'd said cats. Five minutes later, Gran came in for the debrief. She got Ethel on loudspeaker on her phone and they started.

"OK," said Marsham. "Let's go through what we noticed watching it back – anything at all, no matter how small. It could be important."

"Vera's shoelaces were brown with white dots on them," said Gran, looking pleased with herself.

"Sorry, Gran," said Marsham. "What?"

"On the telly," said Gran. "You said to watch closely, and that's what I saw."

"Ah, I see," said Marsham. "OK, well, that's very helpful, thank you, Gran. Did you spot anything else?"

"No, that was it," said Gran.

"Ethel?" said Marsham.

"I thought that Selina's make-up was done very well," said Ethel. "I didn't really notice it when we were there, but seeing her on television I was very impressed with it, though I'm guessing that's not the sort of thing you were looking for Marsham, was it?"

197

"Not really, Ethel," said Marsham. "But don't worry, I didn't see anything, either. We'll just have to be extra vigilant next time."

"Yes," chimed in Gran. "Like hawks with super bionic eyes. Don't worry, we'll crack this case, I'm sure of it." She coughed lightly, then stood to go.

Suddenly, something hit Marsham like he'd been kicked by a donkey wearing diving boots.

"Coughing!" he yelped.

"Just clearing my throat, dear, nothing to worry ab—"

"No. In the show! I think instead of using our eyes, we should have been using our ears! Hold on."

Marsham walked over to his desk and flipped his laptop open. He found the show online, and clicked on it. He moved the tab on the play bar along, speeding past the introductions, and then let it go just before Naomi's general knowledge round.

"There," he shouted about halfway through her round. "Did you see that? She just asked for a question to be repeated because someone in the audience coughed. I didn't think anything of it when we watched the show downstairs, or when I was there."

"I'm not sure I think much of it now," said Gran.

"Nor me," said Ethel.

"Well, it might be nothing," said Marsham. "But there were definitely loud sneezes during two of Dionna's questions, but she didn't ask for either of them to be repeated."

"Oh yes, I remember the sneezes," said Ethel. "The person who did them was quite near to us, and I didn't want your gran to catch a cold."

"I was worried about *you*, Ethel dear," chuckled Gran. "But I don't think I heard the sneezes when we watched the show on television, though."

"That's because they did those retakes, remember?" said Marsham. "At the end of the round they recorded Selina saying some questions again, and that's the version they used for the show on television."

"Ohhhhhh," said Gran, though Marsham wasn't too sure she understood.

"They must have decided not to do that for Naomi," continued Marsham. "Maybe to make it seem more dramatic, or perhaps they couldn't edit it out."

Marsham's mind was racing now. Maybe Naomi's hearing wasn't so good, but *he'd* nearly asked for a question to be repeated in his round because of coughing, so either Dionna had super hearing or perhaps something else was going on.

"Why is it important, though?" said Gran.

"Well, as I said, it might be nothing," replied Marsham. "But if someone knows the questions already then not hearing them that well wouldn't be a problem, would it? Let's watch Dionna's round again."

They went back to Dionna's round and Marsham noticed something else. When Dionna was asked the question that she got wrong, the one that Marsham thought was quite easy, for the tiniest moment she seemed to be about to give the correct answer. Her lips closed together to make the M of Managua. Then she appeared to change her mind and give a different answer.

It could have been nothing, but something about it didn't seem quite right. Perhaps she was thinking that it might look suspicious if she got all the questions right, so purposely got one wrong.

Thoughts were still racing round his mind, but then one of them made it to the finishing line before all the others: "Gran, what's your sneezing like?" said Marsham.

"My sneezing?" she said in disbelief.

"Your fake sneezing, to be precise," said Marsham. "You see, I have a theory, and I want to test it by getting you to sneeze quite loudly while Selina is reading one of Dionna's questions."

"Really?" said Gran.

"Yes," said Marsham. "Unless you think Ethel would be better for. . ."

"No, no," said Gran quickly. "I can do it. And then Dionna will catch a cold from me and invent a cure for it and make even more money for her business. . . No, hang on, how will that help?"

"Your sneeze should mean that Dionna can't hear the question very well and should ask for it to be repeated. Unless, of course, she already knows the questions, in which case. . ."

"Aaachooo!"

"Bless you," continued Marsham. "In which case. . ."

He stopped, realizing what had just happened. "Gran, that was brilliant, it sounded completely real."

"That's because it was," said Gran. "But how about this one? Ah ah ah ah chooooooooo kkkkkkk oooooo!"

It was, quite possibly, the oddest sneeze Marsham had ever heard.

"How was that?" said Gran. "She'd never hear anything during a sneeze like that."

And neither would anyone else in the studio because their eardrums would have burst, thought Marsham.

CHAPTER 26

"Did you see that Medhansh kid? What a loser."

Marsham tensed up. He was with Nainan and Adrian. They were outside the school science labs waiting for their next lesson to start. There was a group of the cool kids nearby. Tabatha was with them, but if she'd seen Marsham, she didn't let on.

"They're all losers," said a sly-looking boy with a long face and greasy hair that looked like seaweed. "Though Marc is all right."

There was general agreement about this, and then someone said that they also thought Vera was OK. It seemed any brush with celebrity made you acceptable to the cool kids.

"Marc was fierce on his show last week," said another voice. "But now he's all laid back, saying it's too easy for him and he doesn't need to win. He's messing with their heads, I reckon."

Marsham hadn't watched the new episode of *The Q&A Kids*, but if what he'd just heard was correct, it was an odd change of attitude from Marc.

"The other four are total losers, though," said the first person again. "In fact, they should call it *Britain's Biggest Loser*." Cackles of laughter erupted from the group, as if they were spitting rather than laughing.

"Shame your wifi didn't work last night," ventured Nainan, quietly.

Marsham had been expecting this.

"Yeah, I know," he said. "My dad said he's going to get in touch with the company and have a go at them. It was a great show, though, wasn't it?"

"Yeah, I was so right about Marc," said Adrian. "He's definitely going to win."

"You don't know what you're talking about," said Nainan. "Vera's going to walk it. She's cool."

"You're both wrong," said Marsham. "It's Dionna all the way."

"Hey, you said Naomi before," said Adrian. "*And* you said we couldn't change once we'd picked a contestant."

"Nah, you must have misheard me," laughed Marsham. "I definitely said Dionna." Despite the cool kids being nearby, it was good being with his friends.

He had been worrying about speaking to them, but then something changed. He just told himself to *stop* worrying so much and be himself. And now he was. It was almost as if he'd separated himself from Daniel and was normal again. Almost. He still had to concentrate and be careful what he said.

"So what did you think of the questions then?" said Nainan.

"Not too difficult," said Marsham. "I knew most of them."

"Yeah, but you'd be worse than Medhansh at the ice skating," said Adrian, laughing.

Marsham laughed as well, but really he wanted to shout, *No I wouldn't, I did OK at it!*

"Respect to that girl who cheated, though," said a loud, snarly voice from the cool kids table. "That's what I'd do, only I wouldn't be stupid enough to get caught."

Marsham felt his stomach lurch. "Come on, let's go in," he said, pushing open the door of the science lab.

After the lesson, in the playground, he definitely made eye contact with Tabatha, but she looked down and ignored him. Marsham was annoyed. He was seeing her the following morning at the ice rink. Couldn't she at least say hello to him at school?

That evening, Marsham watched the new episode of

The Q&A Kids. Marc was indeed acting as if he was less bothered about winning. Could that have anything to do with the argument he'd had with Dionna?

Marsham decided to forget about solving the mystery for the time being. He had schoolwork to be getting on with, as well as maths and spelling to work on for the show. He hunkered down at his desk and focused.

The following morning he was up early to meet Tabatha at the rink.

"Erm, I think I saw you outside the science lab yesterday," said Marsham.

"Did you?" said Tabatha. "Yeah, maybe, dunno."

"I'm pretty sure," said Marsham. "You were with your friends."

Tabatha didn't say anything, she just flicked her hair out of her eyes.

"You know, you're really good at skating," said Marsham, tentatively. "If you told your friends, maybe they'd come with you one time."

"Dunno," said Tabatha. "It's kind of my thing, y'know, I'm not sure they'd get it. I mean, they'd probably be cool with it, but they . . . they like to have a laugh, and they might find it funny. . . You won't. . ."

"Of course I won't tell them," said Marsham. "But

I'm sure they'd be OK about it if they're your friends. I mean, why do you hang around with them?"

"I just like being part of that crowd," said Tabatha. "I feel good when I'm with them."

She paused for a moment.

"I, er, I did see you yesterday," she continued. "But, it's just, you know, well, I. . ."

"It's OK," said Marsham, sparing her any embarrassment. "I get it."

Marsham felt strange talking to Tabatha about not being true to herself with her friends when he was doing exactly the same thing, but they'd been getting on well and he felt as if he wanted to understand her a little more.

They had a good training session – she was a great teacher, Marsham was definitely getting better – and then strolled to the bus stop together.

"Oh, I meant to ask," he said. "Could we meet on Sunday morning? I'm going skating with some friends later that day and I want to impress them, so a last-minute extra session would really help."

"Sure," said Tabatha. "Why not?"

Marsham was relieved. He'd broached a difficult subject, they'd talked it through, and Tabatha had still agreed to meet on Sunday morning. Of course, the real reason he wanted an extra session was because the ice-skating round of the show was that day (they were doing the maths round and spelling bee on the Saturday), but he couldn't tell her that.

Maybe in some ways the two of them were quite similar.

CHAPTER 27

"The question is: how?" said Marsham. It was Saturday, the day of the spelling bee and mental arithmetic rounds, and they were at Ethel's house where Marsham was being transformed into Daniel. The nose, eyes, eyebrows and freckles were all done, and Ethel had prepped his real hair for the wig by putting hairpins in it and covering it with a silk wig liner, which made him look bald and a lot older. Ethel was now fitting the actual wig.

"And why?" said Gran.

"And also, when?" added Ethel.

The rest of the week had been pretty uneventful, other than Mum and Dad worrying that Gran had a terrible cold, but she'd assured them it was just an allergy to her new hairspray and had continued dropping nose bombs about every twenty minutes.

Marsham hadn't had too much schoolwork, so he'd spent plenty of time on his spelling and arithmetic. He'd also done some drawing while pretending to skate around his bedroom, and the results weren't too bad. All told, he felt about as prepared and confident as he could be.

"Yes," said Marsham. "If Dionna knows the questions, how is she doing it, why is she doing it, and when is she doing it?"

"What about who?" asked Ethel.

"Well, the who is Dionna," said Marsham.

"Maybe," said Ethel. "But she must have an accomplice or two?"

"Aaaaaaaaaaaaaaaaaaaaachoooooooey!"

"Ooh, very good, Elsie," said Ethel, stepping back from a transformed Marsham as Gran followed up her fake sneeze with an equally loud nose blow.

"Come on then, Daniel," said Gran. "We've got a cactus growers' convention to get to." Gran had moved on to her next hobby.

"You do know that's just the cover story you told Mum and Dad, don't you, Gran?" said Marsham, checking himself in the mirror. His freckles were in exactly the same positions as before. He was very impressed.

"Of course I do, dear," said Gran. "But I would like

to actually go to one some day. I'm sure they're very exciting."

"I'm sure they are," said Ethel. "Come on, time to get going, I'm going to get Mikey Lanston's autograph this time."

Half an hour later, they arrived at the studio building, where they were met by Gloria, who was as bubbly as ever.

"Hey, Team Daniel, how are we today?" she said, beaming.

"*We* are wonderful," said Gran.

"Team Daniel, I like that," said Ethel, who was holding her overflowing bag. "We are a team, aren't we?"

"Yup," said Marsham. "Couldn't do it without you."

"Come on, let's get going," said Gloria. "It's the mental arithmetic round first today, but you've got a bit of time for last-minute revision before we actually start, if you'd like. Then it's the spelling bee after lunch."

She trotted off towards the lifts with Team Daniel behind her.

"Actually," said Marsham. "I'm going to take the stairs, if that's OK. A bit of exercise is good for the brain. I'll see you in the dressing room."

"OK," said Gloria. "Come on, ladies."

The three of them headed off and Marsham started walking towards the stairs, which were just past the canteen, but then doubled back and made his way to the question setters' room. He crouched down, pretending to do up his shoelaces, and stared at the door as if he were trying to penetrate it with his mind.

If Dionna's getting the questions, she must have access to this room. Or is there another way she can get them? Is one of the question setters an accomplice? Or Naomi? Or even Khalid?

Marsham had been there for about two minutes – which, if anyone had been watching, would have led them to believe he was very bad at doing up his shoelaces – when Khalid came hurrying along and almost tripped over him.

"Daniel!" he said, regaining his balance. "What are you doing down there?"

"Sorry," said Marsham, looking up. "I was tying my shoelace."

"Well, it looks done up to me. Good luck today! See you later," said Khalid, opening the door to the question setters' room and going in.

As the door shut, Marsham thought about pressing his ear to it, but if he got caught, claiming his ear had got stuck there probably wouldn't convince anyone. So he headed back towards his dressing room.

He was about to turn into the corridor where the production office was when he heard:

"Aaaaaaaaaaaaaaaaaaaahhhhhhhhhhh! Oooowwwwwwww! Oooooowwwwwwwwww!"

Marsham rushed round to see Gloria outside the office holding an empty coffee cup next to someone who was doubled over in pain. Marsham recognized him as Gavin, the man with the nose ring who'd been outside the canteen on the day of the selection interview. It was obvious that boiling-hot coffee was all over him.

"I'm sorry, I'm sorry!" said Gloria frantically. "Are you OK?"

"I'm fine," said Gavin, though he was clearly not fine.

More people appeared and gathered round offering advice – *honey is good for burns, I heard yoghurt was better, he needs to wrap a wet towel around it, no, clingfilm is what he needs* – until a moment later Khalid appeared. He was holding a folder and didn't look happy.

"What happened?" he asked.

"I was taking a coffee to Selina," said Gavin, wincing as he spoke. "But then Gloria said she would take it and went to grab it and it spilled all over me."

"I didn't mean. . . I just. . . I usually take Selina her coffee," spluttered an embarrassed Gloria. "So I thought. . . I don't know, I didn't think, and. . ."

"OK, fine," said Khalid. "We'll talk about this later. Gavin, go see the medic. And Gloria, take another coffee to Selina."

The two of them slunk off as someone shouted, "Honey! Don't forget, put honey on it!"

"Right, party over," said Khalid. "Back to what you were doing."

The crowd dispersed and, as Khalid strode off, Marsham found himself staring at that folder gripped tightly in his hands. *Was Dionna getting access to it, and, if so, how?*

CHAPTER 28

"Ah ah ah blllloooooooooeeeeccchhhh!"

"Bless you, Gran," said Marsham, entering his dressing room.

"Fake or real?" said Gran, her eyes willing Marsham to answer.

"Erm, fake?" said Marsham.

"Darn it!" snapped Gran, stamping her foot. "How did you know?"

"Lucky guess, I suppose," said Marsham, feeling increasingly anxious about his plan. "Gran, are you sure you'll manage to do a *realistic* sneeze at the right moment, because we could always think of something else?"

"I'll have you know I was the UK's sneezing champion in 1985," said Gran. "Finest sneeze in the land, they said, so I will be absolutely fine, don't you agree, Ethel?"

Ethel didn't say anything. She was staring at her phone.

"Ethel?" said Gran again.

"Sorry," said Ethel, looking up. "I'm watching the new episode of *The Q&A Kids*. It's really good. I've subscribed, and I'm going to join the fan club."

"Right," said Marsham. "But you still want *me* to win and not Marc, don't you?"

"Oh, yes, of course," said Ethel. "But I want Marc to come second. Or first, if you don't win, which I definitely, definitely do want you to."

"Thank you," said Marsham. "Right, I need to get on with some wor—"

"Noooooo! Incorrect! You have to do better, Medhansh! You are a winner, do you hear me? A winner! Start again."

Marsham shook his head. Poor Medhansh. Next door, his mother wasn't going any easier on him today.

"No! That is wrong! Concentrate, Medhansh, concentrate!"

"Arrrrrrchoooooollllllllaaaaaaggghhh!" sneezed Gran.

"Ooooh," cooed Ethel, looking at her phone.

"Right, that settles it," said Marsham, to no one in particular. "I'm off to the canteen. Hopefully it'll be quieter than here."

Marsham left to the sound of another explosion from Gran's nose.

As it turned out, the canteen was quite empty and Marsham was able to nestle in a corner and get on with arithmetic revision. At least he was until someone said, "Hello, mind if I join you?"

Marsham felt a jolt of annoyance, but fixed his face into a pleasant smile and looked up from his work. It was Naomi. Her glasses had slipped down her nose and she was peering over them at him.

"Yes, of course," said Marsham.

Naomi pushed her glasses back up and eased her wheelchair into the table so that she was opposite Marsham. She glanced at the sheets of paper spread out everywhere, covered in sums.

"I can't look at another number," she said. "Nothing more is going in. I find it's always best to stop when you get to that point."

"Well, maybe I will when *I* get to that point," was what Marsham wanted to say, but instead he said, "Yeah, I know what you mean."

"How are you finding it? The show?" said Naomi.

"It's tough," said Marsham, gathering together the papers. "There's a lot, and the skating is a bit of a curve ball. And, you know, you and the others are really clever."

"Yeah, yeah," said Naomi, nodding in a way that suggested she had something else on her mind. "Phillips is a Welsh name, isn't it? Is that where your family is from?"

"What?" said Marsham, caught off guard.

"Originally, I mean," said Naomi.

"Oh, erm, yeah, yeah," said Marsham. "My dad's dad was from Swansea."

"I see," said Naomi, nodding. "And your dad is actually in Ecuador at the moment, with your mum."

"That's right, yes, they're, erm, botanists," said Marsham, a sense of panic creeping up on him. "They're researching toadstools."

"Oh, so if they work with fungi they're mycologists, then?" said Naomi, her tongue licking the corner of her mouth.

"Yes, of course," said Marsham. "Myco-botanists, in fact." He desperately hoped that such a thing existed.

"Fascinating," said Naomi. "And your schooling sounds interesting."

"Does it? It's just a local school near to where I live," said Marsham, feeling as if he was being interrogated. *What was going on?*

"Oh," said Naomi, a look of serious intent on her face. "I thought you said in your film that you were homeschooled."

Aarrggh! screamed Marsham inside his head. It was so easy for everything to come toppling down; a little mistake like that and Daniel's cover would be blown.

"I'm sorry, I misheard you," spluttered Marsham. "I thought you were asking about schools near to my house... Oh, sorry, I've just remembered, I need to get something for my grandmother. Great chatting to you."

"Yes, it was," said Naomi thoughtfully.

Marsham grabbed his papers and pens and scurried out.

That had been really odd. Why had Naomi asked all those questions? Had she worked out that he was in disguise? Or did she also suspect someone was cheating and that it was him?

Whatever it was, the way Marsham had reacted – like a startled gazelle – would only have increased any suspicions she might have.

"Where's Gran?" asked Marsham back in the dressing room.

"Hmm?" said Ethel, who was still glued to Marc and Paul's *The Q&A Kids* on her phone.

"Gran. You know, that strange woman who hangs around with us?"

"Oh, she went to get Mikey Lanston's autograph for me," said Ethel. "It's ridiculous, really, but I'm quite shy about asking for things like that, so she said she'd get it for me. Isn't that nice of her?"

"Yes, she's good like that," said Marsham.

Knock knock.

"Come in," said Marsham. "Oh, you have. Hi, Gloria."

"Hi, we'll be ready for you soon. I hope you'll be ready for us."

"As ready as I'll ever be," said Marsham. "Is, erm, everything OK, you know, after the coffee incident?"

"Oh, ha ha, that," chuckled Gloria. "Yes, no harm done, Selina got her coffee."

"Right," said Marsham, thinking it was odd that Gloria thought Selina getting her coffee was more important than Gavin's burns.

"What are you watching, Ethel?" asked Gloria.

Ethel showed Gloria her screen. For a moment it was as if Gloria was trying to focus, but then she seemed to go into some sort of trance. Her lower lip dropped down and the corners of her mouth curled upwards in the hint of a smile. She tilted her head to one side and her eyes became watery and glazed.

Ethel looked at Marsham. He shrugged his shoulders.

"Gloria?" he said after a few seconds. "Do you know the order we're going in today?"

Gloria didn't move. It was as if she hadn't heard him.

"Gloria," said Marsham, louder.

"What?" said Gloria. "Sorry, I was miles away. So yes, probably five minutes, OK? I'll be back for you then."

After Gloria left, Marsham turned to Ethel. "That was weird."

"No, it wasn't," she replied. "She likes Paul. A lot."

"Don't be silly," said Marsham. "She just went into a little daydream. It must be tiring doing her job, she probably switched off for a moment."

"You wouldn't understand," said Ethel. "It's a girl thing. I can tell."

"Got it!" said Gran, bursting in, brandishing a piece of paper. "What a nice man that Mikey Lanston is. Can't say the same about his daughter, though."

"Vera's not a nice man?" joked Marsham.

"She was shouting rudely at him, telling him to do this, do that, get this, get that," said Gran. "She probably takes after her mother. Aaaaaannnd..."

"Yeesssss?" said Marsham, bracing himself.

"I did a sneeze while Mikey was signing his autograph, as a test," said Gran. "They didn't say anything, but the look she gave me. Oooh, it was like I'd thrown a bucket of wet fish over her."

"She could be the cheat," said Ethel.

"Or she could just be under a lot of pressure like the rest of us," said Marsham. "Gran, I don't know the order today. Dionna could be first, so make sure you're ready, OK?"

"I was born ready," said Gran. "Ready is my middle name."

Marsham smiled weakly.

"More importantly, are you ready, Daniel?" asked Gran.

"Yes," said Marsham.

"Good," said Gran. "Then let's go catch a cheat!"

CHAPTER 29

"Hello, Marsham," said Naomi. "Lovely chatting earlier. You mentioned that your parents were in Ecuador; what region are they working in?"

"Oh, erm, I forget, exactly," said Marsham. "Somewhere quite central."

"Napo province?" said Naomi.

"Yes, that was it," said Marsham.

The finalists were back in the circular studio waiting for Selina to start the show. Why Naomi had leant over to ask Marsham that question was a mystery to him. If she suspected him of something and was trying to unsettle him, she had succeeded.

"Thank you, everyone," said the floor manager. "We are now ready to start recording. Here we go, please, in three, two, one. . ."

The opening titles and music started and then

Selina introduced the show.

"Welcome, everyone," she said, "to *Britain's Smartest Kid . . . on Ice*. It's our second of three shows, effectively the semi-final, and there is everything to play for. Last week our contestants showed us what they were made of over two rounds, but this week we're ramping up the pressure with three rounds. We're kicking off with mental arithmetic, and, first up, it's Marc."

A short film played with Marc talking about how the first week had gone. There was no mention of Liselle – the show was keen to move on from that now – but as Marsham watched, he definitely got the sense that Marc was less confident. That bravado from before had completely gone and he seemed unsure and even a bit rattled. Was that anything to do with his argument with Dionna?

The film finished and Marc made his way to the lectern. He was far from enthusiastic though. He was trudging there as if it were the last thing he wanted to do.

"Hello, Marc," said Selina. "How are you?"

"I'm, er, OK, thank you," he said.

"Wonderful," said Selina. "So, you have fifteen questions and you have five seconds to answer. Question one: what is 324 multiplied by 16?"

Marc closed his eyes for a second.

"5,184?"

"Correct," said Selina.

Sitting in his seat, Marsham shook his head. He'd calculated the answer to be 5,160. He'd have to do better when it came to his turn.

Fourteen questions later, Marc returned to his seat having given eleven correct answers.

Vera was next. From the moment she stood up it was obvious she wasn't in the best frame of mind. She stomped over to the lectern and stood there with a look of grumpy defiance on her face.

As the round progressed, the reason for that look became clear: she really wasn't good at mental arithmetic. She got the first three questions wrong and managed to get just four of the remaining twelve correct. By the end, she was staring daggers, swords, bayonets and shards of white-hot glass at her father. For some reason, she seemed to be blaming him for her failings.

"Well done, Vera," said Naomi as Vera returned to

her seat among the other contestants.

Vera stared at Naomi for a second and then gave her a huge, mock smile that was so rude it immediately stopped any of the others from saying anything to her.

"Now we come to our next finalist, Daniel," said Selina.

Here goes, thought Marsham. His film played and he made his way to the lectern with what he hoped was the right mixture of cool confidence and modesty.

"Welcome, Daniel," said Selina. "How are you feeling today?"

"Very well, thank you," said Marsham. "And how are you, Selina?"

A frisson of laughter zinged around the audience. Marsham didn't quite know why he'd done that, it had just come out.

"I'm fine," said Selina, looking at Marsham and making it very clear that *she* was the one who did the asking. "Here is your first question. What is 411 multiplied by 23?"

Marsham focused and did the calculation in his head.

"Nine thousand, four hundred and fifty" – he leant back and looked upwards – "three."

"That's correct," said Selina. "What do you get if

you take 40 per cent of 350 away from 15 per cent of 2,800?"

"Erm, that would be . . . erm . . . 280."

"That is correct," said Selina.

It was the best possible start, and by question ten Marsham was flying. He'd only given one wrong answer and was relishing the challenge. This was what he was born to do.

"Question eleven," said Selina. "Estimate to within 5,000 the answer to 3,525 multiplied by. . ."

"Aaarrchhoooocccchhhh!"

Marsham jumped.

Oh no, he thought. *Gran's got confused. She's sneezing during my round.*

He glanced over at her, but to his surprise both Gran and Ethel looked as startled as he was. A moment later, he heard what sounded like a trumpet blast as someone on the other side of the audience loudly blew their nose.

It hadn't been Gran.

Someone else had genuinely sneezed.

"I'm sorry, Selina," said Marsham. "Could you repeat the question, please?"

"Yes, I can," said Selina, throwing an angry glance in the direction of the person who had sneezed. "Estimate to within 5,000 the answer to 3,525 multiplied by 96.418."

Marsham's brain got right back on track, and after three seconds he said, "Approximately 340,000."

"Excellent," said Selina. "The answer is, in fact, 339,873.45. Well done."

Marsham allowed himself a tiny moment of relaxation. Not only was he doing well in the round, he now had confirmation that a loud noise from the audience definitely made it difficult to hear Selina. He just had to hope that Gran was ready for action.

"That's correct," said Selina after Marsham's final question. "You gave thirteen correct answers in that round. Well done, Daniel."

A wave of relief washed over Marsham. He'd done well and he'd enjoyed himself. It felt good.

He returned to his seat to be warmly congratulated by three of his fellow contestants. Vera was still simmering from her poor performance so didn't say anything, and Medhansh seemed too tense and distracted to speak.

"Could we have our next contestant, Medhansh, please?" said Selina.

CHAPTER 30

Marsham watched as Medhansh made his way to the lectern like a robot. His whole body seemed to be rigid, and, for some reason, Marsham found himself wondering if that even extended to his little toes.

"Hello, Medhansh, how are you today?" asked Selina.

"Fine," said Medhansh quickly, as if on autopilot.

"Good," said Selina. "Here is your first question. What is 119 multiplied by 48?"

Medhansh stared straight ahead. His eyes were fixed on Selina, but now it was as if his muscles had tensed up so much they just wouldn't move.

"Sorry, you're out of time," said Selina. "The answer was 5,712."

The audience shifted uncomfortably in their seats, almost as if they were also feeling all the tension in Medhansh's body.

"Question two," said Selina. "What is the square root of 196 multiplied by the cube root of 343, divided by the fourth root of 256?"

As the seconds ticked away, all eyes were on Medhansh, the audience willing him to answer.

"24.5. It's 24.5!"

"That's cor..." Selina started to say, but then she stopped.

The answer hadn't come from Medhansh.

"Come on, Medhansh! It's easy! What's the matter with you?!"

The tension in the room had now been shattered by the shrieking voice of Medhansh's mother, who was standing up, screaming at him. Her eyes were bulging and her nostrils were flaring as if they were trying to get away from each other.

"Why are you doing this to me?! You have to win!"

Medhansh's dad tried to get her to sit down, but she shrugged him off. Marsham, and probably everyone else in the room, couldn't quite believe what was happening.

"You can do this, Medhansh, you have to do this, you have to!!" she shrieked.

"Mrs Gupta!" shouted Khalid, rushing out. "Please, calm down!"

"Stop it, stop it, stop it, stop it!"

It was Medhansh. Like a tennis match, everyone now turned to look at him.

"I can't do it!" shouted Medhansh. "I can't do it. It's not my fault you didn't win!"

"It was my title!" bellowed Mrs Gupta. "I was cheated! Cheated! I should have won!"

"It wasn't my fault!" shouted Medhansh, standing up. "And it was *twenty-five years ago!*"

"PLEASE!" shouted Khalid, using the voice he'd used to get order during the interview process. "Please stop and calm down."

Mrs Gupta slumped back down into her seat and started sobbing.

"OK," said Medhansh. "I am calm now, but I have to explain."

"Of course," said Khalid. "But maybe later?"

"No," said Medhansh firmly. "Now. My mother was a contestant on the first-ever *Britain's Smartest Kid* series twenty-five years ago. Her name then was Amyra Ghosh. She did very well, she came second, but there was some controversy about one of her questions. She felt her answer was acceptable, but it was deemed incorrect."

There was a murmur of excited intrigue from the

audience. This was better than a soap opera.

"She was angry then, and she's still angry now," continued Medhansh. "She has never got over it, and, well, you can probably work out the rest. When I was old enough to enter there was no question about it. I thought it might be fun, but I didn't realize how desperate she was for me to win. She put so much pressure on me. Only it was for her, as if somehow my winning would make what happened to her better. But it won't, Mother, it won't!"

"Thank you, Medhansh," said Khalid as Amyra continued sobbing and the audience looked at each other with *well-I-never* faces. "Because your mother shouted out an answer, I'm afraid you'll have to be disqualified from this round. But as for the rest of the competition, at this stage I'm not sure what we're going to do."

"Forget it," said Medhansh. "Good luck to the other finalists, because this is the last you'll be seeing of me."

With that, Medhansh strode out defiantly. His mother let out a final wail and, coincidentally, someone sneezed.

"Time for our next contestant now: Dionna," said Selina, after recording had resumed. (Khalid had called

231

a short break following the "Medhansh incident". Marsham had used it to check that Gran was still happy to go ahead with her "performance", and needless to say, she was raring to go. Now all Marsham could do was hope it was worthy of an Oscar.)

As Dionna's film played out on the screen, Marsham glanced across at her. She seemed composed and focused. Nothing out of the ordinary.

The film finished and Dionna stood up, brushed a hair out of her eyes and walked to the lectern. She looked more like a high-powered, wealthy businessperson than a twelve-year-old kid. Marsham felt himself tense up and started biting his fingernails, something he'd never actually done before.

"Are you OK after our little interruption?" asked Selina.

"Yes, thank you," said Dionna, smiling sweetly.

"Excellent," said Selina. "Here we go. Question one: what is 449 multiplied by 23?"

Dionna thought for a moment and then said, "10,327."

"Correct," said Selina, a word she repeated three more times in quick succession. Dionna was off to a flying start.

By now Marsham had chewed off about half the fingernail from his left index finger and was also tapping his right foot feverishly. When would Gran sneeze? He willed himself to relax and sat back in his seat.

"Question five," said Selina. "Take 451 from 630 and give the answer as a percentage of. . ."

"Arrcchhoooookkkaa!"

Gran had done it. Marsham certainly hadn't heard the end of the question from where he was, but would Dionna give an answer?

"That would be, let me see, twenty per cent, I think," said Dionna.

"Erm, yes, that's correct," said Selina, who, as far as Marsham was concerned, seemed surprised, as if she had been expecting Dionna to ask for the question to be repeated.

Marsham glanced at Dionna. She also looked a little fazed, as if she'd realized too late that she'd made a mistake and should have asked for the question again. Marsham felt himself becoming more certain that his theory was correct.

Dionna continued and surprisingly gave three incorrect answers, though Marsham figured that she'd done that on purpose, much like she'd got the question wrong in the general knowledge round. She finished with a score of twelve, so she'd still had a strong round.

Naomi went last and scored nine, which meant Marsham had won the round! He felt a surge of pride and couldn't stop himself grinning widely. A moment later, though, he panicked that his smiling had somehow dislodged his nose. Thankfully, everything was still in place.

"So, that's the end of our mental arithmetic round," said Selina. "Remember, we only have five contestants now, so the top scorer receives five points and the lowest gets one, which means the leader board looks like this."

```
Dionna     16
Marc       11
Vera        8
Naomi       8
Daniel      8
```

Marsham was still bottom, but so were two others. Either way, he'd made up a lot of ground.

"Next for our finalists, it's the spelling bee," said Selina. "And here's a little taste of the sort of thing they'll be facing."

The audience all waited for something to happen, but instead Khalid came out to address them. "Thank you, everyone," he said. "At this point, when you watch the show on television, there will be a short film of previous spelling bee rounds. However, it's not ready yet, so we can't show it to you now, but if you could stay where you are for a few moments, we have a couple of retakes to do, thank you."

Marsham watched as Selina recorded a short sequence explaining Medhansh's absence. She said that he'd been taken ill and unfortunately had to drop out of the show. That was probably to save his family too much embarrassment, but Marsham guessed the truth would come out eventually.

More interestingly, Selina recorded Dionna's question again, the one during which Gran had sneezed. It was yet another sliver of proof in Marsham's ever-growing theory.

CHAPTER 31

"I know I'm right," said Marsham. "But how's she doing it?"

"Someone must be helping her," said Gran, pacing and stroking her chin.

"Naomi's asking a lot of questions, and she's been hanging around the question setters' room, so it could be her," said Marsham.

"And don't forget Vera's dad," Ethel said. "Maybe Selina *is* helping them."

"But why would he be helping Dionna and not Vera?" asked Marsham. "And Marc has completely changed since the start of all this; something is definitely bugging him."

"It seems that way," said Ethel, combing Marsham's wig. They were back in the dressing room and she'd taken it off to give him a break. They'd only been back a few minutes, as Marsham had had another "reaction" film to shoot after the mental arithmetic round.

"Khalid is the only person who goes in and out of the question setters' room," said Marsham. "We should follow him."

"Just what I was about to suggest," said Gran.

A couple of minutes later, Marsham, now with his wig back on, and Gran were strolling as casually as they could towards the question setters' room.

"What are we going to do when we get there?" asked Gran.

"I don't know," said Marsham. "Just be alert. Wait!"

Marsham stopped. Up ahead, along the corridor, he could see the door to their target room and, once again, there was Naomi! She was beyond the door, further down, reading a book.

"What's she up to?" Marsham whispered to Gran.

Before Gran could answer, the door of the question setters' room opened and Khalid came out, clutching the folder.

Naomi immediately hid behind her book and then, when Khalid had walked past her, she followed him.

"I'm going after her, Gran," said Marsham. "You stay here and keep an eye on the room."

"Right you are," said Gran.

As quietly as possible, Marsham set off after Naomi. Perhaps she and Khalid were in this together, and they were going somewhere he could show her the questions?

Naomi was quick, and Marsham had to keep out of sight, so after he'd followed her round a couple of corners he found himself in an empty corridor. She wasn't there. He had lost her!

Marsham looked around and saw the lifts. The first floor was where the contestants' dressing rooms were and he didn't think she'd be going there, so he pressed the button for the second floor, where Gloria had said the stars' dressing rooms were located.

Getting out of the lift, it looked exactly like the first floor with double doors to Marsham's right. He went through them, then turned left into a corridor when suddenly—

"What are you doing here?"

He'd walked straight into Naomi and they'd both asked each other that question at the same time.

"I asked you first," they both said together. Very awkward.

Thinking quickly, Marsham said, "My gran wandered off and is lost somewhere in the building. She called me and described where she was. I was looking for her and ended up here."

"Yes, I see," said Naomi. It *seemed* as if she believed him.

"What about you?" he asked.

"Oh well, you see, it's kind of a secret," said Naomi. "I mean, a private matter, sort of."

"Oh, I see," said Marsham. "Well, I don't want to be nosy, only it does seem a little odd, you being here, and I did tell you what I was doing, but. . ."

"OK, I'll tell you," blurted out Naomi. "But you must promise not to say anything to anyone."

"I promise," said Marsham, hoping it was a promise he could keep. He also felt a sense of camaraderie with Naomi. He knew all too well how difficult it was to keep a big secret and how strong the desire could be to tell someone.

"It's for my new book," said Naomi. "I've decided it's going to take place at a show like this. I don't want anyone to know yet, as I only came up with the idea at the interview, so I've been trying to do as much research as I can without anyone finding out."

"I see," said Marsham. It certainly *seemed* as if Naomi was telling the truth. "So is that why you were asking me all those questions?"

"Yes, exactly," said Naomi. "Sorry about that. I've

been chatting to everyone. Do you know, Edgar thinks Selina doesn't like the whole ice skating and different-types-of-intelligence thing?"

"Really?" said Marsham, a little surprised that Naomi hadn't worked that out for herself. "But why are you *here*?" he persisted. "In this corridor."

"Ah, yes, right, very good question," said Naomi. "You see, I noticed Khalid always leaves the question setters' room with a folder which I believe contains the questions. But I didn't know where he would take it, so I got my father to follow him earlier, and he told me this is where Khalid goes."

"And where are we?" said Marsham.

"Here," said Naomi, "or at least further down, is Selina's dressing room. Khalid is in there now, and my guess is he's going through the questions with Selina."

"That's what our runner, Gloria, told us," said Marsham, his brain whirring away in the background with all sorts of thoughts. "Well, don't worry, I won't tell anyone, but I should probably find my grandmother."

"Of course," said Naomi. "I need to get back and work on my spelling. I think this next round is going to be tough. See you later!"

Naomi headed off, and Marsham walked further on

down the corridor with thoughts careering around in his mind. Did Dionna have access to Selina's dressing room somehow? Could she even be in there now? Were she, Khalid and Selina all working together for some reason?

Whatever was going on, he was going to get to the bottom of it.

CHAPTER 32

Marsham walked on past Selina's dressing room – it had "Selina Constantin" on it – to a door on the opposite side of the corridor. He tried the handle and it opened. It was another dressing room, and thankfully it was empty. He went in and pushed the door, leaving it open a tiny bit so he could monitor the door to Selina's room. He stood, peering through the crack, and waited.

He didn't know how long he had crouched there, but he was prepared to stay for a while. He was practising spelling the word *miscellaneous* in his head when he heard footsteps. He tensed up and focused.

A moment later he saw Gloria approach Selina's room with a coffee. "That makes sense," he said to himself. He relaxed a little, but then something odd happened. Gloria was about to knock on Selina's door when she stopped. She tutted and bent down to pick something up from the floor.

Whatever it was, it was clearly very small, as she seemed to be holding it between her thumb and forefinger. She glanced around nervously and then pressed the tiny object on to the bottom of the cup. She then lifted the cup up and appeared to be checking that the object was securely attached, before knocking on Selina's door and entering.

A short while later Gloria came back out. She shook her head and wiped her brow, clearly relieved, and then left.

Marsham couldn't quite believe what he'd seen. He was shocked, but he also felt a burst of exhilaration: this was a major breakthrough. He waited another few seconds and then made his way back to his dressing room.

"It's Gloria!" he said the moment he went in, which was a little reckless as she could have been there.

"What is Gloria?" asked Gran.

"I've just seen her taking a coffee into Selina's dressing room," he said.

"I believe she told us that was part of her job," said Ethel.

"Yes, but check this out," said Marsham. "Before she went in, something fell off the bottom of the cup. She picked it up and made sure it was stuck on properly before going in. Khalid was in Selina's room with the question folder for Selina to rehearse the questions. The thing Gloria put on the cup must be some sort of listening device. So when Selina rehearses the questions, whoever is listening – Dionna, presumably – will hear them. I've cracked it!"

"No, you can't be right," said Gran. "Gloria is our friend. She'd never do anything like that."

"Gran's right," said Ethel. "Why would Gloria do that?"

"I don't know," said Marsham. "But I know what I saw. Oh, and ... and ... and ... that explains what happened with Gloria and Gavin. He must have been taking the coffee to Selina, but Gloria tried to take it off him so she could take it! It makes sense now!"

"Maybe," said Gran. "But what are you going to do about it? Tell Khalid?"

"I can't yet, I still don't have any definite proof," said Marsham. "But there has to be a way to do something about it. Come on, think. . ."

For the next few minutes the three of them sat in silence, their brains whirring away inside their heads until Marsham suddenly jumped up and said, "I've got it!"

"Hi, Khalid, could I have a quick word?" asked Marsham outside the production office.

"Is it important, Daniel?" asked Khalid. "I'm very busy."

"It is, yes," said Marsham. "And, erm, it's a little personal."

"Fine," said Khalid. "Come with me."

Khalid led Marsham through the production office to a small room at the back, where there was a desk and two chairs. Khalid gestured for Marsham to sit down, and he did likewise.

"What's the problem?" asked Khalid.

"It's my grandmother," said Marsham. "She has a, erm, boil on rather a delicate part of her body."

"Riiiiigggghhhhttt," said Khalid, clearly wondering why Marsham was telling him this.

"The thing is," said Marsham. "She thinks it might possibly, erm, burst, so she needs to see a doctor."

"Well, we have a medic here," said Khalid.

"Yes," said Marsham. "But she would rather see her usual doctor, you know. She isn't keen on just anyone seeing her . . . erm, her. . ."

"Yes, I understand," said Khalid quickly.

"So would it be possible for me to go first in the spelling bee?" asked Marsham. "And then she could rush off early to see her doctor?"

"Hmm, yes, you could," said Khalid, weighing the matter in his head. "It's not ideal, but we could edit it so no one would notice your absence in the studio. The thing is, though, we've already decided on the order. You were going to go second, after Dionna... But I don't think it matters all that much, and it probably is best that your grandmother sees her doctor, so yes, fine, that won't be a problem."

"Thank you," said Marsham. "Gran and her boil will be very grateful."

Marsham rushed back to his dressing room to tell Gran and Ethel the news.

"He agreed!" said Marsham excitedly. "So if I'm right, this should really scupper Dionna's plans."

"Absolutely," said Gran. "But could you just explain it again?"

"Sure. My guess is that when Dionna listens to Selina rehearsing the questions," said Marsham, "she's

246

only interested in *her* questions and not anyone else's."

"That makes sense," said Gran.

"Dionna will know she's going first. But now that they're changing the order, I should get the spellings she would have got, the ones she'll have practised. And the spellings she should get are the ones I would have got, ones she probably won't be prepared for."

"As long as they use the same questions for you that Dionna would have got," said Ethel.

"Yes," said Marsham. "But why wouldn't they? Everyone's questions are meant to be equally difficult, so it shouldn't matter who gets the first or second set of questions."

"Got it," said Gran. "I think."

"Now, look," said Marsham, "when Gloria comes to get us, act natural, OK?"

"OK," said Ethel and Gran.

"Though, Gran," said Marsham, "you have to pretend you have a boil on your, erm. . ."

"Yes, I know where it is, thank you," said Gran. "Don't worry."

Five minutes later there was a knock at the door and Gloria entered.

"Hi, everyone," she said. "Ready to go?"

"Yes, yes, of course, yes we are, absolutely ready to

go, aren't we, Ethel?" said Gran, acting very much not naturally.

"Oh, we are sooooo ready," said Ethel, also not acting at all naturally. "Really, really, really ready."

"Ha ha, you two are silly," said Marsham, spotting the curious look starting to appear on Gloria's face.

"Great," said Gloria. "And you're OK now, Elsie? After getting lost? Naomi told me."

"Oh, yes, she's fine. I found her," said Marsham, jumping in quickly. He hadn't told Gran what he'd told Naomi and by her look of confusion, she could well have been about to say the wrong thing.

"Awesome," said Gloria. "Come on, let's go."

"I'll tell you after," whispered Marsham as they made their way out.

Soon Ethel and Gran were in the audience in the circular studio with Gran perched on the edge of her seat, grimacing in an exaggerated way every so often because of her "boil". Marsham was in his seat alongside the other finalists.

"Good luck," he said to the others, who all smiled sweetly and wished him the same.

"Here we go, folks," said the floor manager. "In three, two, one..."

"Welcome, everyone, to our spelling bee round,"

said Selina. "The American president Thomas Jefferson said, 'take care that you never spell a word wrong', and whilst I don't believe he was speaking about a spelling bee, it is perfect advice for our contestants today. So, let us commence..."

Selina paused for a moment. Out of the corner of his eye, Marsham thought he could see Dionna ready herself to get up.

"Could I invite Daniel to the lectern, please?" said Selina.

Marsham stood up, but just as he was about to start walking—

"Errr errrr, eccchhhh, ecccchhhh, uccchhhh, ucccchhhhh..."

It was Dionna. She was having a coughing fit and her face was going a deep shade of red.

Khalid and the medic instantly ran over to check on her.

"Are you OK?" asked the medic. "What happened?"

"Uccch, ucccch, I don't, ucch," said Dionna with difficulty. "I don't, ucccch, ucccch, know."

"Deep breaths. Take deep breaths," said the medic.

Dionna did as she was told, and after a short while she calmed down.

"I'm sorry," said Dionna. "I think some water went

down the wrong way, that's all."

"Are you sure?" asked the medic.

"Yes, I'm much better now," said Dionna. "That must have been it."

Marsham looked at the glass of water by Dionna. It didn't look as if it had even been touched.

CHAPTER 33

"Exopthalmic," said Selina. "Having or characterized by protruding eyes. Exopthalmic."

Marsham took a deep breath and focused. This was his fourteenth spelling, so he was already very much "in the zone", but each new one meant he had to clear his mind and start again.

"E-X-O-P," he said, each letter plopping out of his mouth as if it were a letterbox and they'd been delivered in the post. "T-H-A-L-M-I-C."

"Correct," said Selina. "So far you have fourteen out of fourteen. Will you have a perfect round? We shall see. Here is your final word. Taaffeite, a type of mauve gemstone with a hexagonal crystal structure. Taaffeite."

Marsham felt both the pressure of getting a perfect score but also a sense of relaxation knowing that he'd done very well anyway. It mattered and it didn't matter, but it did matter.

"T-A-A-F," he said with confidence, but then, the next moment, that confidence faded like a wisp of air and was replaced by a whirlpool of uncertainty. What was the next letter? It was between two: E or F.

"I need the next letter, please," said Selina.

He tossed the letters around in his head as if they were the opposite sides of a coin and then decided to go for it.

"E," he said.

Beep.

"I'm sorry, that sound means you've made a mistake," said Selina. "Not a perfect round, I'm afraid, but still very impressive, Daniel. Well done."

Marsham wiped his hand across his forehead and then immediately panicked that his wig might have moved, so he quickly made his way to the side of the room to meet Gran and Ethel. As he did so, he felt a sliver of sweat trickle down his back.

"That was brilliant," said Ethel.

"Thanks," said Marsham as he heard Selina introducing Dionna. "Come on, we've got a boil on the boil."

They slipped out and Marsham heard a *beep*. Clearly Dionna hadn't got off to the best of starts.

"Hello, you three," said Mum when they arrived home. "How were the cacti? Not too prickly, I hope?"

"They were succulent, thank you, my dear," said Gran, using a word she'd learnt after looking up cacti on the way home.

"Oh, very clever," said Dad. "And was there plenty for you two to do?"

"There was loads, actually, Dad," said Marsham. "Can't wait for tomorrow, in fact. Someone is bringing in the biggest prickly pear in the world."

"Really?" said Mum. "Well, make sure you don't eat it."

They all laughed, and Marsham felt they'd got away with it, though something seemed a bit odd about the way Mum and Dad were being.

"And it's not too much for you, Gran?" asked Mum. "Looking after Marsham all day?"

"He's no bother at all," said Gran. "Not like that boil, it's giving me all sorts of trouble."

"What boil?" said Dad.

"Ha ha, that was our joke today, wasn't it, Gran?" said Marsham, panicking. "We told someone at the convention that Gran had a boil so that we could, erm, jump the lunch queue."

"So we did," said Gran. "And it worked a treat, we

got right to the front and I had a lovely egg and chips."

Mum and Dad exchanged a look of shared understanding, but that seemed to be the end of the conversation, so Marsham heaved a huge sigh of relief and retreated to his room.

"Hi, Tonks," he said to the ball of fur curled up on his bed. "You don't want to swap lives with me, do you? Mine is quite complicated at the moment."

From the way Tonks continued to purr gently, Marsham assumed the answer was no.

An hour later, Gran came in for a chat.

"It's definitely Dionna," said Marsham.

"So why don't you just tell Khalid?" said Gran.

"Still too risky," said Marsham. "We need to catch her and whoever she's doing this with."

"We need to get the bugging thing off Gloria," said Gran.

"We could intercept her when she's taking coffee to Selina," said Marsham. "Or we could make a lot of noise outside Selina's room so Dionna can't hear her rehearsing the questions?"

"Yes, I could have a sneezing fit again!" said Gran.

Marsham shook his head. "Look, I don't think she's cheating on the skating rounds," he said. "So we have time. I'm sure we'll come up with something, but whatever happens" – Marsham puffed out his chest and put on his sternest face – "she's not going to get away with this."

"That's good, you've really got the hang of the leg crossover!" said Tabatha. "You're a fast learner."

Marsham smiled and definitely detected a little reddening of her face as she smiled back at him, her green eyes widening as she did so.

It was early on Sunday morning, and, as arranged, Marsham had met Tabatha for a training session. She had her blonde hair tied in a bun again and her nails had been painted a deep, dazzling red.

"Shall we take a break and get a drink?" asked Marsham.

"Yeah, great, sure," said Tabatha. "I mean, if you want to, whatever, I'm not bothered."

Now her face was really red and, as they walked over to the café, she didn't seem to be able to look at him. Marsham felt awkward himself, but didn't really know why.

As it was still early, the café wasn't actually open, so Marsham grabbed two glasses of water and they sat at a table.

"Did you see on *Britain's Smartest Kid* that the

contestants have to skate while drawing a picture?" he asked.

"Yeah, stupid idea," said Tabatha.

"It is, yeah," said Marsham. "But my friends have challenged me to do it, and I said I could, so now I've got to do it when I meet them later. I can't lose face, can I? I've brought some stuff. Can we try it when we go back on the ice?"

The excuse felt weak, but Marsham didn't have any better ideas. Luckily, Tabatha didn't seem fazed by the proposal. Five minutes later, Marsham was standing on the ice, holding a clipboard and pencil, ready to give it a go.

"I reckon you can draw better than you can skate," said Tabatha. "So, concentrate on your feet more and just do the drawing from memory, yeah?"

"Good idea," said Marsham. "I'm going to draw my cat, Tonks."

"OK, but keep the skating simple," added Tabatha.

Marsham nodded and set off. Three seconds later he was flat on his back.

"Ooof," he said, picking himself up. "This is not easy."

He set off again and this time he lasted five seconds before tumbling over.

"Let me have a go," said Tabatha.

She took the pencil and clipboard and pushed off with her skates.

"Whooaaaa," she said, wobbling. "This really isn't easy."

She didn't fall over, though, and returned to where Marsham was standing. She'd drawn something, but it wasn't very clear what it was.

"You've just got to really concentrate," she said. "You need your arms for skating, but you can't use them when you're drawing, so you've got to think about it and focus on your feet, right?"

Marsham nodded and took the pencil and clipboard. He took a deep breath and pushed off.

"Ooooooo, aaaaaaaarrrrrrrr, ooooooooo, ooof!"

He'd skated right into the side wall and fallen backwards on to the ice.

"Ha ha ha!" laughed Tabatha. "Sorry, but that was funny."

"Oh no, no, this is no good," wailed Marsham.

"I've got to do it for real later, with loads of people watching."

"It's OK, don't worry about it," said Tabatha, looking confused. "It's just your mates, isn't it?"

An icy coldness invaded Marsham body. He'd panicked and said something stupid.

"Yes, yes, but there's a lot of them, that's what I meant," he said. "And I really want to show them I can do it. Sorry."

Now Marsham was the one whose face had turned red – very red.

"No worries," said Tabatha. She was smiling as she said it, but behind the smile Marsham sensed an unease, as if she knew something wasn't quite right.

It's probably just because I got a bit upset, thought Marsham. *She can't possibly think anything else, can she?*

CHAPTER 34

Marsham, who was now Daniel, was still thinking about what had happened at the local rink when he arrived at the studio with Gran and Ethel.

"Are you OK?" asked Ethel.

"What?" said Marsham. "Yes, I'm fine."

Ethel pursed her lips together and made a face which said, "I know you're not fine", but didn't actually say as much. It had the same effect on Marsham, though, and he was now even more unsettled that she'd read him like a book.

"I think that Vera has got something to do with all the funny business," said Gran. "She's a nasty piece of work."

"Keep your voice down, Gran!" hissed Marsham.

"Hi," said Gloria, walking up to them. "Shall we go to your dressing room?"

"Sure," said Marsham. "Hey, Gloria, how did everyone do yesterday? You know I couldn't stay as we had to take Gran to the doctor – she's much better now, by the way."

"Well, you came top, Daniel!" said Gloria. "Vera was second, then Naomi. Marc was fourth, and then poor Dionna was last."

"Poor Dionna?" said Gran.

"Yes, she didn't tell anyone before filming, but she had a bad migraine," said Gloria. "That's why she didn't do so well. She's still not feeling great today. Right, here we are. I'll come and get you when we're ready to start."

"Thanks, Gloria," said Marsham.

As soon as the door shut, all three of them said, "A migraine?!"

"She's a crafty one," said Gran. "She's covering her tracks. She got caught out yesterday, so she needs a reason for it."

"Maybe," said Marsham. "But why carry on with it today?"

"To make it look more convincing," said Gran. "Oh, I've got her number, all right."

"I hope so, Gran," said Marsham. "I hope we all have. And Gloria didn't seem quite her usual self, did she?"

"She seemed quite sad to me," said Ethel.

"You don't think Dionna is going to pull another 'sprained ankle' stunt, do you?" asked Gran.

Marsham was about to answer when there was a knock at the door.

"Gloria?" said Marsham. "You're back soon."

"Khalid wants to see you in the studio now," she said.

"Okee doke," said Marsham, glancing at Gran and Ethel. "Be there in a second."

"OK," said Gloria. "But don't be long."

"How do I look?" said Marsham once Gloria had shut the door.

"You look amazing, dear," said Ethel. "I've made sure everything is extra secure as it's ice skating today. Nothing is going to get dislodged unless. . ."

"Unless I fall flat on my face at high speed on the ice, I know!" said Marsham. "See you later. . ."

He headed to the studio, where Khalid, Marc, Naomi and Vera were already waiting.

"Where's Dionna?" he asked Marc as he sat down.

"Hi, everyone, I won't keep you long," said Khalid before Marc could answer. "You probably know that Dionna had a bad migraine yesterday. Well, she's still not great today, and we're not sure whether she should skate. However, she's being very brave and insisting that she does."

Marsham looked across at the others, but their faces were giving nothing away.

"She's in her dressing room now," continued Khalid. "And, under the circumstances, we have allowed her to take some medication, and of course the judges will be taking her condition into account. Are you all OK with that?"

"Yeah, that's totally cool," said Marc quickly. The others all nodded in agreement.

"Good," said Khalid. "Then I'll see you all shortly at the rink."

"What a shame for Dionna," said Naomi after Khalid had left. "Though she didn't seem all that bad yesterday."

"Migraines can come on really quickly," said Marc. "I get them. The lights can bring it on."

"Yeah, well, I hope the judges don't go too easy on her," said Vera. "She came top last time and she didn't even skate."

"It was a really bad sprain, though," said Marc.

"Huh, you'd have thought someone with all her money could hire a team of medics to cure her of everything," said Vera, bitterly.

***

Fifteen minutes later, Marsham was at the rink sitting next to Marc, who was tapping his left skate on the ground as if it were an overexcited woodpecker.

"This is going to be tough, isn't it?" said Marsham.

"What? Oh yeah, yeah," said Marc distractedly.

"Have you practised much?" asked Marsham.

"A bit. . . Oh look, it's Dionna," replied Marc.

Marsham looked up to see that Dionna had got out of her seat and was coming over. *Act natural,* he said to himself as a wave of panic engulfed him.

"Hi, Daniel. Hi, Marc," she said quietly. "Marc, would you mind swapping seats with me? The light is quite bright where I am; it's better for me here."

"Course, yeah, no problem," he said, getting up.

"Thank you," said Dionna sweetly as Marc vacated his seat and she sat down. "You don't mind, do you, Daniel?"

"No, not at all," said Marsham. Something felt odd about it, but perhaps it was just suspicion playing tricks with his mind again. "How are you feeling?"

"A little better," she said. "The tablets help. In fact, I have to take one now."

She fished a packet of tablets out of her pocket and went to pop one into her mouth, but unfortunately she

263

missed, and the tablet dropped on to the floor.

"Oh dear," said Dionna.

"Here, let me. . ." said Marsham. He was about to look for the tablet, but before he could do anything Dionna was on her knees, looking for it herself.

Oh well, he thought, and sat back in his seat.

A few seconds later Dionna popped back up again.

"Got it," she said triumphantly. "Seems OK to me. Three-second rule, isn't it?"

Marsham smiled as she swallowed the tablet down with a swig of water.

A moment later, the floor manager called for silence and Selina came out to start the round.

"Welcome, everyone, to today's ice-skating round," she said. "And welcome in particular to our gorgeous ice-skating judges, the wonderful Edgar Brookes-Jocelyn and the sensational Julia Lockwood."

The audience applauded as Edgar and Julia smiled victoriously from their seats. *Clearly,* thought Marsham, *Selina has been told to be extra-specially nice to them this time.*

"As you know," said Selina, "today's challenge for our finalists is to skate whilst drawing a picture, so we're also joined by scientific illustrator Morgan Davies. Welcome, Morgan."

The audience applauded again as a distinguished-looking gentleman with gray hair and thick-framed glasses just about managed a smile.

"Today's challenge is not easy," continued Selina. "But then, we are looking for Britain's Smartest Kid. If we look at the leader board. . ."

```
Dionna 17
Marc   13
Daniel 13
Vera   12
Naomi  11
```

"We can see it's pretty close. So, without further ado, can we have our first contestant today: Vera?"
Vera majestically got up and skated to the centre of the rink. A moment later, Julia also got up and skated out to meet her, doing a breathtaking jump along the way. She was holding a pencil and clipboard.

"Vera," said Julia, as the applause died down. "We would like you to draw a double helix structure."

Vera took the pencil and clipboard and said, "No problem."

Her confidence wasn't misplaced. Those lessons she was having were certainly paying off. Drawing a picture was barely a hindrance as she threw in some new skating tricks – a salchow and a split jump – and even managed to draw a pretty good double helix. The skating judges loved it and gave her 9.6. Morgan said her picture was somewhat lacking in detail, and was rather child-like. He gave her 6.3 for an overall total of 15.9. (Morgan seemed to be completely oblivious to the fact that the picture had been drawn during an ice-skating routine.)

Marc was next. He had to draw a heart with its chambers and didn't do well at all. He nearly fell twice, but just about made it through his routine. He received 8.1 for his skating and 5.6 for his picture, for a total of 13.7.

"And now for our next contestant," said Selina. "Our spelling bee champion, Daniel."

CHAPTER 35

Marsham smiled, trying to look as confident as he could.

He pushed off with his skates, but immediately felt something was wrong. His skates seemed to have a mind of their own and he just couldn't control them. One leg went one way, and the other shot off in the other direction. He made it to the centre of the rink with his left knee on the ice and his right foot at a forty-five-degree angle to his body.

What's going on? thought Marsham. *Maybe I'm more nervous than I thought!*

"Well," said Selina. "It's a good job that part isn't marked."

Too right, thought Marsham, heaving himself upright.

A moment later, Julia skated out to meet him.

"Hello, Daniel," she said. "We would like you to draw a methane molecule, please."

Marsham took the clipboard and pencil.

"Come on," he said to himself. "Keep it simple, it'll be fine."

He put the pencil to the paper on the clipboard and pushed off.

"Whoooaaa . . . ooops . . . yikes . . . eeeek!"

It was definitely not fine. His legs were going off in all directions; he just couldn't get any traction on the ice!

"Ow!" he said, as his right foot twisted under him, and this time his right knee hit the ice.

"Come on, what's wrong with you, legs?" he shouted to himself. There was a collective intake of breath from the audience as they watched the scene unfolding before them in amazement. Last time he'd been reasonably competent on the ice, now he looked like a newborn foal trying to walk.

He managed to get himself upright and started again.

"Oooooooooh, aaaaaaaaaaah!" he shrieked, as both feet went in opposite directions and he did the splits, something he'd never done before, and the clipboard went flying across the ice. Most of the audience were

also ooh-ing and aah-ing, as if they were experiencing Marsham's performance themselves, but some of them were laughing at him.

With an immense effort, he made it back to the centre of the ice to face the judges. He was sweating, despite the cold, which only added anxiety to the confusion and humiliation he was already feeling. He'd just about managed to avoid falling flat on his face, and no one was shrieking that his nose had come off, so he guessed all was well, but he knew he needed to cool down, and quickly.

An uncomfortable hush descended on the audience as the judges collectively gave him 3.5, for effort. It had been worse than disastrous.

"Bad luck, Daniel, but really good effort," said Dionna, gently touching his arm as he sank back into his seat, thanks to a helping – and somewhat embarrassing – hand from Julia.

"Yeah, everyone could see you were trying really hard," said Marc.

"Thanks, thanks," said a still-dazed Marsham. He searched the audience and eventually made eye contact with Gran and Ethel.

What happened? mouthed Gran.

Marsham shook his head. He couldn't understand it.

He felt disorientated. He felt helpless. He felt the same way he did when the kids at school had been mean and laughed at him.

His brain was awash with confusion, but, for the time being, all he could do was sit there and watch as Naomi took to the ice.

She did well, scoring 15.4 overall, and then it was Dionna's turn. She was asked to draw an electrical circuit diagram for a bulb, battery and switch.

If her migraine was still affecting her, it didn't show. Her skating was fairly basic, but her drawing was good, almost as if, Marsham found himself wondering, she'd already known exactly what she had to draw.

"Well done," said Edgar. "Under normal circumstances, we would have scored you 8.5 for that, but, as you have been feeling unwell, we are giving you 8.7." Morgan gave her 6.5, his highest score of the round, so she ended with a total of 15.2.

"Thank you," said Dionna as she returned to her seat.

"Congratulations to all our finalists, that was a very tough round," said Selina. "And congratulations to you, Vera, for another great performance on the ice."

Vera looked smug as the audience applauded. Marsham was just grateful that he hadn't been mentioned.

"So, if we add those scores in," said Selina. "The leader board looks like this. . ."

Dionna	20
Vera	17
Marc	15
Naomi	15
Daniel	14

"It really is very open," said Selina. "Any one of our finalists could still triumph."

Yeah, right, thought Marsham. *Not if one of them is cheating!*

"But that all depends," continued Selina. "On how they do in our final show next week when, once again, we have three rounds: a specialist subject round, a skating round in which they have to give a talk in a foreign language, and a mystery round. Yes, the very last round will remain a mystery until the last moment. The only thing I can tell you, and our finalists, is that they can each choose a teammate for that round. It can be anyone they know, so they will have to select wisely. The rest will be revealed next time, when we crown *Britain's Smartest Kid . . . on Ice.* Goodnight."

There was a bit more filming to do before everyone

filed out, after which Marsham remained in his seat. He felt deflated and confused. He sat there for a few more moments before heaving himself up and shuffling to the boot room. He plonked himself down on a bench and started to pull one of his skates off. It was proving difficult, so he hiked his leg up on to his knee and grabbed the blade

"What the—?" said Marsham.

He looked at his fingers. They seemed to have something on them. He sniffed.

"Oil? Olive oil?" he said.

He ran his finger over the blade again. It was covered in oil! He checked the other skate and, sure enough, it was also covered in oil. That would explain why it was extra slippery on the ice, but how had it got there?

It took him a moment, but then – as if a piano had landed on his head – it hit him.

Dionna!

She had set the whole thing up. The light wasn't bothering her. She'd changed seats with Marc so that she could sit next to Marsham. She dropped the tablet on the floor on purpose. She must have had a spray bottle and sprayed oil on his skates when she was "looking for the tablet"!

Marsham's head was reeling. He didn't know if she'd done it simply because she was furious about the change of order in the previous round and wanted to get back at him or whether she was on to him and wanted to send a strong message to back off.

Either way, thought Marsham, *she is one very nasty person who really will stop at nothing to win.*

PART 5

THE FINAL

CHAPTER 36

"You're very quiet, Marsham," said Mum at supper that evening. "Are you OK?"

"I'm fine," grunted Marsham.

"We had a very busy day at the cactus convention," said Gran. "He's probably just tired."

"Yes, I'm tired," said Marsham. "I might just chill in my room, if that's OK?"

"Fine by us," said Dad.

Marsham stood up and shuffled off to his room.

"What should I do, Tonks?" asked Marsham.

Tonks, who was lying on one of Marsham's jumpers on the floor, said, "I would curl up and have a lovely sleep."

Well, he didn't, but that's exactly what Marsham imagined he would say, and it was good advice. Before long he was indeed in bed, his mind running over the day's events.

After the olive oil discovery, Marsham had barged into his dressing room. "That's it! I've had enough," he had ranted. "I'm going to tell Khalid everything. Everything!"

"What?" Gran and Ethel had yelped at the same time.

Marsham had told them what he'd found out, getting even angrier as he recounted it to them.

"We need to catch her in the act before going to Khalid," Ethel had said.

"Yes, and anyone else who may be helping her. Like Gloria – we don't know how the two are connected!" Gran had added.

Lying in his bed, Marsham could still feel his anger from earlier like it was a wild cat, but, with all the effort he could muster, he managed to put that cat into a box and close it. Before long, he was dreaming of a salad with tomatoes, lettuce, cucumber and ice skates, all covered in an olive oil dressing.

The next morning Marsham woke up with a feeling of dread. That evening his ice-skating performance would be seen by millions on television, and even though he'd done well on the other two rounds, he knew it would eclipse everything. He thought about pretending to be ill and getting Mum or Dad to tell the school he wasn't coming in, but he couldn't bear the thought of deceiving them even more. Sometimes you just had to grit your teeth and deal with whatever was coming. And it came the moment he arrived at school.

"Hey, Marsh!" shouted Adrian enthusiastically, running up and almost bumping into Marsham by the Tree of MAN. "Is your wifi working properly yet? I saw Selina on breakfast TV this morning and she said the show tonight is amazing. We've got to watch it together this time."

"Yeah, yeah," said Marsham. "I saw that. Let's do it, can't wait." He hoped he sounded convincing.

"Hey, did you two see Selina on breakfast TV this morning?" asked Nainan, joining them.

"Hang on," said Adrian, laughing. "I think I'm experiencing déjà vu."

"I reckon someone else got caught cheating," said Nainan.

"Nah, the ice cracked and someone fell through it, that'll be it," said Adrian. "What do you think, Marsh?"

"Oh, I think it's probably, erm, just, I don't know," was all he could say. He so wanted to just have a laugh with his mates and be himself, but he was feeling pretty wretched. "Sorry, I slept badly, I'm really tired. I'll see you in class, I've got to go to the toilet."

He sloped off feeling weary and heavy, but just as he was about to go in to the toilet he saw Tabatha. This time she was on her own.

"Hi, how was yesterday?" she said, smiling at him.

"Oh, erm, it was just a boring Sunday, really," said Marsham. Tabatha made a confused face.

"I thought you were showing your friends that you could skate and draw at the same time?" she said. "Like on that show?"

"What?" said Marsham, immediately feeling the weight of his mistake as if it were a giant coconut that had fallen off a tree and clonked him on the head. "No, I mean, what I meant was, I . . . I got into trouble with my parents and they wouldn't let me go. Sorry, I really need the toilet. I'll see you at the rink tomorrow morning."

He rushed into the loo and sat in a cubicle with his head in his hands. He was desperately trying to give himself a pep talk, but all he kept hearing inside was, "I'm not sure I can keep this up much longer."

Marsham kept his head down for the rest of the morning and made sure to yawn a lot whenever Adrian and Nainan looked at him. At lunchtime he lied to his friends yet again and said he was seeing their history teacher, Mr McBroom, to discuss a project. In fact he went back to the toilet cubicle, but even that didn't help. He heard two kids come in and talk loudly about the show. They even mentioned Daniel and said he was the biggest dork of them all. Their laughter cut through Marsham like a giant buzz saw.

For the rest of the day Marsham sat miserably in a corner and didn't speak to anyone. Nainan and Adrian knew something was up, and he knew they knew, but no one said anything, and at the end of the day he slunk off home as miserable as he'd ever been. If this was what being famous was like, he didn't want any part of it (and Marsham wasn't even the famous one!).

CHAPTER 37

"Come on, Marsham!" shouted Dad. "It's about to start."

Marsham, who was up in his room, had no intention of watching the show. But he knew his parents would wonder why not, and he had just about talked himself into grinning-and-bearing-it when an email had come through to Daniel entitled, "Breakfast TV Interview".

Dear Daniel,

Following Selina's interview earlier on *Wakey Wakey Britain*, the producers have asked if all five of our contestants could appear on the show tomorrow morning. Isn't that wonderful?

Please ask your parent/guardian to sign and return

the attached permission form and then be ready to be picked up at 6 in the morning. It's an early start, but you are needed in the *Wakey Wakey Britain* studio at 7 a.m.

Khalid and the team

A pick-up at six would mean having to be at Ethel's by five at the latest to be transformed into Daniel. Then, after the interview, he would have to get back there so she could turn him back into Marsham, and *then* he still had to go to school. It had tipped him well over the edge and made up his mind for him.

"It's OK, Dad!" he shouted. "It's on record, I'll catch it later, I've got homework to do!"

He could almost see Mum and Dad making a "what's up with him?" face at each other, but he didn't care. Marsham also didn't care when Nainan's FaceTime call came through. He just declined it.

As it turned out, he did *hear* the show, sort of. From downstairs, he heard Mum's gasps and exclamations, which must have been her reactions to Daniel's performance.

He'd definitely made the right decision not to go through it all again.

"So, Tonksy," he said, "any thoughts on my specialist subject for the final?"

Tonks lifted his head up and looked at Marsham.

"Of cooouuurrrsseee," he said. "Thanks, Tonks, that's a great idea!"

"What's a great idea?" said Gran from outside his room. "Can I come in?"

"Oh, nothing, Gran," said Marsham, getting up and opening the door. He didn't feel like telling anyone yet.

"You know, it wasn't that bad," she said, smiling. She was wearing a navy-blue cardigan and when she smiled, Marsham could see how much she looked like Mum. They both had the same kind, open face and small upturned nose.

"I could hear Mum's gasps of horror from up here," said Marsham.

"OK," said Gran. "But at least our plan is working. It's Daniel who will be getting famous, or rather infamous, for his ice-skating antics, not you. No one knows your secret, do they?"

"No," said Marsham. "But it's. . ." He was about to tell her how difficult he was finding it, but he didn't really see the point. Instead he told her about the breakfast TV interview.

"Ooh, don't you worry," said Gran. "Ethel is an early

bird and Mum and Dad will be fast asleep; your mother always was a sound sleeper. It'll be fine."

Gran's relaxed confidence made Marsham feel a little better, and, as it turned out, she was right. They slipped out of the house and into a cab at four thirty and were at Ethel's in plenty of time. Marsham felt tired and nervous, but Ethel was in a good mood and listening to her and Gran nattering away helped take his mind off everything. At six, a car arrived and took him to the studio.

The other contestants were all there when he arrived and they were put in a room together to wait for their interview. It felt odd, them all being together outside the studio building. The truth was, they barely knew each other, so it was somewhat awkward having to socialize, but they managed to make small talk.

Their interview had been planned for seven thirty, but there had been a big story overnight about the prime minister having given everyone in the Houses of Parliament nits because he'd caught them off his children, so they were pushed back to eight thirty. Marsham had messaged Gran to tell her to contact school and make up some story about why he would be in late.

Eventually, though, all five of them were on a sofa

being interviewed by the show's hosts, Stewart Bick and Charlotta Lynch.

Vera seemed to be very keen to speak; she clearly had her heart set on becoming a celebrity like her father, and Naomi was also pretty chatty. The interviewers were especially interested in Marc because of his online show and Dionna because she was currently in the lead, so Marsham was able to make the occasional comment in agreement with someone else or just laugh along when something vaguely humorous was said.

Nonetheless, it was very hot in this studio and Marsham could feel himself beginning to sweat. His scalp was also getting quite itchy and he was starting to pray that it would all be wrapped up soon when Stewart said, "So, Daniel, I've got to ask, because we've had so many messages about it: what happened on the ice?"

Suddenly Marsham was the centre of attention, and not just in the studio, across pretty much the entire nation.

"I-I-I," spluttered Marsham. "I don't know, it was very hard drawing as well as skating and I think I got into a muddle and I wasn't sure what the methanol molecule looked like. No, it wasn't methanol was it, it was erm . . . erm . . . oh, my mind's gone blank. . ."

"Well, whatever it was," said Charlotta, "it certainly caused you all sorts of problems. Take a look."

"What? Oh no," said Daniel.

The next moment a clip of Daniel's ice-skating round was being played again. He couldn't bear to watch it, but he could hear his shouts and shrieks. He felt himself getting hotter and hotter. His face was going a deep shade of red and now his scalp was itching horribly. Worse still, his nose felt odd. *Was it slipping off?*

"Daniel, you really are a great sport," said Stewart when the clip had finished. "How are you feeling about the final now, though, and in particular the skating round in which you have to give a talk in a foreign language?"

"Yes, it's going to be, I mean, you know, it's another difficult. . ." Marsham was babbling now. He was incredibly aware of his nose. It really felt as if it was moving. His heart was beating so fast it felt like a machine gun and even his hands were sweating. In fact, the only part of him that was dry was his mouth. It was all clammy and sticky and he could barely speak. ". . . roond, I mean round – round, yes, round, it's. . . I'm sorry, sorry, I really really need the toilet, sorry, sorry. . ."

To the amazement of everyone, Marsham then got up and ran out of the studio, tripping over a camera cable and falling into a camera operator, making him yank his camera upwards so that for a moment, the only thing the viewers at home saw was the ceiling of the studio.

If Marsham had had a nightmare about how the interview would go, it could not have been worse.

CHAPTER 38

"Don't you worry about it, love," said Ethel, removing the wig from Marsham's head. "It'll all be forgotten soon and people will be talking about something else."

"Yes," said Gran. "And like we said before, Marsham is not Daniel, so he can go about his business as usual."

Marsham looked at himself in Ethel's mirror. It didn't matter to him that Daniel was a different person. It was still him. He was the person who had been made to look foolish on the ice and he was the person who had run out of a live television interview saying he needed the toilet. It was awful.

After the interview Marsham had stayed in the toilet for quite a while. His nose was fine, but his pride was deeply, deeply wounded. Eventually he had come out and faced the others. They were all very nice. Marc said he understood how difficult it was being on television,

Naomi said she'd needed the toilet as well and Dionna told him she knew he was hurting now, but in time he would learn from this experience and be a better person for it.

"But Daniel still has to go back and take part in the final," said Marsham to Gran and Ethel forlornly. "I really don't think I can do it now."

"Nonsense," said Ethel. "Everyone makes mistakes; it's how you respond to them that is important. You should go back with your head held high and show them what you're made of."

Marsham sighed. That felt like the most difficult thing in the world to do at that moment.

Ethel finished up and Marsham dragged himself to school – Gran had told them he'd had a dentist's appointment. He arrived at morning break and it was immediately obvious that people were talking about what had happened and watching clips of it on their phones. Laughter was erupting all around him. It was meant to be a happy sound, but it only made him feel sad. He felt enveloped in a bubble of dejection.

He kept his head down and was looking around for a secluded corner when a voice said, "Oi, where were you this morning?"

He looked up and saw Tabatha standing in front of

him. Marsham felt confused, but then a small glimmer of realization dawned on him – he'd completely forgotten that he had been meant to meet her at the rink! He didn't think he could feel any worse, but in that moment he felt as if he had finally hit rock bottom.

He was about to make yet another excuse when something happened inside him and his brain suddenly lurched completely the other way.

"Right, that is it," he exclaimed. "Come with me."

Marsham marched off in the direction of The Tree of MAN.

"What? Where are you going?" said Tabatha.

"Come on," Marsham shouted back.

Sure enough, as he approached the tree, Marsham could see Adrian and Nainan there.

"Hi Ade, hi Nain," he said.

"Hey, Marsh," said Nainan. "Did you see Daniel on breakfast TV this morning? It was—"

"Yeah, yeah, I saw it," interrupted Marsham.

"What am I doing here?" said a breathless Tabatha, arriving at the tree.

"Nainan, Adrian, this is Tabatha," said Marsham.

"Er, hi, Tabatha," said Nainan.

"Yeah, hi," said Adrian.

"All right?" said Tabatha.

"OK, listen," said Marsham. "I didn't see Daniel on breakfast TV this morning."

"But you just said—" spluttered Nainan.

"I didn't see it," continued Marsham, "because I was there. *I am Daniel.*"

There was a stunned silence for a moment, then Adrian said, "*You* are Daniel?"

"Yes, I am," said Marsham. "Tabatha, tell them what we've been doing."

"We, er, we've been ice skating," said Tabatha.

"Right, now, watch the interview from this morning again," said Marsham. "Actually, don't, get up a clip from *Britain's Smartest Kid*. Not the ice skating. OK, any one. But look at Daniel really, really closely, and while you're doing that, ask yourself why his interests are military history and graphic novels and why I asked you to borrow some books, and why his parents are in Ecuador and why my internet was mysteriously broken and why – this is just for you, Tabatha – why I said I wanted to learn to skate and draw, and any other questions about things that have felt strange over the past few weeks."

Marsham stood back as Adrian, Nainan and Tabatha watched a clip of Daniel on Nainan's phone. He felt like a scientist observing an experiment where, when all the parts came together, there would be an explosion. It took about eight seconds.

"Oh my goodness!" cried Adrian.

"I don't believe it!" shouted Nainan.

"It really is you!" said Tabatha.

"This is amazing, Marsham," shouted Adrian. "What, why, when... I mean, how come... it's YOU?!"

"OK, calm down," said Marsham. "I'll explain." And he did. He told them absolutely everything, including what he'd found out about Dionna and Gloria. It felt amazing. The relief was so overwhelming, it almost made him cry. It was like a fast flowing river, taking away all of his worries.

"But look," said Marsham. "You can't tell anyone, OK?"

"Of course," said Nainan.

"Sure," said Adrian.

"Tabatha?" said Marsham.

Tabatha was deep in thought; she seemed to be trying to work something out. Then she asked the most difficult question of all.

"But why?" she said. "Why are you Daniel? Why couldn't you just enter the competition as Marsham? I don't understand."

Marsham looked at Tabatha and realized that he

didn't want to start lying again, so he told the truth. He didn't say that it was her friends who had been horrible to him and made him feel bad about being clever, he just talked about a group of kids who had been mean, but it was obvious that she knew who he meant.

"I . . . I understand now," she said. Then it was as if *her* brain lurched in another direction and she suddenly added, "Hey, do you want to meet at the rink later to make up for the session we missed today?"

"Yes, please," said Marsham. "That would be great."

"So what are you going to do about Dionna?" said Nainan.

"Yeah, you can't let her get away with it," said Adrian.

Marsham smiled at his friends. As he'd been telling them about her and what she'd done, he'd realized that he had enough to deal with just being Daniel. It wasn't his job to catch a cheat; that's not what he'd gone on the show for. He'd made another big decision.

"I'm going to tell Khalid," he said.

CHAPTER 39

"Hi, I'm home!" Marsham shouted as he entered the house, slinging down his school bag. There was no response, which pleased Marsham. He was still buzzing after telling Adrian, Nainan and Tabatha the truth, but he could sense his determination to tell Khalid about Dionna waning a little. An awkward conversation with Gran might not help; he needed to stay resolute.

He went up to his room and sat in front of his computer. He took a deep breath and thought about what Dionna had done. He could feel the anger well up, but now it was less bubbly and explosive, and more like a solid block. He also felt a strong sense of injustice. Of course everyone else was going to find his skating performance funny, but they didn't know what was really going on!

Yes, thought Marsham. *It's the right thing to do*. He

started typing out an email.

> Hi Khalid, sorry to bother you – again! – but I really
> need to talk to you in private. I promise it's nothing to
> do with my gran this time, or about what happened
> on television this morning, but it is important. Can I
> come and see you?

He very nearly signed the email as "Marsham", but noticed just in time and changed it to Daniel. He sat back in his chair and looked at what he'd written.

I shouldn't try and outwit Dionna and whoever else is helping her myself, he thought. *It's much better to tell Khalid and let him sort it out. Yes, I'm definitely doing the right thing.*

He leant forward and hit the send button.

Whoosh!

There was no going back now.

"Hi, Daniel," giggled Tabatha.

"Shhh!" hissed Marsham.

"Oh, don't worry," said Tabatha. "There's not that many people here, and anyway, it's quite a common name."

Marsham smiled and relaxed.

It was later that afternoon and they were at the ice

rink. There had been no reply from Khalid yet, though Marsham had checked about thirty times.

They got their skates on and took to the ice.

"That's good, just keep your right leg straight when you lift it," said Tabatha.

"I will," said Marsham. "But it's hard, like trying to stop a snake from wriggling."

Tabatha smiled. In fact she'd been smiling a lot during their session. Marsham guessed that she liked having a secret "famous" friend.

"What language are you going to speak in, on the show?" said Tabatha.

"Espanol, señorita," said Marsham.

"What?" said Tabatha

Marsham smiled. "Spanish," he said.

"Oh, that's good," said Tabatha. "I mean, I think. Is it?"

"It's not too bad," said Marsham.

They continued skating together for another fifteen minutes. It was the first time Marsham had had fun in a while.

They finished up and headed out of the rink.

"That was really good," said Tabatha as they walked towards the bus stop. "Your skating has improved a lot."

"Well, I've got a great teacher," said Marsham.

Tabatha blushed and was about to say something else when a voice behind them on the street said, "Hello, what's going on here, then?"

They turned round. It was the sly-looking boy with a long face and greasy hair that looked like seaweed. Marsham immediately tensed up.

"Billy," said Tabatha in a much higher pitch than normal. "What are you doing here?"

"Just hanging out," said Billy. "But what are *you* doing with this loser?"

Before Tabatha could say anything Marsham said, "We've been ice skating, actually."

"Ice skating?" said Billy. "Why would anyone want to do that? It's stupid."

Tabatha looked down at the ground.

"It's not stupid!" snapped Marsham.

"Yes, it is," said Billy. "Come on, Tab, say goodbye to this loser and let's go meet the others."

"He's not a loser!" shouted Tabatha suddenly. "You're the loser, Billy! He's really really clever. And he's going to be skating on television!"

There was a moment of silence and then Tabatha gasped, sucking in air like a vacuum cleaner in reverse.

"Oh, no, I didn't mean..." she said, eyes wide, turning to Marsham. "I'm sorry, I'm sorry."

She started to run away.

"Tabatha," shouted Marsham. "It's OK, come back!"

But Tabatha wasn't coming back.

Billy smiled meanly and said, "See you later, loser," before walking away, chuckling to himself.

Marsham sloped off home feeling glum and anxious. He found Gran in the kitchen and told her that he'd sent an email to Khalid.

"Good for you," said Gran. "That's what I would have done in your shoes, but you did the right thing not rushing into it."

"But Khalid hasn't got back to me yet," said Marsham.

"Oh, he has now," said Gran.

"What?" said Marsham. "I just checked a couple of minutes ago."

"Well, check again," said Gran.

"OK," said Marsham.

Gran waited patiently.

"Oh, wow!" he said. "He has! How did you know?"

"I didn't," said Gran. "I was just playing, but sometimes it works out like that. Come on, then, what does it say?"

"Hi, Daniel," said Marsham, reading the email aloud. "Yes, I saw the interview on breakfast TV. If you do want to talk about it, we have a counsellor here who you can chat to. As for your other matter, I could fit you in late afternoon tomorrow, say about five?"

"Wonderful. Do you want me to come with you?" asked Gran.

"I'll be OK, thanks," said Marsham. "But I'll need to change into Daniel."

"Don't worry, I'll get agent Ethel on the case," chirped Gran. "Though, actually, there is something else I wanted to talk to you about."

"What is it, Gran?" said Marsham.

"You know Selina said you could have a teammate in the mystery round?"

"Yes, Gran," said Marsham.

"Have you decided who yours is going to be?"

"I have," said Marsham as Gran's eyes lit up. "It's going to be ... *Tonks.*"

"Tonks?" said Gran. "But he can't even speak, and he doesn't... Oh, you're joking, aren't you?"

"Yes," said Marsham, smiling. "I don't know who it's going to be. I haven't decided yet. But when I do, you will be the first to know."

CHAPTER 40

"Don't worry about Billy," said Adrian. "He's a useless slimeball, he won't work it out."

It was break time on Wednesday morning and Marsham was with Adrian and Nainan at the tree. He hadn't seen Tabatha around. In fact, he wondered whether she'd even come to school today. She hadn't answered any of his texts either. He felt concerned that she thought he was angry with her, but if anything, it was the opposite. She'd been defending him, sticking up for him, and it had made him feel pretty good.

"Yeah, Billy can't even dress himself," said Nainan, laughing. "It'll be fine."

Marsham smiled, but he wasn't so sure. Billy would definitely have told the others in his group, and who knows what they would have thought? Even if they didn't believe it, it was a good story, and rumours like that could spread rapidly. He'd also sensed a few people looking at him oddly during the morning, as if they were studying him and trying to work something out. He might be wrong, but it was unsettling.

Ade and Nain are right, he told himself. *It'll be OK.* He tried to sound definite and firm, but he wasn't convincing himself.

He spent the rest of the day trying to keep his head down, but now people were definitely looking at him. In fact, even some of the teachers seemed to be staring at him and on a couple of occasions someone walked up to him, about to say something, but then ran away giggling.

Worst of all, he spotted Billy and his friends laughing at him and shaking their heads. That could have been because Billy had seen him with Tabatha, but was there more to it?

"Have you heard anything?" he said to Nainan at the end of the day.

"No, nothing," said Nainan far too quickly. Adrian was at football training again.

"Are you sure?" said Marsham.

"Well, a couple of stupid things," said Nainan, a little embarrassed. "But nothing really."

"What things?" said Marsham.

"Oh, you know, like you and Tabatha are going to get married, and, erm, that you're a superhero with an alter ego."

Marsham shook his head as a look of concern melted over his face.

"Hey, this is just a school," said Nainan. "Remember there was that rumour last month about Ms Potter having been an Olympic weightlifter when she was younger? It was just a laugh, no one really believed it."

"That's because it wasn't true," said Marsham. "But this is."

As soon as he got in he dumped his bag and rushed round to Ethel's house, where Gran was waiting for him.

"I once tried to cheat in an exam," said Ethel as she fitted the wig on to Marsham's head.

"Did you?" said Gran. "You are a devil. What happened?"

"Well, I wrote the answers on my lower leg," said Ethel. "And then I dropped my pencil so I could look at them when I bent down to pick it up."

"That is clever," said Gran.

"Yes," said Ethel. "But what wasn't so clever was banging my head on the desk when I sat back up. I nearly knocked myself out, and when the teacher came over she saw that I'd written on my leg. I got into an awful lot of trouble."

"Cheats are a little more sophisticated these days," said Marsham.

"But that doesn't mean they should get away with it," said Ethel. "Right, you're done. Go tell the director and expose that cheat."

"He's the producer, Ethel," said Marsham. "But I will, and thank you."

Marsham, now Daniel, checked himself in the mirror, and, as ever, Ethel had done a great job. He set off for the studio.

"Hi, Daniel," said the receptionist when he arrived. "Take a seat. Khalid won't be too long."

Marsham sat down in the reception area. It was a little odd being there on a non-show day; the whole place was quieter, but Marsham could still sense that he was at the epicentre of some huge television machine.

Fifteen minutes later, Marsham was still sitting in reception and was beginning to think that Khalid had forgotten about him when a runner he'd vaguely seen before, a girl with short brown hair and wearing dungarees, appeared.

"Hi, Daniel," she said. "Would you like to follow me?"

Daniel stood up and followed the girl to the production office. She took him to the room at the back, the one he'd gone to when he'd told Khalid about Gran's "boil".

The door was open and he could see Khalid sitting at his desk.

"Hi, Khalid," said Marsham.

"Hi," said Khalid. "Come in. Shut the door behind you, please."

Marsham did so and sat down.

"Thanks for seeing me," said Marsham. "I know how busy you are, but I've found out something very important and I thought you should know."

"I see," said Khalid. "Well, before you start, I have also found out something rather important."

"Oh, really?" said Marsham.

Could Khalid already know about Dionna and the bug on the coffee cup?

"Yes, really, Daniel," said Khalid. "Or should I call you Marsham?"

Marsham was stunned. "What?" he said, his heart racing. He was suddenly very hot.

"It's been brought to my attention that you are not

who you say you are," said Khalid. "Marsham Lucas, I believe, is your real name?"

Marsham couldn't speak. He sat there with his mouth open, feeling as if everything had been turned upside down.

This really wasn't how he had expected the meeting to go.

"But, but. . ." Marsham spluttered. "How do you know?"

"I'm not going to reveal that, and I don't want to know why you did it – some silly prank, no doubt," said Khalid. "But I take it you don't deny it?"

"No, no, I don't," said Marsham. "But I came to tell you that someone's cheating and I know how they are d—"

"I'm sorry, do you really expect me to believe that?" interrupted Khalid firmly. "Is this another one of your games, then? You're the one who has duped us. This scandal is going to make us a laughing stock, so why should I believe a word you say?"

"Because it's true!" shouted Marsham. He sounded desperate. This was all going wrong.

"How gullible do you think we are, Marsham?" said Khalid loudly. He was doing his best to keep his emotions in check, but it was clear he was finding it difficult. His face was red and he looked exasperated. "If someone really was cheating, we would have discovered it ourselves by now, like we did with Liselle. This has been a difficult enough series and now this! What you've done could throw the whole future of the show into question. Disqualifying you will only leave us with four contestants, but we have no choice. We'll announce it just before we film the final episode this weekend. I think it's best if you leave now."

Khalid looked away to his computer, and Marsham knew that was that. It was over for him. And the worst thing about it was that Khalid was right. He *had* duped the show, and now that they'd found out, he felt heavy and wretched and wanted to cry, something he hadn't done for a long time.

Marsham stood up. "Bye then," he mumbled, but Khalid didn't look up.

The journey home was agony. Marsham's emotions were playing havoc inside him and, worst of all, when the show announced his disqualification, Mum and Dad would find out everything.

He arrived home and put the key in the front door. He hoped he could sneak up to his room unnoticed, but the moment he walked in, Gran pounced on him.

"What happened? What happened?" she said. "Is she

going to be disqualified?"

Now Marsham wanted to cry more than ever.

"No," he said. "I am."

"*You* are?!" said Gran.

Marsham couldn't look at Gran. He felt ashamed and angry and upset and also, somewhere inside, part of him was saying this had been her idea.

"They know I'm not Daniel, they know I've been lying to them, they're going to announce it before the weekend. I'm out."

"But how did they find out?" asked Gran. She sounded shocked.

"He wouldn't tell me," said Marsham. "But. . . Oh, I'm such an idiot!"

"It's OK, Marsham," said Gran. "Don't be so hard on yourself."

"I told Adrian, Nainan and Tabatha that I was Daniel," said Marsham. "Then she told someone else. Well, not exactly, and she didn't mean to, but I think everyone at my school knows now. I didn't think anyone would tell Khalid. I thought it would just be a stupid school thing, but I was wrong. Khalid thinks I was trying to ruin the show. He's really angry."

"Life can be unfair at times," said Gran. "But usually things work out for the best."

"I can't see that happening here," said Marsham. "I'm going upstairs."

Marsham trudged up to his room and lay on the bed. He glanced at his phone. Nothing from Tabatha, but loads of messages from Adrian and Nainan. He switched it off. He was done. The last few weeks had been not just a rollercoaster, but a rollercoaster, a merry-go-round, a Wurlitzer and a ghost train too. It felt as if it had been non-stop, but now it was time to get off and give up.

He shut his eyes and tried to sleep, but a couple of minutes later he heard a familiar "phrruupp" as Tonks came into the room and jumped up on to the bed. It was as if he knew Marsham needed him at that moment.

"Hi, Tonks," said Marsham, stroking him. "I've got myself into a bit of a mess. All I did was go and see Khalid to tell him the truth about what was really going on with Dionna, but..."

Marsham stopped. Two words stuck in his head like they'd been bolted and superglued in there.

The truth.

It was time to tell the truth, but this time it would be the whole truth and nothing but the truth.

CHAPTER 41

"So, Marsham," said Dad. "Why did you want to talk to all of us?"

It was later that evening and Marsham had called a family meeting. The four of them were sitting around the dining table. Mum was wearing a bright orange cardigan and smiling at him. Dad had a shirt on and was running his hand over his bald head every so often. Gran was sitting next to him in a grey jumper.

"I – er – I have something to tell you," he said.

Gran gave his arm a supportive squeeze.

Do it quick, like ripping off a plaster, he thought to himself. He took a breath and said quickly, "I'm the contestant on *Britain's Smartest Kid* called Daniel Phillips. I put on a disguise and entered as him."

He looked at Mum and Dad, searching their faces

to gauge their reaction as they let this announcement sink in.

"So..." said Dad, "there was no beekeepers' conference or cactus convention?" He sounded shocked.

"No," said Marsham. "Gran made them up because she's been coming to the show, and—"

He stopped. Mum and Dad were smiling at him.

"You knew!" he said.

"Well," said Mum. "We knew you and Gran were up to something, but we didn't know exactly what."

"Yes," said Dad. "But we thought we'd let you get on with it and tell us when you were ready."

"But then, erm, Daniel had quite a bad skating round," said Mum. "And he was quite upset, so someone might have told us." She was looking at Gran.

"Yes, well, I was feeling a little guilty because the whole thing had been my idea," said Gran. She seemed quite embarrassed. Marsham had never seen her like that before. "But I told them not to say anything to you just yet."

"And even though it was a good disguise, something felt quite *familiar* about Daniel," said Mum.

"Ooh, you never said anything like that *before* you knew," said Gran.

Mum smiled.

"But now something has happened," said Marsham. He could feel a build-up of emotion, as if he was heading to an unknown point where he didn't know what would happen. It was scary. "I ... well, erm, Daniel has been disqualified," he said.

"What? Why?" gasped Mum and Dad at the same time.

"The show found out I was in disguise," said Marsham. "But *I* had already found out that someone was cheating, so I went to tell the producer. But because I'd lied to them he wouldn't listen, and he disqualified me."

"Whoa, wait a minute," said Dad, his serious face now looking even more serious. "Start at the beginning."

So Marsham told them the whole story.

"Dionna shouldn't be allowed to get away with it," said Gran angrily when he'd finished.

"No, she shouldn't," said Dad. "But I can understand Khalid's point of view. You have deceived them, Marsham."

"Yes, you have," said Mum. "And all because you didn't want to be famous. How ridiculous is that?"

Marsham felt his chest tighten and a pulse of

adrenalin shoot round his body.

The whole truth.

"That isn't why I did it," he said, tears welling up in his eyes.

Marsham could feel the tension in the room ramp up about a thousand notches. Or maybe that was just how it felt to him. This was the secret that he'd lived with for the longest time. He took a deep breath.

"I did it because I didn't want people at school to know that I'm clever. They ... they made fun of me for being clever when I first started at Aylestone Vale, so ... so I started to hide it. That's why I only get average marks and grades. But I didn't want you to know about it because I didn't want you to get involved and maybe ... make things worse. I'm ... I'm sorry. Are you angry?"

Marsham didn't know quite what he'd expected. Anger, disappointment, punishment, shame, sadness? What he didn't expect, though, was to see his mother with tears in *her* eyes, looking at him with kindness. Her orange cardigan seemed to be making her face glow.

"No, Marsham," said Mum, looking at him. "We are the ones who are sorry. We should have realized and together we could have found a way to help you – a way that you were comfortable with."

Marsham felt a tear slip out of his eye. "I've really screwed up. Khalid is furious at me because it's really embarrassing for them. And they're going to have to announce it before the weekend, then everyone will know what I did. . ."

Marsham got up and left the room. If he'd stayed a moment longer he would have burst into tears and quite possibly never stopped.

CHAPTER 42

The following morning Marsham was up early, but he wasn't going to the rink. He slipped out of the house quietly and made his way to the studio building, arriving there just after eight.

At first he looked for somewhere to hide, but then he realized that he wasn't in disguise, so no one knew who he was. There was a small wall to one side of the building so he sat there and waited. He had no idea when Khalid got in, or if he was even going to be there that Thursday morning, but he had to see him and this seemed to be the only way.

He'd tossed and turned all night going over everything. There was a lot to sift through, but what came back to him time and time again was the fact that he had deceived the show. His favourite show. Worse still, he might have destroyed it for ever. *You could have thrown the whole future of the show into question,* that's what Khalid had said.

And then the worst part of all: Khalid thought it might have been just a silly prank. Marsham couldn't live with that. He had to tell Khalid why he'd done it. It probably wouldn't make any difference, but at least Khalid would know the truth.

An hour and a half later, Marsham was still sitting on the wall. He'd called the school and, putting on the deepest voice he could to try and sound like Dad, had told them his son had a doctor's appointment that morning and would be in later. Another lie. The last one, he hoped.

Marsham was cold and hungry. He was wondering how long he was going to give it, maybe another hour or so, when he saw Khalid heading towards the entrance of the building. He was wearing a big overcoat and carrying a backpack. He was hurrying and looked like a man with a lot on his mind. Marsham stood up and intercepted him.

"Khalid?" he said.

Khalid stopped suddenly; his prominent chin seemed to be looking down at Marsham.

"Yes?" he said. He clearly didn't recognize Marsham.

"It's me," said Marsham. "Daniel. Marsham."

Khalid shook his head. "Look, Dan— Marsham," he said. "I'm really very busy and I have nothing more to say to you. I've spoken to the television channel and they agree that we have no option but to disqualify you."

"I know," said Marsham. "And it's the right thing to do. What I did was wrong, it was a mistake, but I promise you it wasn't a silly prank. Please, just give me two minutes so I can explain, that's all I need."

"Oh, for goodness' sake," said Khalid. "Look, I'm meant to be in a meeting with Selina. I can give you two minutes, but that really is it. Follow me."

Khalid walked into the building with Marsham following him. He strode straight to the production office and into his room at the back.

"Ah, hello, Khalid," said a voice when he entered. It was Selina. She was already there. "And who's this? Are we already auditioning contestants for next year?"

"This. . ." said Khalid, "is *Daniel*."

"Hello, Selina," said Marsham. "I'm actually Marsham."

"Yes, I believe so," said Selina coldly. "What are you doing here? I thought we'd seen the last of you."

"He was waiting outside," said Khalid. "He says he wants two minutes to talk to us."

"Well," said Selina. "The clock is ticking."

Marsham sat down and composed himself.

"First of all," he said. "I'm sorry I disguised myself. It was wrong and I shouldn't have done it."

"Thank you for that apology," said Khalid, a little curtly.

"But I didn't do it for a silly prank, or to ruin the show," continued Marsham. "I did it because ... because ... people made fun of me at my school for being clever. I got really good marks in my first week and the headteacher announced it to the whole school. Then these kids started being horrible to me, they called me names, teacher's slug and others, and they made noises and then it felt as if the whole school was doing it. I hated it, it was horrible, and it felt as if they were taking away something I loved."

Khalid coughed and Selina shifted a little in her seat, but Marsham wasn't finished.

"Here, being smart is considered amazing, but for some reason it's not cool to be clever at my school. So from then on I made sure I only got OK marks and became an average kid. No one bothered me then. But the truth is, I love being clever. I am clever, that's why I love this show so much, so when my grandmother

came up with the idea of entering in disguise, I guess. . .
I guess I just couldn't resist showing the world who I
really am . . . if you see what I mean. It was wrong, I
know, but it really, really wasn't a silly prank. I now
realize that, to me, it was the most important thing in
the world."

Khalid sat back in his chair and took a deep breath.

"Look, I'm genuinely sorry for what you've been
through, but it doesn't change things," he said. "Even if
we hadn't found out, it would have come out eventually,
and that would make the show look pretty stupid, which
is not a good look for a show such as ours."

"I understand," said Marsham. "I just wanted you to
know the truth, that's all. I've had enough of lying and
deception. That's also why I wanted to tell you about
the cheating."

"Yes, that," said Khalid. "Believe it or not, we did
investigate and we haven't found any evidence of
any . . . *more* . . . cheating."

"I wasn't making it up," said Marsham.

"No, well, I'm sure you weren't, exactly," said
Khalid. "Maybe the incident with Liselle made you
think something else was going on and you believed
it was, but I assure you we are satisfied with our
investigation."

"I see," said Marsham forlornly. "Well, I guess I'll go now then."

He started to get up.

"Hang on," said Selina. She'd been pretty quiet, a look of serious contemplation on her face. "Khalid. Marsham's story is my story. I used to be scared to show how intelligent I was. I knew all the answers at school, but I wouldn't put my hand up. I was shy, I didn't want to draw attention to myself and open myself up to ridicule. It took a long time for me to be myself and be proud of who I am. And I'll bet it's the same for thousands, if not millions, of people."

"Yes, it could well be," said Khalid. He sounded awkward. Marsham guessed Selina had never spoken about this to him before. "So what are you thinking?"

"Marsham," said Selina, "it took a lot of courage to tell us the truth today, but are you brave enough to tell the whole country?"

"What do you mean?" asked Marsham.

"Either way, this situation is going to have to be explained," said Selina. "So why don't we film you, as Marsham, saying what you just told us? Then we put it on the show's website, and people will understand why you did it. And they'll also understand why we have let you stay in the competition. Would you be comfortable with that?"

"Stay in the competition?!" said Khalid and Marsham at the same time.

"Well, of course," said Selina. "Even if he misrepresented who he was, he has been playing the rounds fairly, right? And we can't let the bullies win, can we, Marsham?"

Marsham felt both terrified and excited at the idea. He was also reeling from hearing that Selina had been just like him once. He nodded.

Selina turned to Khalid. "What do you think?"

Khalid was quiet for a moment, deep in thought. "I'm not sure," he said eventually. "I think it needs something else. I think *you* have to be in the film as well, Selina."

Selina looked at Khalid, then over at Marsham. A moment later, her face broke out into a huge smile.

"Marsham," she said. "We're going to be quite a double act."

CHAPTER 43

"What? Why aren't you going to tell us what happened?" shouted Nainan, sounding put out.

"Because you'll find out soon enough," said Marsham.

It was lunchtime and Marsham, having just made it back to school, was walking towards the school canteen with Nainan and Adrian. Incredibly, Selina had said there was no time like the present and, after a short chat about what they were going to say, they'd shot the film there and then. It was going to be released later that day.

"Nah," said Adrian. "I reckon nothing happened and you're still disqualified."

"Nice bit of reverse psychology, Ade," said Marsham. "But it won't work."

"Erm, excuse me," said a voice.

The three of them turned to see two girls from the year above behind them. They were acting a little coy and shy.

"Yes?" said Nainan.

"Is it true?" said one of the girls. She was quite small, with bangles on her arms and neat dark hair. "About you being on television, but, like, in someone else's body?"

Marsham and his friends laughed. This was what happened with rumours. They became bent out of shape until the real story almost disappeared.

"Well," said Marsham. "I *was* taken over by aliens and they transported my brain into another person for an experiment, but it's over now and they've gone back to their planet."

The girls rolled their eyes, smiling.

"OK, yes, it's true, I'm on *Britain's Smartest Kid*, and until now I've been in disguise."

"That's super cool. Well, good luck, we'll look out for you!" said the dark-haired girl, and they walked on.

"So, you're really keeping shtum?" said Adrian.

"Yup, come on, let's get some food, I'm starving," said Marsham.

They headed off to grab some lunch. Marsham was in a pretty good mood after what had happened with Khalid and Selina, but he was still concerned about Tabatha. With the rumour having spread far and wide now, she was probably feeling even worse. He had texted her, but if she wasn't reading his messages, she wouldn't know that it was all working out for the best.

He looked around for her, but she was still nowhere to be seen. And for the time being, there wasn't anything Marsham could do about it.

Ping!

Marsham checked his phone.

"OK. You ready?" he said.

He was in his room with Mum, Dad, Gran and Ethel. He hadn't told them anything yet either, but that "ping" was an email from Khalid telling him the film had been posted on the show's website.

"Yes, we're ready, Marsham," said Mum. "Though I'm not sure what we're ready for."

"You'll see," he said. He was excited and nervous, but in a good way.

Marsham got the website up on his computer and, sure enough, there was now a big headline: "An important message from Selina".

Marsham clicked on the link and Selina appeared

on the screen.

"Hello," said Selina. "I'm Selina Constantin, the host of *Britain's Smartest Kid . . . on Ice.* You probably think of me as a very intelligent person. And that's true, and I'm proud of how intelligent I am, but that wasn't always the case. When I was at school, I hid my intelligence. I didn't want people to know I knew most of the answers. I was scared they might make fun of me. If I was just an average kid, nobody would notice me and expect anything of me. It was easier that way. And it stayed that way for a long time, until I overcame my fear and learnt to be who I am. But my experience is not unique. There are others like me, and I'd like you to meet one of them."

The camera panned right to find Marsham standing there.

"Hello," said Marsham. "I'm Marsham Lucas. Like Selina, I believed it would be easier to hide the fact that I know things, and that I actually enjoy learning. At school, other kids bullied me and made me feel bad for doing well in class. But at home I loved answering questions on quiz shows, so I applied to be on *Britain's Smartest Kid . . . on Ice.* Only, I didn't apply as myself. . ."

On-screen, Marsham took a breath.

"I applied," he continued, "as Daniel Phillips."

At that point the screen split in two, and a picture of Daniel appeared in the other half.

"I didn't want anyone from school to see me on the show and realize I actually know quite a lot and that I enjoy a challenge, so I disguised myself as Daniel Phillips. It was wrong, and I am sorry. I didn't think about what it would mean for the show if I was found out, which I have been. *Britain's Smartest Kid* is about celebrating cleverness, but my actions were stupid and have risked the credibility of the show. I fully accepted that I should not continue."

Daniel Phillips now disappeared, leaving only Marsham on the screen.

"But, having heard my story, the producers have given me another chance, as long as I carry on as myself, Marsham Lucas. So now everyone knows exactly who I am, a boy who likes learning things and finding things out and answering questions, and that makes me very happy because now, just like Selina,

I can also be myself."

Selina then entered the screen again.

"Well done, Marsham. It's a very brave thing to admit being vulnerable, and to admit being wrong," she said. "So if you're in a similar situation to Marsham, remember this: bullies only make people feel unhappy and insecure because that's how they feel themselves. It's sad that some people feel they have to take it out on other people, but if it is happening to you, speak to someone who can help you stand up to them by being the person you really are. But most importantly, don't forget to watch the final of *Britain's Smartest Kid . . . on Ice* this Monday evening. I have a feeling it's going to be amazing."

Then Selina and Marsham high-fived.

The film ended and Marsham looked at his family. Dad had a huge smile on his face, and Gran was winking at Marsham, but Mum had tears in her eyes. Was she crying?

"Mum, I'm sorry," said Marsham. "I didn't mean to upset you."

"I don't think your mum is crying because she's sad, Marsham," said Ethel.

"Of course not," said Mum, sniffing a little. "Marsham, I'm so proud. Come here."

Mum opened her arms and Marsham went in for the biggest cuddle ever. He emerged a few seconds later, a little dishevelled, but feeling all warm and mushy.

"So, Marsham, what is the show going to do about this cheat?" asked Dad.

"Nothing, I'm afraid," said Marsham. "Khalid told me they looked into it, but couldn't find evidence of any cheating. I mean, we don't have any actual evidence either, do we? And there's only one show left anyway."

Marsham shrugged and looked resigned to whatever would happen. The others were silent. There was a sense of helplessness in the room.

"But," Marsham said, a smile growing on his face that sent a small rocket into the atmosphere and instantly changed it. "I know who it is and how she's doing it. So, what do you think, Gran, Ethel? Reckon we can stop her ourselves?"

"You betcha," said Gran.

"I'm down with that," said Ethel, which made the others look at her in some disbelief.

"I've also made some other decisions," said Marsham. "My specialist subject is going to be cats, and I've decided who my teammate is going to be."

"Oh, yes?" said Gran, looking interested.

"Gran, I hope you don't mind," said Marsham, "but

I would like it to be Ethel."

"Oh my goodness," said Ethel.

"That's if *you* don't mind, Ethel," said Marsham. "You've done so much for me, you even lent me your house!"

"Well, that's very kind," said Ethel, clearly a little thrown. "But I'm not really very clever. I don't think I'll be much use to you."

"Ethel, you're a genius," said Marsham. "Even my own parents didn't recognize me. You are super-intelligent in your own way. And, truthfully, it's not about winning any more, it's about having fun. You've spent most of your life behind the camera making other people look great, and you love celebrities and film and television. Now it's your turn to be the star."

Ethel was blushing.

"Well, in that case," she said. "How can I refuse?"

"Great," said Marsham. "You don't mind, do you, Gran?"

"Of course I do," said Gran, laughing. "I will be very jealous, but it's a lovely thing to do, so I think I can just about stomach it."

"Excellent," said Dad. "So, Marsham, how do you feel now the whole world knows your secret? Could be a fun day at school tomorrow?"

"Weird, nervous, a bit scared," said Marsham, "but mainly OK. It's out now and there's nothing I can do about it; I'll just have to see what happens."

CHAPTER 44

"Wish me luck, Tonks," said Marsham.

"Meow!" said Tonks, which was good enough for Marsham.

He didn't want any fuss, so he left early that morning without checking his phone or any social media. In fact, he hadn't looked at anything the previous evening, which might have been why he'd slept well. It definitely felt as if a weight had been lifted, but as Marsham got closer to school he felt the nerves kick in.

He ducked into a café and sat at a table drinking a hot chocolate until it was time to go in.

As he set off, he realized he was slouching, almost as if that weight was trying to re-attach itself.

"No," he said to himself. "I am who I am, and I'm going in as I am."

Wondering if that actually made any sense, he lifted

his head up and strode purposefully through the school gates and into the playground.

He could instantly sense people looking at him, and that weight began hovering around again . . . but then something amazing happened:

A girl he didn't know started clapping. Then someone else did, and then another person, and another, and another, until eventually everyone in the playground, including teachers and parents, was applauding him. Some of them were even cheering.

Marsham felt himself blushing. He didn't quite know how to react, but then he saw Adrian and Nainan charging towards him with huge smiles on their faces.

"Marsh, you were amazing!" said a breathless Adrian.

"I couldn't believe it," said Nainan. "Wow. It's gone crazy online, you must have been getting millions of messages."

"I haven't actually looked," said Marsham, bashfully.

"*What?!*" screeched Adrian. "You're famous! Everyone is talking about you, they think what you did is great. You've probably missed loads of invites to be on telly and everything!"

"I didn't know what to expect," said Marsham. "I thought. . . I don't know what I thought, really. I just wanted to come clean and stop lying about it."

"Hey, we've got a famous friend," said Nainan. "That makes us famous, too, doesn't it?"

"Yeah!" said Adrian. "We'll probably get asked to be on *I'm A Celeb* or something."

"Yeah, right!" said Marsham, laughing. It all still felt very strange, but he was starting to enjoy his new-found "fame".

"Hello, boys," said a voice.

They looked up. It was Ms Potter, the headteacher.

"So, Marsham," she said, a stern look on her face. "You were absent yesterday morning and we got a call saying you were at the doctor's."

"Ah, yes," said Marsham, suddenly panicking. "You see ... it, well, erm ... what happened..."

Ms Potter's face suddenly broke out into an enormous smile. None of them had ever seen her look so happy.

"Marsham Lucas, I am very proud of you," she said, beaming. "What you did took great courage, but I also have to apologize to you. This school has a zero tolerance policy towards bullying and we let you down. Rest assured, we will do our utmost to ensure something like this never happens again."

"Thank you, Ms Potter," said Marsham.

"You're welcome, Marsham," she said. "Now, there's someone else who would like to have a word with you."

Ms Potter moved to one side. Marsham hadn't noticed that someone had been standing behind her. It was Tabatha.

"Hi, Marsham," she said, blushing.

"Tabatha, hi," said Marsham. He felt happy and relieved to see her. "I was worried about you. Are you OK?"

Adrian, Nainan and Ms Potter melted tactfully away, leaving the two of them alone together.

"I wasn't," said Tabatha. She looked down at the ground. "I was really, really upset. I thought I'd ruined everything. I felt so stupid. And angry. And I wasn't just angry with myself. I realized I was angry with Billy and all of them. They're idiots. They're not my friends."

She looked up at Marsham. "It's like you said, you've got to be yourself, who you are, and do what you love."

"I did say that, didn't I?" said Marsham, nodding his head. "But I wasn't quite living up to it, not really. I'm trying to now, though."

"Well, when I saw your video," continued Tabatha, "I realized it was all going to be OK because you were brave and told the truth." She blushed again and scuffed the ground with her left foot.

"But so did you," said Marsham.

"What do you mean?" said Tabatha, taken aback, a look of confusion on her face.

"You told Billy that he was an idiot and I was clever and I was going to be skating on television," said Marsham. "It was all true, and you said it because ... well, because you were defending me."

"I guess that's right," said Tabatha, smiling now.

"And then the show found out and I told them the truth and I made that film," continued Marsham. "And I don't think any of it would have happened if it wasn't for you."

"Wow," said Tabatha, her eyes lighting up.

"Hey, you look different," said Marsham, suddenly noticing.

"Oh yeah," said Tabatha. "I'm not wearing so much make-up. I only wore it to fit in with those other kids, but that isn't me any more. The real me never liked it anyway."

"Neither did the real me," said Marsham. "That's why I'm wearing less as well."

Tabatha looked at Marsham for a minute and then the penny dropped and she laughed.

"You know those kids made faces at me when I came in today," she said. "But I went up to them and told them I didn't care and I love skating and I've been helping you, only I didn't know it was you, well, I did, but I didn't know it was the other you, do you know what I mean?"

Marsham smiled and nodded.

"Ahem." Adrian had cleared his throat nearby. "The bell's about to go, we'd better head in," he said. "Though me and Nain were just talking and, you know, now you are going to be in the final, can we get tickets?"

Marsham smiled. "I'll see what I can do," he said. "I might know some people. Come on."

"Hang on, one more thing," said Tabatha. "I'm sorry I didn't reply to your messages or anything, but I thought I could make it up to you. You've missed a lot of skating training this week, and you've got a big performance coming up. If you've got time, we could go to the rink after school. Would that be OK?"

"I'd like that very much," said Marsham as they made their way into the building and more cheers rang out all around the school.

CHAPTER 45

Arriving at the studio building for the final, now with Mum and Dad as well as Ethel and Gran, Marsham got a real taste of how famous he'd become. Just the day before he'd sat on a wall outside the exact same building and no one had taken any notice of him. Now he was met by a bank of photographers and journalists, as well as a considerable number of "fans" wanting his autograph and a selfie.

He'd checked his messages and looked online earlier, and there were indeed plenty of offers to appear on various shows. But he'd really needed to work on his Spanish and his cat knowledge, so he'd turned them all down.

The film had obviously caused quite a storm, though; he hadn't been expecting to be met by quite so many people. He got through it as best he could – he stopped for quite a few selfies and had his picture taken a lot – and entered the building.

Once inside, he got a similar reception to the one he'd got at school. People didn't exactly cheer and applaud, but they told him how impressed and touched they'd been by his story and patted him on the back. And that included one person in particular.

"Well done, Marsham," said Dionna outside his dressing room. She was dressed immaculately as ever. Her brown hair was full and shiny. "I'm really proud of you. Good luck today. See you later."

"Thanks, you too," said Marsham as Dionna flitted off towards her room.

Marsham waited a few seconds, then said, "That's her."

"She seems so nice," said Dad.

"It's always the nice ones," said Mum.

"Let's not talk about it here," said Marsham.

He opened the door and they all went inside.

"It's weird not wearing the wig and make-up," said Marsham. "Feels wrong somehow."

"Sometimes it's not easy being yourself," said Ethel. "But I'm sure you'll get used to it."

"So what's the plan?" said Dad.

"Don't worry, Dad," said Marsham. "We've got it

sorted." He smiled at Gran and Ethel conspiratorially. They smiled back.

Knock knock.

"And I think we're about to go into action pretty soon," said Marsham. "Come in."

The door opened and in bounded Gloria.

"Hi, Marsham, I... Oh, hello, who's this?" she said.

"Gloria, this is my mum and dad," said Marsham.

"Hi, good to meet you," said Gloria. "Your film was great, Marsham. Sooo inspirational."

"Thanks, Gloria," said Marsham.

"We'll be starting in about twenty minutes," she said. "It's the specialist subject round first. Is there anything any of you need?"

"Gloria's a runner," said Gran. "But that doesn't mean she runs, it means she gets drink and food and things."

"I see," said Mum. "Thank you, Gloria, but we're fine for now."

"No worries," said Gloria. "I'll be back later, see ya."

"Gran, Ethel, you ready?" said Marsham once Gloria had left the room.

"Never been readier," said Gran.

"OK, let's go," said Marsham. "But remember, wait for my signals."

Marsham went out into the corridor just in time to see Gloria walking around the corner. Keeping his distance, he followed and saw her go into the production office. Now that she was in there, Marsham could wait and watch the entrance, until she came out again. There were loads of people coming and going. A lot of them said hello to him and congratulated him again, but he still managed to keep an eye on the door.

He got his phone and messaged Gran.

You and Ethel go to Selina's dressing room now.

Five minutes went by, during which time other runners came and went with various drinks and snacks, until eventually he saw Gloria appear holding a cup of coffee.

Marsham dropped back further and watched as Gloria headed off. He messaged Gran again.

She's on her way. Good luck.

Marsham could see Gloria at the end of the corridor. She was definitely heading to Selina's dressing room. If Gran and Ethel did their jobs well, Dionna certainly wouldn't be able to cheat on the specialist subject round.

Feeling satisfied and excited, Marsham went back to his room.

"Hi Mum, hi Dad," he said.

"Well, hello there," said Mum. "Are you going to tell us what's going on?"

"Well, Gran has taken Ethel to get Selina's autograph, only, when they're in her dressing room getting it, they might have a little accident and spill a cup of coffee."

"Oh dear," said Dad.

"Don't worry," said Marsham, smiling. "They'll get her a brand new cup."

"I see," said Mum. "And the reason they're doing this is. . .?"

"Because there's a bugging device on the bottom of the original cup, and when Selina rehearses the questions in her room, Dionna listens," said Marsham. "But I really have to get on and learn more about cats now, and practise my Spanish for the skating round."

With that, Marsham sat down and opened a book called *The Encyclopaedia of Cats*. He couldn't really concentrate, though. He was desperately hoping for Gran and Ethel to return with news of a successful mission.

Five minutes later, his desperation had increased, and after another five minutes had passed he was beside himself. *Where were they?*

Marsham couldn't stand it any longer, so he went out into the corridor. He paced up and down for a while and then strode off in the direction of Selina's dressing room.

When he got there, the door was shut and there was no sign of anyone.

"Gran? Ethel?" he hissed.

"Down here, Marsham," said a voice.

Marsham looked up and saw Gran's head poking out from a door further along the corridor.

"Why are you still here?" he said.

"We're waiting for Gloria," said Ethel. "Like you said."

"But, she should have been here ages ago," said Marsham. "Are you sure she hasn't gone in?"

"Definitely," said Gran. "Someone else went in, but it was a man."

"What did he look like?" said Marsham.

"He had quite short hair," said Gran.

"And he had an earring in his nose," said Ethel.

"Gavin," said Marsham. "It must have been Gavin. Did he have a cup of coffee with him?"

"Yes," said Gran. "But you told us to wait for Gloria, not someone called Gavin. That's what we've been doing."

Marsham cast his mind back to when he was

watching the door of the production office. Yes, Gavin had definitely walked out carrying a cup of coffee.

What on earth was going on?

CHAPTER 46

"I don't get it," said Marsham, as they hurried back to his room. "Gloria always takes Selina her coffee ... unless. . ."

"Unless what?" said Ethel.

"Unless she put the bug on another cup and gave it to Gavin," said Marsham, excitedly. "That must be it! That argument they had when she spilled the coffee must have worried her, that's why she got him to unwittingly take it in."

"But he went in ages ago," said Gran. "Dionna will know the questions by now."

Marsham stopped. What Gran had just said hit him as if he'd been slapped with a soggy, sand-filled sock.

"You're right," he said, deflated. "There's nothing we can do now."

"You could go to Selina's room and show her the

bug on the bottom of the cup," said Ethel.

"Yes!" said Marsham, suddenly excited, but then a moment later, the excitement turned to uncertainty. "Wait, no. What if he didn't have the bugged cup? Maybe something went wrong with the plan. Or the bug could have fallen off again. I really don't want to cause any more trouble on the show."

"No, that wouldn't be good," said Gran. "Come on, let's go back and re-group."

"You two go on," said Marsham. "I'm going to wait here for a minute."

"What are you going to do?" said Ethel.

"Nothing," said Marsham. "I just want to be alone."

When Gran and Ethel had gone, Marsham walked along the corridor to Dionna's room and stared at her door. *Maybe I should just barge in and confront her,* he thought. *But she'd probably just deny it.*

He felt as if he'd been on a long journey and come to a very disappointing end. He meant what he'd said about it not being about winning any more, but he didn't want to lose this way.

He knew he wasn't actually going to storm into Dionna's room, though, so he turned to go back to his room when Marc came out of his, holding a notebook. He looked fraught and miserable.

"Oh, hi, erm, Marsham," he said. "Great video."

"Yeah, well," said Marsham. "I just wanted to do the right thing. I felt bad about what I'd done, but at least now I can be myself. You know, maybe it's true, sometimes honesty is the best policy."

Marc looked at Marsham for a moment. Then he seemed to go through a transformation, as if he'd suddenly woken up from a deep sleep.

"You know something, Marsham?" said Marc, brightly. "You're right. Thank you!"

Marc turned and went back into his room with a spring in his step.

What was that all about? thought Marsham, but he didn't have any time to ponder it. The next moment, Vera's door opened and her dad, Mikey, came flying out.

"Go now!" shouted Vera from inside. "There isn't much time! Go!"

Mikey threw a somewhat pathetic smile at Marsham and scurried off down the corridor.

Back in his dressing room, Marsham was still a little downcast.

"Hey, come on," said Mum. "You're playing as Marsham now and you're going to show everyone just how clever Marsham is."

"I know, Mum, I know," said Marsham.

"And we know you'll do your best," said Dad. "Which is all you can do, isn't it?"

"I know," said Marsham. "And I will try, but when someone else is cheating, my best is not going to be good enough, is it?"

"What's going on?" said Marsham as he arrived in the reception area a few minutes later with Gloria and his family, along with the other finalists and their families. They had all heard a commotion and come to look.

"It was a joke! I was joking!" shouted Mikey. "Come on!"

The two security men holding him didn't seem to think it was funny. They definitely weren't laughing as they threw him out. Neither was Khalid, who was standing nearby, along with a crowd that had gathered

Gloria shrugged, but the next moment Vera came steaming past shouting, "What are you doing? Why are you throwing my dad out?!"

"If you'd like to come to my office, Vera," said Khalid. "We can talk there."

"No!" she shrieked. "I demand you bring him back right now!"

Khalid sighed. "Vera," he said. "I'm afraid your

father tried to – how should I say this – *cajole* Selina into telling him some of your questions for this round. So, under the circumstances, I think it's best he leaves."

"You're lying!" yelled Vera. "He would never do that!"

"That must mean you're calling me a liar, then," said a voice.

Everyone turned to see that Selina had joined the throng.

"Of course not," said Vera sulkily.

"Good," said Selina. "I did wonder why your father was so friendly. I had hoped it was because he enjoyed my company, but it seems he had other motives."

"Yeah, well, I don't know anything about it," said Vera.

"Of course you don't, my dear," said Selina. "I did remember that celebrity quiz show we were on together, though. As I recall he finished bottom with no points. Perhaps he wasn't able to get the host of *that* show to let him see the questions, either. Shall we go?"

Vera silently snarled as everyone trooped off together.

"How exciting," said Naomi to Marsham.

"More good stuff for your book?" Marsham replied under his breath.

"Absolutely," said Naomi. "I'll change her name,

of course, but a character who's desperate to improve her family's reputation by winning a quiz show after her father does terribly on a different one, I think that would work very well."

"Do you really think that's why Vera got her father to do it?" asked Marsham.

"Oh, I don't know. What I'm talking about is purely fiction," said Naomi, smiling knowingly at Marsham. "Good luck today."

Arriving in the circular studio, Marsham was surprised to see that Marc and Dionna weren't there. He'd presumed they were following behind everyone else, but clearly not.

Khalid also seemed concerned and sent some runners off to find them.

"Are we the only three left, then?" said Marsham.

Vera just scowled and muttered, "Hopefully," but Naomi said, "I think not. Look!"

Marsham looked up to see Marc striding confidently in, followed by Dionna, whose face resembled a grizzly bear who had stepped on a nail. She was clearly fuming, and not doing a very good job of hiding it. *Had they had another argument? And if so, what about?*

They sat down, and, after the floor manager had

counted Selina in, she was finally able to start the show.

"Welcome, everyone," she said, "to the final of *Britain's Smartest Kid . . . on Ice*. Tonight we will crown our winner, and find out who will be getting the one hundred thousand pounds and that trip to the Nobel Prize ceremony. But whoever it is, on behalf of everyone on the show, can I congratulate our finalists? This has been an . . . *interesting* series, but they have all done exceptionally well."

The audience applauded politely, though two people were shouting and whooping above everyone else. Marsham looked up and saw Adrian and Nainan in the audience. They looked so happy and excited, he couldn't help grinning hugely.

"We're starting tonight," continued Selina, "with our specialist subject round. But first, let's remind ourselves of the scores."

Dionna	20
Vera	17
Marc	15
Naomi	15
Marsham	14

"Just six points separate them all, it really is very open.

So, could I have our first contestant, Marc, please?"

Marc stood up and smiled to the audience before making his way confidently to the lectern. His specialist subject was *The Simpsons* and, after fifteen questions, he'd scored ten points.

Vera was next. She answered questions on the works of Philip Pullman and scored just seven points. It felt very much as if she'd given up and lost the fight. Naomi's topic was the Vikings, and she proved to be quite an expert, scoring thirteen points.

"We now come to our fourth contestant," said Selina. "And you could say this is his first appearance on the show. Marsham Lucas."

Marsham stood up and was surprised, and a little embarrassed, to be greeted with warm and loud applause from the audience.

"Marsham," said Selina. "You have chosen to answer questions on cats. Are you ready?"

"Yes," said Marsham.

"Here goes," said Selina. "Question one: what is the collective noun for cats?"

"Clowder," answered Marsham.

"Correct," said Selina. "Question two: all cats are born with what colour eyes?"

"Blue," said Marsham.

"Correct. Question three: what is a cat doing when it is smurgling?"

"It's kneading the ground with its paws," said Marsham.

"Correct."

And so it went on. By the final question Marsham had only given one incorrect answer.

"And so we come to question fifteen," said Selina. "The prime minister of the United Kingdom has an official resident cat. By which title is it known?"

Marsham thought for a moment. He was pretty sure he knew the answer.

"The Chief Mouser," he said.

"Correct," said Selina. "Marsham, you have scored fourteen points. Well done."

As the audience applauded, Marsham walked back to his seat, thinking that Tonks would be very proud.

Yes, he thought. *I'm in the lead, but not for long: the next contestant is Dionna.*

CHAPTER 47

"And our final contestant in this round is the current leader, Dionna," said Selina. "Will she still be leading after her round? We shall see. Dionna. . ."

Dionna made her way to the lectern. She hadn't said a word to anyone so far and still seemed unhappy, to say the least. However, in the full glare of the cameras, she managed to rearrange her face into a smile of sorts.

"Dionna, you have chosen the rivers of Europe as your specialist subject," said Selina. "Are you ready?"

"Yes," said Dionna.

"Here is your first question. What is the longest river in Europe?"

"The Volga," said Dionna.

"Correct. Question two: which river drains almost twenty per cent of the land area of France and enters the Atlantic Ocean at the Bay of Biscay?"

"The Loire River," said Dionna.

"Correct."

Marsham groaned inwardly. Two out of two. Even if Dionna only got a couple of questions wrong, she would still get enough points to stay well on top.

"What is the source of the River Isar?"

"Erm, I . . . erm. . . Is it the Black Forest?" said Dionna.

"No, the Tyrolean Alps," said Selina.

Hmm, thought Marsham. *Is she just acting? Or did she really not know the answer?*

"Question four: Saale, Mulde, Ohre and Vltava are major tributaries of which river?"

"I . . . I . . . I don't know. Pass," said Dionna.

"The Elbe," said Selina.

Now Marsham was sensing something unusual. *She doesn't know the answers.*

Thinking back to the first two questions, Marsham felt that he could have answered them correctly, so it was no surprise that Dionna could too, but now that things were getting more difficult, she was clearly struggling. Had she done any revision at all, or had she been relying entirely on cheating?

Eleven questions later, Marsham had his answer.

"So we come to your final question, Dionna," said

Selina. "Where is the confluence of the Rhone and Arve rivers?"

"Vienna?" said Dionna.

"No, I'm afraid the answer is Geneva," said Selina. "So, at the end of that round you have scored eight points. Thank you, Dionna."

That says to me, thought Marsham, *that she had done some revision just in case, but not enough. Something's gone wrong with her plan, but what? And why?*

"What an exciting round," said Selina. "Congratulations to Marsham, he gets five points. Naomi, you score four, Marc is next with three, Dionna you get the two points and Vera you have one."

The audience applauded as Vera did her best to style it out in an "I don't care any more" way, while Dionna was giving nothing away with a face of solid concrete.

"So, putting all those scores into the leader board," said Selina. "The current positions are as follows. . ."

Dionna	22
Naomi	19
Marsham	19
Vera	18
Marc	18

"Dionna is still leading," said Selina. "But with two rounds to go, anyone could still win."

It certainly looks that way, thought Marsham. *I just hope it's true.*

"As you know," said Khalid to the audience after Selina had done some retakes, "we're doing all three rounds today, so we'll have a short break and then head over to the rink for our skating round in about fifteen minutes. Thank you."

Dionna was up and out in a flash, while Vera slumped down into her seat as if she was going to stay there for ever.

"Well done, Marsham," said Marc. "Great round."

"You certainly know your cats," said Naomi. "But Dionna doesn't seem very happy, does she? I wonder what's up with her."

Marsham looked at Naomi. *Did she know, or was she just fishing for information?*

"She's probably got another migraine coming on," said Marc, chuckling. "Or maybe her ankle is still hurting. See you later."

"I don't see what's so funny about a migraine or a sprained ankle," said Naomi, but Marc had already left.

"Beats me," said Marsham, getting up. "See you on

the ice."

Back in the dressing room, everyone was very excited and intrigued.

"I'll bet the bug didn't work," said Dad. "That'll be it."

"I'm not sure," said Mum. "She's tricksy. Maybe she purposely had a bad round to make it look as if she's not cheating."

"She's become a pretty good actress, then," said Ethel.

"Come on, let's get to the rink," said Marsham, buzzed up and already focused on his next task. "I am going to double, triple, quadruple check my skates today." He flung open the door.

"Hello," said the person standing outside.

"Tabatha!" shouted Marsham. "What're you doing here?"

"I wanted to see you do the tricks and stuff that I taught you," she said. "Make sure you do them right. Your gran got me a backstage pass; she said it was a present for helping you."

Marsham smiled and was about to say something when Gloria pitched up.

"Ready?" she chirruped, breezily.

"And raring to go," said Marsham. "Come on, everyone."

Marsham did indeed quadruple check everything

before taking his seat by the rink. If Dionna tried anything this time, he'd be more than ready, but when the other contestants turned up, she was three seats away from him and didn't ask to change places with anyone. She did seem calmer and back to her normal self, though, unlike Vera, who, if anything, had gone into an even deeper sulk.

Once everything was ready, Selina introduced the round. A spotlight fell on her that illuminated the top half of her body. It was somewhat unusual and the audience sensed that something was afoot. "Good evening, everyone," she said. "Just before we start, I would like to take this opportunity to say something to our skating judges, Edgar and Julia."

The audience fell into a hush.

"For a while now, I have been, well, to be blunt, rude," continued Selina. "You see, I wasn't keen on testing physical intelligence. I wasn't entirely sure about it as a notion, but more importantly, I suspected it was just a gimmick to increase the show's ratings at the expense of quite possibly humiliating our contestants. But I was wrong and I apologize. Our contestants embraced the challenge and threw themselves into it in the same way they throw themselves into every challenge. Consequently, they have inspired me – and I know a lot of others out there watching – to expand my horizons and think differently about intelligence."

Selina paused and cleared her throat.

"Ultimately," she continued, "as someone who values intelligence very highly, I suppose I felt inadequate. It challenged me. And so. . ."

Selina stood up and took a step forward on to the ice. The audience gasped. *Selina was wearing ice skates.*

She pushed off and, a little unsteadily, skated to the centre of the rink, where she stopped.

"Well, I don't think that's going to win me any prizes, but it's a start," she said. "Now on with the show, I'm very excited to see what our contestants will do tonight. And I look forward to Edgar and Julia's truly valuable and insightful assessments."

The disbelieving silence lasted another half second and then the audience broke into applause. Edgar and Julia were smiling at Selina; they were clearly satisfied with her apology.

Selina then called for the first contestant, Naomi.

Naomi skated to the centre of the ice. When she was in position, Edgar skated out and waved a French flag, which was the language Naomi was going to speak in. Then, she was ready to begin.

"Bonjour mesdames et messieurs," she said as she set off. *"Aujourd'hui je vais vous parler de la tour Eiffel."*

She then proceeded to impart some facts about the Eiffel Tower while performing her routine. Marsham thought her skating was safe and competent, and it seemed the judges agreed, giving her a score of 8.4. Crucially, though, she didn't make any language mistakes, so she didn't lose any points.

"Our next contestant is Marsham," said Selina.

Checking his skates one last time, Marsham made his way on to the ice. This time he got to the centre without any wobbles and stood there as Edgar circled him carrying a Spanish flag.

Marsham glanced into the audience and found Tabatha. She was sitting with the others. A huge smile wriggled across her face.

"Buenas tardes a todos," he said. *"España es un gran país de casi 50 millones de habitantes."*

He pushed off and immediately went into a split jump. The audience gasped and applauded as he continued speaking in Spanish.

Marsham felt great as he skated around the ice. He threw in more

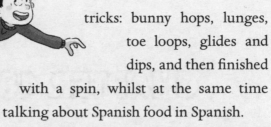

tricks: bunny hops, lunges, toe loops, glides and dips, and then finished with a spin, whilst at the same time talking about Spanish food in Spanish.

He came out of the spin with a little wobble and shouted, *"Ole!"*

The audience applauded and Marsham could see that seven people in particular were out of their seats, giving him a standing ovation.

"Well," said Edgar, "that was an impressive routine. Not everything was perfect, but you really pushed yourself, so we have given you 9.6."

The audience applauded again and Marsham waited to find out how he had done on his Spanish.

"A very good score, Marsham," said Selina. "And I can tell you that you only made one linguistic mistake, which means your overall score is 8.6."

Marsham headed back to his seat thinking: *Fantastico!*

CHAPTER 48

"Dionna, you're our next contestant," said Selina. "Could you take your position, please?"

Dionna made her way to the centre of the ice. Marsham felt himself tense up, but didn't exactly know why.

Edgar came out carrying a German flag and then Dionna started her routine.

As she skated and talked, Marsham felt himself relax a little. She wasn't a bad skater, but he knew he was better. He was also pretty certain that this round, at least, was a fair fight, and one that, if his judgement of her skating was correct, he would win.

"Well done, Dionna," said Julia. "A solid performance. Perhaps we might have expected a little more by now, but all things considered you did well. We have given you 8 points."

"A good score, Dionna," said Selina. "And you didn't make any mistakes during your most informative talk on lederhosen, so eight is your final score for that round."

Dionna returned to her seat. Marsham watched her the whole way, but her face was like a closed shop. No one was getting in to find out what was behind the door.

The next contestant was Vera. As soon as she started it was clear it was a case of all or nothing for her. She threw herself around the ice like a firecracker, chucking in complicated moves that would have been difficult for a professional skater. Sometimes they came off, other times she was all over the place. She didn't actually fall over, but she did a very good impression of a windmill at least three times.

Her talk in Italian was littered with screeches and yelps as she tried to regain her balance and consequently she ended with a total score of 2.7. When it was announced, she bowed deeply and made a rude gesture to the audience. All or nothing had turned into nothing.

Marc was the last to go, and he seemed to be really enjoying himself on the ice. His talk was also in Spanish, and all was going well until the end when he attempted quite a big jump. He completely messed up and finished on his backside, but he stood up quickly with a big smile on his face as the audience applauded.

He only made one language mistake and ended up with a score of 7.7.

"Thank you to our contestants for a wonderfully entertaining round," said Selina. "Let's see what those scores have done to the leader board."

Dionna	25
Marsham	24
Naomi	23
Marc	20
Vera	19

"What a contest," said Selina. "There is everything to play for in our final mystery round, when we will find out who'll be crowned Britain's Smartest Kid . . . on ice!"

"Are you absolutely certain you want me as your teammate?" said Ethel back in the dressing room. "I mean, you could actually win!"

"I could not be certainer," said Marsham. "In fact, I am the certainest I have ever been about anything."

Knock knock.

"Come in!" he shouted.

The door opened and someone who looked like Gloria came in, but unlike the usual sparky Gloria, this one was very different. Her make-up was a little smeared around her eyes and she could barely raise a smile.

"Would anyone like a drink?" she said, forlornly sniffing.

"Is everything OK, Gloria?" said Marsham.

"Yes," she said unconvincingly. "It's just a cold."

"That came on quickly," said Mum. "You seemed fine earlier."

"I know what you'd like," said Ethel. She got out her phone and took it over to Gloria. "Marc and Paul posted a new episode of *The Q&A Kids*," she said. "It's very good. Look."

Gloria took one look at it and promptly burst into tears.

"What's the matter, dear?" said Gran.

"I'm such an idiot," she wailed. "How could I have been so stupid?!"

The others all looked at each other. This was a surprising turn of events.

"I loved him and I thought he loved me too!" cried

Gloria. "That's what he said and I believed him. I really did."

"Who said he loved you?" asked Marsham.

"Marc said that Paul loved me," said Gloria, her face now a mess of make-up, snot and tears. It wasn't her best look. "He said we'd be together for ever."

"I see," said Marsham, a little unsure how best to deal with this.

"Oh, my dear," said Mum, putting an arm round Gloria.

"Marc's just told me that it wasn't true," sniffed Gloria, snuggling into Mum. "He made it up. He just said it so I would help him."

"Help *him*?" said Marsham.

"Oh, I shouldn't have said that," mumbled Gloria.

"It's OK," said Marsham. "We'd worked out what you were doing. Well, we thought we had. But we thought you were bugging the coffee for Dionna."

"No!" said Gloria. "Marc asked me to do it, I don't know anything about Dionna. Oh, I'm so stupid!"

"Marc and Dionna must be working together," said Gran.

"That would explain why I saw them arguing," said Marsham. "But, Gloria, now you know the truth about Paul, you can stop doing it."

"It's too late!" wailed Gloria, collapsing in tears again. "I've already done it aaaaa haaaaa haaaa haaaa..."

"It's OK," said Mum, drawing Gloria into her chest.

"It's not OK," said a slightly muffled Gloria. "It was wrong, and I'm going to confess. I'll tell Khalid everything."

"Are you sure?" said Marsham.

"Yes, it's the right thing to do," said Gloria. "But, erm, I was thinking that I could try and make it up to you by ... erm ... telling you what the mystery round is."

There was silence for a moment.

Then Marsham said, "Thank you, Gloria. I understand why you said that, but I don't want to know. I'm not going to cheat. I might not win, but at least I will have played fairly."

CHAPTER 49

"Welcome to the final round of this year's competition!" said Selina. "As you know, it's a mystery round. But before we reveal the mystery, our finalists have been joined by a teammate of their choosing. So arise, please, teammates."

The teammates, who were sitting next to their contestants, all stood up.

"Joining Marc is his older brother and co-host of *The Q&A Kids*, Paul," said Selina. "Alongside Vera is rocket scientist and Noble Prize winner Dr Susannah Lawrence. With Dionna is Cambridge University Professor of Business Studies Sir Michael Radbil. Naomi's teammate is Booker Prize winning author Karen Stanton and, erm, Marsham has chosen his gran's friend Ethel. Welcome to all of you."

"This is scary," said Ethel, sitting down as the audience applauded.

"You'll be fine," said Marsham. "But I'm not sure about Dionna. Something is up with her, look."

Ethel glanced over at Dionna. She had a frown running across her forehead and was shifting her position every few seconds.

"Well, now we have met the teammates," said Selina. "I think it is time to reveal the subject of this round."

As soon as Selina stopped speaking, a large television screen was wheeled on to the set and placed in front of the contestants.

"Fear not," said Selina. "We are not going to test your knowledge of television; rather, this round is all about *emotional* intelligence."

An undercurrent of intrigued chatter flittered around the audience.

"For example, have a look at this face," said Selina

On cue, a face appeared on the television screen. The lips were tightly closed together, the eyebrows were furrowed and the nostrils were flared.

"Is it expressing sadness, pride, anger or fear?" said Selina.

"He's angry," whispered Ethel.

"The correct answer is anger," said Selina. "Though I don't know what he is angry about. So, you'll now be shown fifteen faces. For each one you have to decide which of the four options on the keypads you've been given describes the expression. The only other difference in this round is that you will all be playing at the same time."

"Oh my goodness," said Marsham suddenly. "I've figured it out!"

"What?" said Ethel.

"Even if Dionna knew what this round was she won't be able to cheat," said Marsham. "There's no way she could have seen the faces beforehand – she only had an audio listening device in Selina's dressing room. That means this is now a completely fair fight to the end!"

"Good luck, everybody," said Selina. "Here is your first face."

A picture of a man with his eyes wide open, his eyebrows arched and his mouth open appeared on the screen.

"Is this person expressing a) fear, b) interest, c) surprise or d) compassion?" asked Selina.

"He looks scared to me," whispered Marsham.

"No," said Ethel. "He's surprised."

Marsham looked at Ethel and for the second time in as many minutes had a realization.

"Wow, you might just be the best teammate in the world!" he said.

"Well, I've worked closely with a lot of people over the years," whispered Ethel. "And directors are often telling actors to show their feelings, but I think it was something I was born with as well."

He pressed "C" on his keypad and sat back, waiting for the next face.

This time the man's eyebrows were pulled inwards, his eyes were almost closed, his nose was wrinkled at the bridge and his tongue was sticking out.

"He looks like he's eaten something disgusting," said Ethel, before Selina had even given the options.

"Is this person expressing a) contempt, b) pain, c) sadness or d) disgust?" asked Selina.

Marsham smiled and pressed "D". He had no idea how the others were doing, but playing the round with Ethel he knew he was going to get a good score.

"So we come to the final question," said Selina.

A face appeared on the screen of a woman gazing downwards with her head tilted forwards and her chin tucked into her neck.

"I'd say she's done something naughty," said Marsham.

"Couldn't agree more," replied Ethel.

Marsham smiled. Sure enough, option "B" was shame. He pressed it on his keypad.

"That concludes our final round," said Selina. "But whose face will be expressing joy when we announce the scores, I wonder? Let's find out which one of our finalists is going to be crowned the winner of *Britain's Smartest Kid . . . on Ice!*"

Tension flooded the room as everyone waited for the results.

"Here we go," said Selina. "Vera, you and your partner got nine correct answers. Well done."

Vera managed a sneer-smile as the audience applauded.

"Marc, you two got eleven right."

Marc seemed pretty happy with that and high-fived Paul.

"I'm going to get Paul's autograph afterwards," whispered Ethel.

"Naomi, you and Janine also got eleven right," said

Selina. "But Marc was a little quicker on the keypad. A very good score nonetheless."

Naomi smiled broadly. It seemed as if she was just happy to be sitting with a famous author.

"Dionna, we now come to you and Sir Michael," said Selina.

Marsham glanced over. Dionna was perched on the edge of her seat, clenching her teeth and gripping the armrests. She wasn't just uptight, she was up, up and away tight.

"I can tell you," said Selina, "that you got twelve correct."

"Yes!" said Dionna, punching the air.

"Has she won?" asked Ethel.

"Not yet," said Marsham. Now all that talk of not wanting to win had flown out of the window. He had meant it at the time, but now that it was between him and Dionna, Marsham didn't want to lose.

"Finally," said Selina, "we come to Marsham and Ethel."

Marsham couldn't speak. His lips were pursed together as though they'd been velcroed and he felt his heart go into overdrive.

"Marsham," said Selina, "I can tell you that you got . . . all fifteen correct!"

A gasp went round the audience as people started to work out what that meant.

"What's happening?" said Ethel. "Did we win?"

"No," said Marsham. "But we didn't lose, either. It's a *tie*."

CHAPTER 50

A shroud of anticipatory silence enveloped the audience.

Dionna's four points in that round and Marsham's five meant they were both on twenty-nine points.

"Well, it looks as if we have a tie," said Selina. "But, all is not as it seems."

Marsham felt himself gripped by something. *Could it be that they had found out about Dionna? Were they about to disqualify her?*

He shot a look across at her. She was giving nothing away.

"It hasn't happened very often on the show," said Selina. "I think the last time was eight years ago, but we like to reward excellence, and, as you'll see if you peruse the rules on our website, if any contestant plays a perfect round, they get an extra point."

Selina seemed to punch home the word "point". It clearly landed with a thump in Dionna's stomach. She let out a groan and crumpled back in her seat.

"And so, having scored fifteen out of fifteen on that last round, Marsham, you have earned an extra point, which means, congratulations, *you are the winner!*"

The audience erupted in applause and cheers. If anyone was trying to work out the expression on Marsham's face now it was a mix of surprise, joy, excitement, disbelief, relief and uncertainty.

Had he heard Selina correctly?

"Marsham, please come and collect your trophy."

He had!

He was just standing up when an anguished wail burst forth.

"Nooooooooooooooooooo!"

It was Dionna.

Khalid started to make his way towards her when he was overtaken by Dionna's mother, somehow walking very quickly in her stilettos. She looked, frankly, terrifying.

"Dionna!" she snapped. "Stop it! Stop it now! Whatever has got into you?"

"I need that money," wailed Dionna, clearly distraught. "I haven't invented anything new for ages, my business has got no money; I had to win!"

"I wonder if we should maybe take this somewhere else..." said Khalid, but Dionna's mother wasn't listening.

"For goodness' sake," she continued in a slightly more conciliatory tone. "You tried your best to win and you nearly did, now come on..."

"I didn't..." said Dionna, "... try my best to win!"

"Whatever do you mean?" said her mother.

"I think I can answer that," said a voice.

The focus now shifted to a young woman who had walked out from behind a camera. It was Gloria! She looked very meek and small.

"And so can I," said another voice. It was Marc! He walked out to join Gloria.

Khalid looked exasperated, but defeated. "Just keep recording," Marsham heard him say into his headset microphone.

"Sorry, Paul," said Marc, looking over at his brother.

It's OK, mouthed Paul.

Marc took a deep breath and said, "Dionna cheated to try and win the money, and I helped her. Once she knew I was going to be on the show she hacked into my brother's emails. She's very good with computers."

Marsham thought back to the "Top Secret" email

he'd received at the start of the competition.

"She found some embarrassing emails Paul had sent to a girl he liked," continued Marc. "Really sloppy stuff. But the girl rejected him, so he sent her some really angry emails. Dionna got them as well."

A murmur of shock went round the audience.

"She threatened to make the emails public," said Marc. "She blackmailed us, basically. It would have ruined Paul; it probably still will. And *The Q&A Kids* . . . it's taken a long time to make it so successful."

Everyone was rapt now; you could hear a pin-shaped

feather drop. Dionna was sitting with her head in her hands.

"We needed a plan," continued Marc. "That's when we remembered Gloria. She was something of a superfan. She kept sending us messages – well, mainly Paul – and she told us she was working on this show. So we came up with the idea. It wasn't very nice, and I'm not proud of it."

Marc looked at Gloria. She nodded and took over.

"I was in love with Paul, and Marc told me that Paul was also in love with me," said Gloria, blushing. "He

said we'd be together for ever if I did this small thing for him. I believed him."

Marc looked down at the ground.

"He said Paul had been on a couple of quiz shows before, so he knew how they worked. He knew that the host always rehearsed the questions beforehand, so. . ." Gloria stopped for a moment. She shut her eyes and looked upwards, steeling herself. Then she brought her head back down and continued. "So I made sure that it was me who took Selina her coffee because . . . because there was a bugging device attached to the bottom of the cup."

A gasp went round the audience.

"Oh my," said Selina, a hand clutched to her chest.

"That's all I knew," said Gloria.

"It's true," said Marc. "Gloria didn't know anything else, but the bug meant that we could listen to Selina rehearsing. You probably won't believe me, but we only wrote down Dionna's questions. Neither Paul or I listened to mine. Then I took them to her."

"No!" shouted Dionna's mother. "Is this true?"

"Yes, I'm afraid it is," said Marc. "She also didn't really have a sprained ankle, there wasn't a spider in her room, and she didn't have a migraine either. She also put oil on Dan— er, Marsham's skates in the drawing round; that's why he did so badly. She didn't have to tell me these things either, but she did. She was boasting about doing them."

There was silence for a couple of seconds, then Khalid said, "Is that it? Please let that be it."

"Oh, one more thing," said Marc. Everyone could hear Khalid groan. "Liselle wasn't lying. She did get an email telling her to cheat. Dionna made it look as if it had come from the show, then she made it disappear so there would be no evidence. Liselle shouldn't have been disqualified."

"Oh, whoop dee doo," said Vera, loudly and sarcastically.

There was another couple of seconds of silence, then Khalid strode out.

"Right, well, there's a lot to take in," said Khalid. "And we will digest everything over the next few days and weeks, I'm sure, but for now: Marc, you're disqualified; Dionna, you're disqualified; and Gloria, you're fired. Dionna, I'm not sure if this is a matter for the police, but I'm sure they will be investigating. I suggest you all leave now."

A weeping Dionna was helped up by her mother and the two of them left to boos and jeers from the audience, followed closely by Marc, Paul and Gloria.

"Now," said Khalid. "I believe we have a winner to reward. Selina?"

"Go on, Marsham," said Ethel. "This is your moment."

"No, I couldn't have done it without you, Ethel!" he said. "Come on!"

The two of them walked to the centre of the room, where Selina presented Marsham with the winner's shield.

"Congratulations," she said as she handed it over. "And, of course, don't forget, you're going to the Nobel Prize ceremony in Sweden, and you win one hundred thousand pounds!"

Marsham took the shield and, together with Ethel, they held it aloft. He'd done it, and he felt amazing! He looked out and found Mum, Dad, Gran, Tabatha, Adrian and Nainan in the audience. They were all beaming.

"Well done, Marsham," said Khalid, coming over after the cameras had stopped filming. "You do know this is just the beginning? Newspapers will want to talk to you, TV shows, you might even get asked to be on *Strictly Come Dancing*!"

Marsham smiled. He couldn't quite take everything in.

"I'm kidding about that last bit," said Khalid.

"Though, you never know. I suggest you go back to your dressing room now and relax a little. You deserve it. Oh, and by the way? Make sure you send me the name of whoever did your disguise make-up. We're always on the lookout for standout talent like that."

Marsham must have nodded because a few minutes later he was back in his room with everyone shouting and cheering. It was unbelievable, and he was finding it quite exhausting.

Knock knock.

"Marsham!" shouted Tabatha, who had answered the door. "It's Naomi!"

Marsham went over. "Hi, Naomi," he said.

"Well, thanks for nothing," she said, looking cross.

"Sorry, what?" said Marsham.

"I'll never write a story as good as that!" she said. "Now I'll have to find something else for my next book."

"I'm sorry, Naomi, I, er. . ." He stopped. Naomi was grinning.

"I'm joking! It's been an absolute blast," she said. "There are always other stories. I really came to say congratulations, you deserved it."

"Thank you," said Marsham. "Do you want to come in?"

"No thanks," said Naomi. "I don't want to intrude

on your celebrations with your family, and your girlfriend."

"Oh, she's not my girlfriend," said Marsham, turning beetroot.

"Sure she isn't," said Naomi, grinning. "See you!"

Marsham smiled and shook his head. It had been quite a day.

"Marsham, come here!" shouted Mum.

Marsham trotted back into the room and sat down.

"I just want to say," said Mum, "that we are *so proud* of you."

"We are," said Dad. "You are amazing."

"But you do know, no matter how clever you are," said Mum, "we would still be proud of you."

"I know," said Marsham.

"That said, though," said Dad. "I do quite like the idea of my son being Britain's Smartest Kid."

"ON ICE!" shouted everyone else.

ACKNOWLEDGEMENTS

Acknowledgements, ackshmoledgements. This bit is more than acknowledgements, though I may just have set a new world record for using the word acknowledgements so many times in such a short space. This is about thanks. Gratitude. Big ups. Because, believe it or not, I didn't do this all on my own. I actually paid someone else to write it for me. No, okay, that's not true, I'm joking. I did write it, but without the people I'm about to mention, you wouldn't be reading it now, so I owe them big time.

First up there's Linas, Sarah, Jessica and everyone at my publisher, Scholastic. They read my words, edited my words, copy-edited my words and proofread my words, and in so doing, made them much better. It's a great skill and they do it brilliantly. And also to Liam for the brilliant cover, and Hannah and Ellen for the publicity and marketing around the book.

Then there's James Lancett who drew the illustrations. He's done a fantastic job, just as he did with my previous book (*Britain's Biggest Star...Is Dad?* – still available) and, once again, I am bowled over by his talent.

Thanks also to Sallyanne Sweeney and Ivan Mulcahy, they're my literary agents, which sounds a bit posh and hifalutin, and maybe it is, but that is who they are and I love them and am deeply grateful for all they do for me.

I'd also like to mention here the book that inspired me, which is How Children Fail by John Holt. I first read it when I was studying to be a teacher (yes, I was a teacher once) and it immediately struck a chord. Who knew that almost thirty years later it would play a part in the creation of this book?

Finally, thanks to all my family (Sophie, Ruby and Art), friends (too many to mention), acquaintances (far too many to mention) and complete strangers (I don't know their names) who I blathered on to about the idea for this book and tested various plot twists and parts of it on. Just for not telling me to shut up, I am grateful.

ABOUT THE AUTHOR

A long, long time ago, Ivor studied Psychology at Manchester Polytechnic because, surprise, surprise, he wanted to be a psychologist. In fact, he didn't just want to be a psychologist, he wanted to be the next Sigmund Freud, who was possibly the most famous psychologist of all time. Ivor then became a primary school teacher because he'd decided he wanted to be an Educational Psychologist.

However, around the same time he also started going to see a lot comedy. That was because his brother (David, some of you may have heard of him) was starting out as a comedian. Ivor enjoyed watching comedy and wondered whether he could write some jokes, so he got together with a friend who wanted to be a comedian and did just that. Astonishingly, when she told the jokes, some people laughed, which made Ivor think he wasn't too terrible at it. He also started sending off articles to magazines and they liked them and printed them, which also helped Ivor think he wasn't too bad at writing.

About a year and a half later, Ivor decided to stop teaching and become a full-time writer. He continued writing for comedians and magazines, but then he got a job writing on a TV show. That was in 1997 and Ivor spent much of his time thinking, *well, this won't last, I'll have to get a real job soon.*

Incredibly, twenty-five years later, he is still writing for TV shows and this is his nineteenth book, all of which now makes Ivor think, *maybe, just maybe, I could be a writer.* And so could you. Ivor didn't start writing until he was thirty-one, which is really old, so you never know. Why don't you give it a try?

ALSO BY
IVOR BADDIEL